LOVE SONGS FROM A
SHALLOW GRAVE

Also by Colin Cotterill

The Coroner's Lunch
Thirty-Three Teeth
Disco for the Departed
Anarchy and Old Dogs
Curse of the Pogo Stick
The Merry Misogynist

LOVE SONGS FROM A SHALLOW GRAVE

Colin Cotterill

Quercus

First published in Great Britain in 2010 by

Quercus
21 Bloomsbury Square
London
WC1A 2NS

A CIP catalogue record for this book is available
from the British Library

ISBN 978 1 84916 995 0 (HB)
ISBN 978 1 84916 045 2 (TPB)

10 9 8 7 6 5 4 3 2 1

Printed and bound in Great Britain by Clays Ltd, St Ives plc

Having arrived at this, the seventh in the Dr Siri series of mysteries, I would like to thank all of you who have taken the trouble to write to express your affection for the good doctor, and to all our fans who have journeyed with us through 1970s Laos.

For making this instalment particularly special, I would like to thank Bert, Bounlanh, Judy, Art, Mac, Leila, Lizzie, Laurie, my lovely Jess, Bob, Bambina, Dad, Tony, Kay, Martina, Charlotte, Jack, Jim, Martin, Valérie, and the entire Williams family, especially Heather.

But, in dedication, this volume is for the spirits of the Khmer who perished under Pol Pot and the resourceful souls who survived. 'There's always someone worse off than you, unless you're Cambodian.' (Dr Siri Paiboun, 1978)

ATTENTION: Judge Haeng Somboun
C/O: Department of Justice,
People's Democratic Republic of Laos

FROM: Dr Siri Paiboun

RE: National Coroner

DATE: 13/6/1976

RESUMÉ:

1904   Plus or minus a year - years didn't have such clear boundaries in those days. Born in Khamuan Province, purportedly to Hmong parents. I don't recall it myself.

1908   Whisked off to live with a wicked aunt.

1914   Dumped in a temple in Savanaketh and left to the will of the Lord Buddha.

1920   Graduate from the temple high school. No great feat.

1921   Buddha investment pays off: shipped to Paris by kindly French sponsor intent on making something of me. The French make me start high school all over again just to prove it wasn't a fluke the first time.

1928   Enrol at Ancienne Medical School.

1931   Meet and marry Bouasawan in Paris and join the Communist Party for a lark.

1934   Begin internship at Hotel Dieu Hospital. Decide I might want to become a doctor after all.

1939   Return to Laos.

1940   Frolic in the jungles of Laos and Vietnam. Reassemble broken soldiers and avoid bombs.

1975   Come to Vientiane hoping for a peaceful retirement.

1976   Kidnapped by the Party and appointed national coroner. (I often weep at the thought of the great honour bestowed upon me.)

Sincerely,

Dr Siri Paiboun

CONTENTS

1

HAPPY BIRTHDAY, DR SIRI

I celebrate the dawn of my seventy-fourth birthday hand-cuffed to a lead pipe. I'd had something more traditional in mind; a few drinks with my new wife, some gay mo lum *music on the record player, shellfish plucked fresh from the Mekhong. But here I am in Hades and not a balloon in sight. My ex-room-mate, a grey-faced youth in his early twenties, is chained by the ankle to the far end of the same pipe. They dragged the boy in during the night and we struggled to communicate. We scratched for words to share. But, as soon as he understood that we were different animals in the same abattoir, tears of despair carved uneven grooves down his bloody cheeks. I could do nothing but sit back against the flaking plaster and watch the life drain from him. He didn't live to greet the new day. When the sun finally sneered through the wire mesh of the window, it cast a shadow like a fisherman's net across the body. The corpse lay trapped, expired from the effort of untangling itself from all this unnecessary misery. But his soul was free. I envied him that.*

I am Dr Siri Paiboun, the national and only coroner of the People's Democratic Republic of Laos, a medical man, a humanitarian, but I'm still unable to summon an appropriate emotion. I listened through the night to the sobs and screams of my unseen neighbours. I didn't understand the words they cried but I knew people were being killed all around me. I scented their essence and saw their fleeing spirits. I am well aware that I will soon be joining them. Yet the overriding thought in my mind is that I didn't have the foresight to say goodbye or thank you to the people I love. That sounds corny, I know, but what's wrong with corny? It has its place.

I wonder whether they might know instinctively. Really. I wonder whether they've been able to see through this crusty, annoyingly stubborn exterior to the warm and fluffy Siri that nestles barely visible inside me. If only I could squeeze the hand of Madame Daeng one final time, ruffle the newly permed hair of Mr. Geung, sniff the cheeks of Nurse Dtui and her milk-scented baby, and slap Inspector Phosy on the back. If only I could raise one last glass with my best friend, Civilai. But those opportunities will never come. The amulet that protected me from the malevolent spirits was ripped from my neck, stolen by one of the teenaged guards. I am exposed. Once the ghosts are aware their enemy is unprotected, they will circle me like hungry jungle dogs and close in for the kill.

All things considered, at this almost final analysis, I am stuffed.

The woman read from the carbon copy in front of her. The sheet was of such proportions as to defy filing and of such poor quality that it was almost inevitable the words would be sucked back into the fibres like invisible ink returning whence it had emerged. The clerk had a pleasant voice, soothing like honey balm, and the two old men opposite stared at her luscious lips as she spoke.

'Of course, it isn't finalised,' she smiled. 'But it will certainly read something like this.' She coughed. 'The People's Democratic Republic of Laos would have it known that Dr Siri Paiboun, National Coroner, Hero of the revolution and lifetime member of the Communist Party, passed away on the second of May, 1978. Dr Siri had fought tirelessly and fearlessly for the revolution and was—'

'Fearlessly first,' one of the men interrupted.

'I'm sorry?'

'It would be better to have "fearlessly" before "tirelessly", then nobody would be in doubt he'd not been tired out by the lack of fearing.'

'Absolutely,' the second man agreed.

'What? Hmm. I'm not sure I understand that,' the girl confessed and made a note on the pad beside her. 'I'll mention it to Comrade Sisavee. It is only the first draft but, to tell the truth, we called you in to check on the factual, rather than the syntactical elements of the eulogy. We have people to deal with all the technicalities in later versions. I'll read on if I'm—'

'And, "was struck down dead" has a more heroic ring to it,' the second old man said. 'That's factual.'

'Struck down?'

'Rather than "passed away",' he added. '"Passed away" makes it sound like bodily wind, a collection of stomach gases on their way out. Do you know what I mean? We're talking about heroism here. Heroes don't just "pass" like flatulence in a strong breeze.'

'With or without scent,' added the second man most seriously.

The clerk glared from one old gentleman to the next, then back to the first.

'Are you playing with me?' she asked, sternly.

'Certainly not, sweet young lady,' said the skinnier of the two men. He was bald as a *boule* with a long camel-like throat sporting an Adam's apple so large it might well have been Adam's original. 'This is a most serious affair.'

3

'No playing matter,' agreed the first.

Still uncertain of her ground, the young lady pressed on. 'The nation will never forget the contribution Dr Siri made to the development of this great nation, nor can—'

'That's two nations,' said the bald man.

'Oh, do let her finish,' said the other. 'Didn't she tell you they have a department that handles syntax? Probably an entire ministry.'

'The Ministry of Getting Words Right?'

'Or it could be a branch of the Ministry of Making Things Up and Bamboozling People.'

The clerk was miffed. She slapped the paper onto the wooden table top and drummed her fingers on it noisily. She seemed to be wrestling down a darker inner person. Her voluptuous mouth had become mysteriously unattractive.

'I don't think either of you appreciate what a great honour this is,' she said at last. Her eyes watered. 'Anybody else would be proud. Dr Siri, I'm particularly disappointed that you would take all this so lightly. Given your record, it's a wonder your name is on the list at all.'

Siri raised the thickets of coarse white hair he called eyebrows and scratched at his missing left earlobe.

'To be fair, you're not giving me much time,' he said. 'How can I take life seriously when I'm forced to squeeze all those remaining pleasures into a mere twelve days? And look at this. You're passing me away on my birthday, of all occasions. The happiest day of the year.'

'That's odd, Doctor,' she said through clenched teeth. 'I thought I had explained myself very clearly.'

'Tell him again,' said ex-politburo member Civilai. 'He's elderly.'

'As I said,' she began, slowly, 'the actual date of your death will be filled in later.'

'In the event of it?' Siri said.

'Exactly.'

'So you aren't actually expecting me to . . .'

'No!'

The transparent north-eastern skin of her neck revealed an atlas of purple roads heading north in the direction of her cheeks. The men admired her composure as she took a deep breath and continued.

'You will pass away naturally, or otherwise, as your destiny dictates. At that stage we will delete your date of birth and substitute it with your date of death. When that happens we will issue the announcement. Is that clear now?'

'And I will become a hero,' Siri smiled.

'It probably won't be instantaneous . . . in your case.'

The Department of Hero Creation, the DHC, was housed in a small annexe of the propaganda section of the Ministry of Information. Based loosely on a Vietnamese initiative already in place, the DHC was responsible for identifying role models, exaggerating their revolutionary qualities, and creating a fairy story around their lives. A week earlier, Dr Siri and Comrade Civilai had received their invitations to attend this preliminary meeting. They'd heard of the DHC, of course, and seen evidence of its devious work. Everyone over seventy who'd done the Party the great service of staying alive was under consideration. If selected, school textbooks would mention their bravery. Histories would be written detailing their supernatural ability to surmount the insurmountable and carry the red flag to victory. Siri and Civilai could hardly pass up a chance to scuttle such a nefarious scheme.

'What is my case?' Siri asked.

'What?'

'You said, "in your case", suggesting I have some flaw.'

'Don't hold back,' Civilai urged the clerk.

'It's really not my place to—'

'Go ahead,' Civilai prodded. 'We won't tell anyone.'

She seemed pleased to do so.

'We are aware of the Doctor's . . . problems with authority,' the clerk said. She was now ignoring Siri and talking directly to Civilai. 'But history has a short memory. It has a way of smudging over personality faults, no matter how serious they might be.'

'Voltaire said that history is just the portrayal of crimes and misfortunes,' Siri said.

'And why should I care what a wealthy seventeenth-century snob aristocrat has to say about anything?' she snapped. 'Don't you have thoughts of your own, Doctor?'

Siri smiled at Civilai who raised his eyebrows in return. The old friends were constantly on the lookout for fire, intelligence and passion within the system and, when found, it brought out their untapped paternal instincts. Wrong century, but most cadres wouldn't have known Voltaire from a bag of beans. Their early evening visit to the Ministry of Information had not been a waste of time after all.

Following a politburo decree, the words Minister and Ministry had been liberated from the dungeon of anti-socialist political rhetoric and new ministries mushroomed. There was infighting within each ministry as departments and sections vied for its own ministerial status. Everyone wanted to be a minister. The secretarial pool at the new Ministry of Justice had put in an application to become the Ministry of Typing, and the head clerk, Manivone, put her name down to become the Minister of Changing Ink Ribbons. Dr Siri had helped her with the paperwork and it had taken several bottles of rice whisky to get it right. Of course, they hadn't submitted the form. The system didn't have a sense of humour.

There was nothing inherently funny about the People's Democratic Republic of Laos in the nineteen seventies. The socialists had taken over the country three years earlier but the fun of having a whole country to play with had soon drained away. Euphoria had been replaced by paranoia and anyone who didn't take the republic seriously was considered a threat. Dissidents were still being sent to 'seminars' in the north-east to join the ranks of officials from the old regime who were learning to grit their teeth and say 'Yes, Comrade'. But Siri and Civilai, forty-year veterans of the struggle, were tolerated. They posed no threat to the status quo and their rants against the system could be dismissed – with sarcastic laughter – as senile gibberish. But there was nothing senile or gibberitic about these two old comrades. Their minds sparkled like a March night sky. Given a chance, they could out-strategise any man or woman on the central committee. To find a young crocodile with a good mind amongst that flock of flamingos was a rare delight to them.

'You're quite right, of course.' Siri bowed his head to the clerk. 'Forgive me. I'm prone, like many men my age, to presuppose that young people have no minds. I assume they'd all be impressed with my bourgeois philosophy. You are obviously a cut above the rest.'

'And you aren't going to win me over with your flattery, either,' she replied.

'Nor with pink mimosa, nor sugared dates, no doubt,' Siri added. He thought he noticed a germ of a smile on her lips. 'You really have to see the funny side of all this, you know?'

'And why is that?' she asked.

'You really want me to tell you?'

'Yes.'

7

'Well, I'm tempted to suggest you fabricate people's experiences here. I noticed, for example, that your DHC has Comrade Bounmee Laoly charging into battle armed with only a machete at the age of sixty.'

'A lot of people are still very active at sixty.'

'I know that, but I also happen to know from personal experience he was already blind as a bat when he turned fifty. He couldn't find a machete, let alone brandish one.'

She blushed, 'I—'

'All we ask,' Civilai took over, 'is, should this great honour of herohood befall us – hopefully not posthumously – that we earn it from merit, not with the aid of major reconstructive surgery from Information.'

'We'd like people to remember and respect us for what we are,' Siri said.

'Warts and all,' Civilai added.

Siri and Civilai sloshed and slithered hand-in-hand through the rain to the ministry car park. A cream Citroën with a missing tail light and a sturdy Triumph motorcycle were the only two vehicles. They were parked in muddy water like boats. Drowning grass poked here and there through the brown gravy.

'Smart lady,' Siri said.

'She certainly put us in our places.'

'Nice lips.'

'Exceptional.'

'They did remain clenched when you mentioned your warts, though.'

'They did.'

Civilai opened the unlocked door of his old car and sat behind the steering wheel. Siri climbed into the passenger seat. They sat for a moment staring at the unpainted side wall of the building. As the concrete absorbed the endless rains, Siri fancied he saw the outline of New Zealand stained there, or it could have been a twisted balloon poodle. Following a disastrous year of drought, the farmers had smiled to see the early arrival of the 1978 rains. It was as if the gods had awoken late and, realising their negligence, had hastily attempted to make up for the previous year. The rain fell heavily and ceaselessly – three times the national average for April. The Lao New Year water festival celebrations – a time to call down the first rains of the year – were rained out. The earthen embankments of the new rice paddies were washed flat, the bougainvilleas had been rinsed colourless. The earth seemed to cry, 'All right. Enough.' But still it rained. It was nature's little joke. Like the Eskimos with their four million words for snow, the Lao vocabulary was expanding with new language to describe rain.

Today the water hung in the air like torn strips of grey paper.

'What is that?' Civilai asked.

'What's what?'

'That noise you're making.'

'It's not a noise. It's a song. I have no idea where I heard it. I can't get it out of my head.'

'Well try. It's annoying.'

Siri swallowed his song.

'What do you think they've got on me?' he asked. 'I mean, the DHC.'

'Huh,' Civilai laughed. 'I knew it. You *do* want to be a national hero.'

'I do not. I'm just . . . curious.'

'About your warts?'

'Yes.'

'Oh, where do I start? How about your abrasive personality?'

'Personalities change. And history has a way of smudging my character, don't forget.'

'So I heard. All right . . .' Civilai beeped his horn for no apparent reason. 'There's the spirit thing.'

'How could they possibly know about that?'

'They probably don't know the specifics. Not that you actually chat with ghosties. I doubt they know that. But they must have heard the rumours. This is a small country. People like Judge Haeng must have accumulated a good deal of circumstantial evidence of your supernatural connections.'

'But no proof. By its very nature he can't have accumulated evidence.'

'No.'

'Then they don't have anything.'

'All right. Well, they probably don't like your Hmong campaign, either.'

'It's hardly a campaign.'

'You walked up and down in front of the Pasason News office with a placard saying "WE NEED ANSWERS ON THE PLIGHT OF OUR HMONG BROTHERS". People have been shot for less. You seem to have it in your mind that the government has a policy to intimidate minorities.'

'It does.'

'Well then. With that attitude I can see the central committee making little pencil crosses beside your name, can't you?'

'Things have to be sorted out before it's too late.'

'You're right. If I were the Minister of Pinning Things Onto Chests I'd make you a Knight of the Great Order of Valour right away. Sadly, I'm just a retired has-been.'

They sat silently for another moment, watching the moss grow.

'Thirsty?' Civilai asked.

Siri twisted around on his seat. The leather squeaked under his bottom.

'Perhaps just the one.'

To celebrate their impending hero status, Siri and Civilai partook of one or two glasses of rice whisky at a cigarette and alcohol stand behind the evening market. The proprietor was nicknamed Two Thumbs. A dull sobriquet, one might argue, no more spectacular than a fellow called One Bellybutton or Ten Toes. But Two Thumbs' uniqueness lay in the fact that both of his thumbs were on the one hand. Nobody could explain it. It was as if one of his thumbs got lonely in the womb and swam across the narrow channel of amniotic fluid to keep company with its twin. It was the talking point that attracted smokers and drinkers to his stall. There was nothing else remarkable about him. In fact, he was almost completely devoid of personality, as dull as laundry scum.

The drizzle continued to fall and the old grey umbrellas that offered respite from the hot sun did little to keep out the determined night rain. The straw mats upon which they would normally sit cross-legged had assumed the consistency of freshly watered post office sponges. So the old men each sat on small plastic bathroom stools with a third stool between them as a table. A fourth and final stool offered a perch for their bags and shoes. Two Thumbs sat on a regular chair with his cigarette display case parked upon two building blocks to his left, and his drink selection – actually rice whisky and slightly cheaper rice whisky – neatly displayed in the body of an old TV cabinet to his right. He sat watching over his three-umbrella establishment like a eunuch keeper of the crown jewels, silent and threatening.

'Tell me again why we come here,' Civilai asked.

'The ambiance,' Siri told him.

'Right.'

'And, for this: Hey! Two Thumbs!' Siri called. He and Civilai hoisted a thumb each. Two Thumbs gave them a two-piece thumbs-up with his left hand. It was his party trick. They never tired of it.

'Great!' they shouted, and threw back their drinks. They were on their second bottle and it was a wicked brew only two degrees short of toxic. They splashed their feet like children and wondered what diseases might be lurking there in the dirty ground water.

'I blame the Chinese,' Civilai decided.

'For the rain?'

'For everything. They're responsible for all our ills.'

'I thought that was the French.'

'Huh, don't talk to me about the French. I hate the French.'

'That's most ungrateful of you. They did educate us.'

'Educate? They certainly didn't educate me. I educated myself, little brother. Like you. We just used their schools and their books . . .'

'And their language.'

'And their language, granted. But we used them. We educated ourselves in spite of the French. But the Chinese. They're sneaky bastards. I mean, really sneaky. The French . . . you have to admire the French.'

'I thought we hated them.'

'Hate? Yes. But you can admire people you hate. I admire their tactics. They steamroll in, shoot everyone, take over and treat us all like dirt. You see? You know where you stand with oppressors like that. But the Chinese? All through the war they were building roads. A damn war going on all around them and they have seven thousand military engineers and sixteen thousand labourers up there in the north building roads.'

'That's good, isn't it?'

'Good? Good? It's devious, is what it is. You think they were up there building roads so we could move troops?'

'Yes?'

'No, sir. They were building roads 'cause they knew one day they'd own us. They were putting in their own infrastructure, damn it.'

'Are you sure you'll be able to drive home?'

'No problem. The roads are all canals right now. I just wind up the windows and float home. Where was I?'

'Discussing how to make a good pie dough.'

'Right. Right. So, "the monstrous plot". That's what the Vietnamese call it. The monstrous plot. They've got that right. Those Chinks have got their eyes on us. They're carnivores. As soon as the timing's right we'll all be speaking Chinese and eating the sexual organs of endangered animals. You mark my words. And what's all this Voltaire crap?'

'I suspect you've changed the subject.'

'What do you think you're playing at, quoting Voltaire at a hero interview?'

'I've chanced upon one or two insightful books. I thought a quotation might help in my self-destruction.'

'Oh, I see. One minute you want to be a hero. Then you don't. A hero has to be decisive, Siri. Into that phone box, on with the tights and the cape. Go for it, I say. Whether or not we deserve it is irrelevant. We either vanish into superfluity or we go down in history. Take your choice.'

'Voltaire said the superfluous is a very necessary thing.'

'You're plucking my nostril hair, aren't you?'

They raised their thumbs to the proprietor who responded obediently.

'She did have spectacular lips though, didn't she?' Civilai recalled.

'They took me back, I tell you.'

They waved at the people two mats away who were celebrating a birthday. The group had a glazed bun with a candle in it. These were frugal times.

'I probably shouldn't tell you this . . .' Civilai began.

'Then don't.'

'They've fixed the projector.'

'At K6?'

'They got someone in from the Soviet Embassy. Now, there's another sneaky oppressor, the Russian overlords. Damn these subtle invaders. Good electricians though. Said it was a fuse problem. Fixed it in a minute. And . . .'

'What?'

'There's a showing tomorrow afternoon.'

'You weren't going to tell me.'

'It's invitation only. All the big nobs will be there. Half the politburo. I only got a ticket 'cause the foreign minister is in Cuba.'

'What's showing?'

'Siri, you can't go.'

'What's showing?'

If there were two greater film buffs in Laos they had yet to surface. Since their school years in Paris, mesmerised by the magic of Clair, Duvivier and Jean Renoir, Siri and Civilai had been addicted to the images on the silver screen. Wherever they happened to be they would seek out a cinematic projection. They could happily sit through anything, from the dullest training film such as last week's *The*

Maintenance of Dykes, to a Hollywood blockbuster with Vietnamese subtitles. The old boys had seen them all. And, most certainly, once the scent of cinema was in Siri's nostrils, there was no way they could keep him out.

That annoying song had been playing in his head all the way back but Siri made it home just before the curfew. Across the road on the bank of the Mekhong river, Crazy Rajid, Vientiane's own street Indian, sat beneath a large yellow beach umbrella. He returned Siri's wave. Siri was surprised to find the shutters ajar at the front of their shop. A hand-written sign taped to the shop's doorpost read, 'All welcome in our time of sorrow.' Siri had known Madame Daeng since long before she became a freedom fighter against the French and a spy for the Pathet Lao. But she and Siri had been married only three months. Both widowed, they had recently found one another and a peculiar magic had entered their lives. Not a day went by without wonder. And this odd situation was certainly a wonder. He looked cautiously inside the shop and found a trail of lit temple candles leading across the floor and climbing the wooden staircase. He smiled, locked the shutters, and began to extinguish the candles one by one. Beyond the contented clucking and cooing of the chickens and the rescued hornbill in the back-yard, there was no sound.

He reached the top balcony and entered their bedroom. Madame Daeng sat all in white at the desk with her head bowed. Her short white hair was an unruly thatch of straw. Their bed was illuminated with more candles and surrounded with *champa* blossoms. He laughed, walked across the room and put his hand on his wife's shoulder but she pulled away.

'Don't touch me,' she said. 'I'm in mourning.'

'It's all right. They said I don't have to die right away. They can pencil me in later.'

'I don't believe you. You're the spirit of my heroic dead husband come to taunt me. Be gone with you.'

She waved a lighted incense stick in his direction.

'You do realise there's something disturbingly erotic about all this, don't you?'

'You're an ill man, Dr Siri.'

'And you're a most peculiar wife, Madame Daeng. Do I have time for a bath before I'm laid to rest?'

It was some time around two a.m. when Daeng awoke and sensed that her husband wasn't sleeping. The night clouds had blanketed the stars and moon. Across the river that trolled grimly past the shop, Thailand was enjoying one of its customary power failures. There were no lights skimming across the black surface of the Mekhong. All around them was a darkness so deep it could never be captured in paint. She spoke to her memory of the doctor.

'Not tired?' she asked.

She heard the rustle of the pillow when he turned his head.

'No.'

'That nightmare again?'

'No, I haven't slept long enough to get into a nightmare with any enthusiasm. Daeng?'

'Yes?'

'Do you think I'm hero material?'

'Of course I do.'

'I mean, seriously.'

'I mean seriously, too.'

'They said I have faults.'

'A hero without faults is like an omelette without little bits of eggshell in it.'

He was silent for a few seconds before,

'An omelette with eggshell isn't—'

'I know,' she laughed. 'Look. It's the middle of the night. What do you expect? I'll have a better example for you in the morning. But, yes. You're not only hero material, you're already a hero. It doesn't matter what the idiots at Information say.'

'You're right.'

'I know.'

They listened to the darkness for a while.

'Oh, and by the way,' Daeng said. 'I forgot to mention, Inspector Phosy came by earlier. He wants you to get in touch with him. Said it's urgent.'

'Why didn't you tell me that when I was still dressed?'

'I didn't want you running off and deserting me in my hour of need. Plus, I don't get the feeling it was that type of emergency.'

'What do you . . . ? Oh, you mean the other type.'

'I swear he's turning into a Vietnamese. If it was police business he'd be here banging on the door. But I doubted it was. Everything in his personal life is suddenly urgent.'

'Why on earth does he need to consult me on domestic issues? You were here. Why couldn't he ask you for advice?'

'He's a man, Siri. You lot still aren't ready to admit in front of a woman that you're clueless.'

'How did I ever make it through seventy-three-point-nine years without you?'

'I think I got here just in time.'

'I've a good mind to invite you to the cinema tomorrow.'

'We haven't got a cinema.'

'K6. They've fixed the projector. There's a film showing in the afternoon. A romance, according to Civilai.'

'And we have tickets?'

'Not exactly.'
'I rather saw that as a yes or no question.'
'Then, yes.'

2

THE TRAIN FROM THE XIANG WU IRRIGATION PLANT – THE MOVIE

Dr Siri and his good lady waltzed in through the double doors with such confidence and aplomb that the quiet usher didn't dare ask to see the tickets they didn't have. There were polite, nostalgic greetings from the old politicians who stood in the side aisles mingling. There wasn't one of them who hadn't tangled with Siri at one time or another, so their offers of, 'We must find some time to get together so our wives can become acquainted' had as much life expectancy as storm ants. The women looked down their noses at Daeng's ankle-length *phasin* skirt. There was an accepted socialist mid-calf standard these days which supposedly allowed freer movement to labour for the Party. Daeng had refused to cut her beautiful old skirts and, had anyone asked, she would have reminded them you couldn't do much hard labour in a skirt whatever its length.

Had he been a more diplomatic sort, a man of Siri's calibre would have soared heavenward through the ranks of these old soldiers. A forty-eight-year Communist Party member-ship and a degree in medicine from Europe had to count for something. But there wasn't a person in the room he hadn't belittled or insulted. A man with no mind to compromise is condemned to sit in the back stalls watching the stars on the screen. So, after a few brief and unnecessary bites at conversation, Siri and Daeng seated themselves in the eighth row chewing on sweet chilli guava and waiting for the show. There was a mumbled comment from the projectionist and the audience, very noisily, took to its seats. Civilai arrived late. As it was impolite to push his way along the rows to an empty place, he accepted a supplementary fold-up chair from the usher and sat to one side. He didn't seem particularly surprised to see Siri and Daeng. Siri casually mentioned to Daeng that their friend had his shirt buttoned incorrectly.

Although the gathering was missing a president, a prime minister and three politburo members, if a person happened to have anti-communist leanings and a large bomb, this would have been a particularly fruitful place to explode it. The room was a Who's Who of leading cadres, high-ranking officials, ministers, Vietnamese advisors, and foreign ambassadors. Judging from the turnout, it appeared there was a large population of dignitaries starved of entertainment.

The main feature was a Chinese film entitled *The Train from the Xiang Wu Irrigation Plant*. The cultural section of the Chinese embassy had gone to a good deal of trouble in first translating, then applying Lao language subtitles to several of their popular films. In a back room, half a dozen Russian-language spectaculars, also with Lao subtitles, lay waiting for their opportunity to bedazzle the Lao leaders. For the cinema fan, being a political ping-pong ball had its benefits.

The lights were doused and a small window someone had forgotten to board over was quickly patched. The conversations subsided to a mumble. Siri held his breath waiting for that magical sound that announced the coming; the clack, clack, clack of the film through the projector. And there it was. The screen was blasted with light and the film leader numbers began to flash before them. If Civilai had been beside him, they would have counted aloud together, 'eight . . . seven . . . six.'

Following what feels like a day and a half of credits, the film finally opens in a busy urban train station. The vast majority of extras milling about on the platforms are in uniform. Everything on the screen is either spearmint-chewing-gum green or stale-tobacco brown. Even the train standing in the station seems to have been spray painted to reflect the green/brown ambiance of the scene. Suddenly, there's a flash of red, a small communist flag rises above the heads of the sombre crowd. We pan down to see a hand clutching the bamboo stick that the flag is attached to. It works its way forward like a bloody shark-fin churning through a green-brown sea. At last we see that holding the flag is a stomach-curdlingly beautiful young lady, Ming Zi, in the uniform of the Chinese People's Revolutionary Army. She anxiously scours the faces of the passengers alighting from the train. A slightly off-key string orchestra is somewhere behind her, lost in the crowd. Her face is a live pallet of clearly recognisable emotions: elation, frustration, false hope, disappointment. Until we finally cut to her alone on a porter's cart. We zoom in to a close-up of the flag on her lap. Tears fall onto it like raindrops, staining it drop by drop – through the magic of special effects – from brilliant red to chewing-gum green. To add insult to her injury, the porter steps up to Ming Zi and reclaims his cart. The broken-hearted girl walks forlornly along the deserted platform as the sun sets in the sky behind her. It is an uncommonly chewing-gum green day in Peking.

Siri squeezed Daeng's hand, his eyes already damp with sympathy for his heroine. It promised to be an eleven-tissue movie. But they were barely ten minutes into it when a side door opened and a uniformed Vietnamese entered the theatre. He walked brazenly into the bottom right-hand corner of the screen and stood there like an extra staring into the audience. Some of its members told him to sit down. But he was obviously not interested in the film or the admonitions. He located the person he'd been searching for, pushed along the row and leaned into the ear of a broad man with a tuft-of-grass haircut. By now, all eyes but Siri's and Civilai's were on the drama in silhouette. Ming Zi had been abandoned. The seated man nodded and turned his head to search the audience. The Vietnamese stood to attention mid-row caring not a jot that he was ruining a perfectly good film. But, by now, everyone sensed the urgency of his mission. To Siri's utter dismay, the broad man pointed to the doctor and rose from his seat. The soldier shouted in Vietnamese above the soundtrack, 'Doctor, come with us.'

Siri remained in his place, attempting to concentrate on the story on the screen. There was nothing he detested more than not being allowed to watch a film to its natural conclusion. In his mind there was no emergency so great as to deprive a man a cinematic climax. The broad man and the soldier had pushed their way to the far aisle where they both stood looking at the doctor.

'Doctor Siri,' the broad man barked.

'I think you'd better go,' Daeng whispered in Siri's ear.

'And insult the director?'

'Well, darling, we're only ten minutes into the film and I'd wager the director's artistic integrity has already been compromised by Chairman Xiaoping. And, besides, it might be a medical emergency.'

Heads were beginning to turn in Siri's direction.

'Damn it,' he snarled. 'All right. But I expect a detailed blow-by-blow account of the whole thing later.'

'In colour,' she promised. Siri huffed and bobbed and bowed his way to the end of the row.

He followed the two men precariously across a walkway of wooden planks on bricks that criss-crossed the flooded sports field. The two men introduced themselves as they walked but neither could be described as friendly. The stout man was called Phoumi, and he was the Lao/Vietnamese head of security at K6. He insisted that he'd met the doctor before but Siri had no recollection. The uniformed Vietnamese officer said his name was Ton Tran Dung and that he was the officer in charge of the Prime Minister's team of bodyguards. Following six assassination attempts, the politburo had decided to assign an elite ten-man Vietnamese army unit on twenty-four-hour watch over the Lao leader. They were supported by a counterpart team of ten Lao People's Liberation Army personnel. Siri had sought out none of this information and wasn't all that interested. His mind was still firmly entrenched in the mystery of how the lovely Ming Zi was ever going to find her lost fiancé.

But, as they walked through the American streets of K6, he soon became enthralled by this small corner of Lao Americana. Forty acres of suburban USA had been plonked down in the middle of rice fields and fenced in to keep out (or, Civilai argued, *in*) the riff-raff. There was certainly a cultural force field around the place. During the height of the Vietnam War, the United States Agency for International Development had four hundred personnel in Laos, three times that if you counted the CIA, but nobody ever did. Their role was mostly economic, juggling five-hundred million aid dollars. There were some showcase development projects, and seemingly endless refugee relief programmes.

LOVE SONGS FROM A SHALLOW GRAVE

Over a million Lao had been displaced by the civil war in the north and the royalist ministers, spilling in and out of the rotating door democracy, had been too busy amassing fortunes to find time for actual aid work.

So, USAID served as a surrogate Ministry of the Interior, and where better to return to after a hard day of running a country than a little slice of the American dream right there in the third world? K6 had its own high school, commissary, stables, scout hut, tennis court, and youth club. But most of all, K6 had gardens; neat napkin lawns and pretty flowerbeds and fences around houses that would be perfectly at home in the suburbs of Los Angeles. The christening of K6 had always baffled Siri given that the place had been planned, designed and built by and for Americans. He'd always expected they'd call it Boone City or Tara or Bedford Falls. But no, K6 it had been named and K6 it remained today.

Once the Americans were evacuated in seventy-five, almost the entire Lao cabinet selected themselves a home on the range and moved in. Other regimes might have burned the compound to the ground as a show of anti-US sentiment, but the Pathet Lao retained an admirable practical streak. Initially it was an act of arrogance as much as a desire for western living, although some of the politburo members seemed to be getting a little too comfortable with their washing machines and barbecues. Some had rescued the rose bushes and tomato plants and weren't ashamed at being seen mowing their own lawns.

Siri and his guides turned left on 6th Street whose sign was far more pretentious than the street itself. The words 'No Thru Road' were stencilled on a short board opposite. The drainage system was doing a good job of keeping the roads flood-free. There were only four ranch-style houses on the cul-de-sac. Each of them was undergoing repossession by Mother Nature. It was into the first of these jungle bungalows that Dung led Siri and the security chief. Twice, Siri had asked what it was all about and twice he'd been ignored. He wasn't in the best of moods. The constant drizzle had soaked into his bones. They walked through the open front gate and turned, not to the house, but towards the carport. An overhead fluorescent lamp flickered and buzzed like a hornet in a jar. It was mid afternoon. Siri wondered why they hadn't turned it off.

At the rear of the carport was a small wooden structure, two-by-two metres, two-and-a-half metres tall, with a sloping concrete tile roof. A Vietnamese security guard stood at ease in front of it with his pistol holstered. Major Ton Tran Dung nodded at the soldier who produced a torch from his belt and handed it to his superior officer.

'There's a light inside,' Major Dung said, 'but the bulb appears to have burned out. It was the smell that alerted our patrol.' Siri had picked up on it even before they turned into the street. It was an odd combination of jasmine and herbs and stewed blood.

'Our protocol is that if anything odd comes up, they're to contact me directly,' Dung said. 'So I was the first one to go into the room. I came over as fast as I could, noticed the heat and the scent of blood, then I opened the door and that's when I found her.'

Chief Phoumi grabbed the torch from Dung and grimaced as he did so. Siri noticed a bandage beneath the cuff of the man's shirt. Phoumi used his other hand to pull the wooden handle. An overpowering stench appeared to push the door open from the inside. Siri felt a wave of warm air escape with it. Inside, the box was dark, lit feebly by what light could squeeze through a small air vent high in one wall. But it created only eerie black shapes. Phoumi turned on the torch and he and Siri stepped up to the doorway. The beam immediately picked out the naked body of a woman seated on a wooden bench. At first glance, she appeared to be skewered to the back rest by a thin metal pole that entered her body through the left breast. A trail of blood snaked down her lap to the floor.

'Do we know who she is?' Phoumi asked Dung.

'Yes, sir. Her name is Dew. She was one of the Lao counterparts on the bodyguard detail. New girl. She went off shift at seven yesterday evening. Didn't report in for duty this morning. And—'

The major gestured that he'd like to talk privately.

'Excuse us, Doctor,' Phoumi said, and walked towards the house where he huddled with the Vietnamese. He'd taken the torch with him so all Siri could see by the natural light through the door was a bloodied towel, crumpled on the floor at the girl's feet. Instinctively, he knew it was important in some way. The two men returned and Phoumi handed Siri the torch.

'All right, Doctor?' was all he said.

Siri was fluent in Vietnamese and he was used to the brusqueness of the language, but he was struck by how unemotional these men had been.

'Yes?' Siri said.

'Perhaps it would be appropriate if you inspected the body. Just to be sure, you know?'

'To be sure she's dead, you mean?' Siri smiled. 'She's got a metal spike through her heart. I think you can be quite sure she won't recover.'

'Then, time of death, physical evidence, anything you can come up with will be useful.'

Siri shrugged and walked carefully into the room.

Although he'd suspected as much, it was obvious that this was a sauna, albeit a small, hand-made variety. He'd sampled one himself during a medical seminar in Vladivostok. In a Russian winter the sauna had been a godsend, but, in tropical Laos where a five-minute stroll on a humid afternoon would flush out even the most stubborn germs, it seemed rather ludicrous. An old Chinese gas heater stood in the middle of the floor surrounded by a tall embankment of large round stones. A bowl of dry herbs and flowers sat beside it on the wooden planks. Siri presumed it had once contained water or oil but, if so, the liquid had evaporated away. Moisture and pungent scents still clung to the ceiling and the walls.

There were two benches – one low, upon which the body now sat, and one opposite about fifty centimetres higher. Siri placed the torch on the floor and knelt in front of the victim. He put his hands together in apology before beginning his examination. The weapon, which from outside had appeared to be a metal spike, was in fact a sword. To be more exact, it was an épée. Siri knew it well. His high school in Paris had provided after-hours classes in swordsmanship. It was a course the doctor had failed – twice. He hadn't been able to come to grips with all that delicate prancing and twiddling when the underlying principle must surely have been to kill the opponent or be killed. Despite the fact that he'd continuously overpowered his sparring partners, he'd ultimately been expelled from the class. The instructors had cited his two-handed running charge and his cry of 'Die, you bastard,' as reason enough to deny him a passing grade.

Yes, the weapon here with its broad-bulbed hand guard was certainly an épée. He couldn't recall having seen one in Laos before. It entered the woman's chest between the fourth and fifth ribs. It had most certainly punctured her heart. The trail of blood had drained from the wound, down her stomach, across her thigh and into a large puddle on the wooden floorboards at her feet. He felt her joints. Rigor mortis begins to show after two hours and peaks at twelve. Judging from the stiffness, it was Siri's educated guess that the poor woman had died somewhere between ten p.m. and two a.m. As he seldom carried his rectal thermometer to the cinema, that was as close as he could get for now.

He reached behind her and confirmed that the sword had been thrust with such force that it had impaled her against the wooden bench. The serene expression on her face and her relaxed sitting position told Siri that she was either looking forward to the experience of dying, or that the attack had come as a complete surprise. There were no indications she'd been shocked to see the weapon, or made any effort to save herself. Her eyes were closed and there was a curl at the corner of her mouth that could once have been a smile. He was about to turn away when he noticed a fresh scar on the inside of her right thigh. There was very little bleeding, which suggested it had been inflicted after her heart had ceased to beat. It was in the shape of an N or a Z, hurriedly carved on her skin.

Which brought him back to the towel that lay at her feet. It was stained with blood but the corners confessed to its original whiteness. Siri couldn't see how it fitted into the scenario. Whose blood was this? Did the assailant attempt to staunch the flow? Or, during the attack, did the murderer injure himself? Siri turned to the seat opposite. There were no bloodstains. This was presumably where the murderer had sat, he and his victim both naked, enjoying a sauna on a rainy Friday night. He tried to imagine the scene. They would have put their clothes outside under the carport to keep them out of the steam. In that case, the carport light would have been turned off or they'd have risked being discovered. So why turn it back on again when it was all over? And where were her clothes? And, the twenty-billion-kip question, where, in a box with two benches and a gas heater, would you conceal a ninety-centimetre-long sword? He began to test the wooden slats of the walls to see if there was a secret compartment, but Phoumi poked his head into the room.

'Doctor? Have you finished examining the body?' he asked.

'Yes, I was just—' Siri began.

'Good. Then I think you can tell us your findings and we'll handle everything else.'

Siri shone the torch into the security chief's face.

'I assume, by "handle everything" you mean contact the national police force so they can conduct an inquiry?'

Phoumi laughed rudely.

'They'll be informed of the findings, of course,' he said. 'But this whole area is under my jurisdiction, and the victim is a member of our security team. We'll take care of it.'

Siri abandoned his search and stood in the doorway.

'This may look like a foreign country,' he said. 'But the fact remains we are still in Laos and the victim is a Lao.'

Phoumi's smile, his body language, and especially the way he reached for Siri's arm and squeezed it were all so conde-scending Siri had a mind to knee him.

'Then, if it is indeed a Lao problem,' the chief said, 'I suppose we should let the Lao Prime Minister decide what is appropriate. You will take his word on it, I assume?'

'He's home?' Siri asked.

'His house is a few blocks from here.'

Siri knew where the PM's house was. He'd been there a number of times. But that wasn't an answer to the question he'd asked. He walked out of the sauna and sat on the step.

'Well, of course, the word of the Prime Minister is more than enough for me. Let's go and see him.'

He swore, if Phoumi laughed again . . . If he flashed those 'everybody's friend' perfect teeth just one more time, Siri would run inside, remove the épée from the corpse and find a warmer scabbard for it.

'Doctor, surely even you understand that the PM can't just receive unscheduled visits,' said the security head. 'Even with an appointment it could be two or three days. I tell you what, I'll go and see him and bring his response. That good enough for you?'

In fact, Siri understood a lot of things. He understood, for example, that the PM had given up his ticket to the movie that afternoon because he was on an unannounced visit to the USSR. He'd left for Moscow the previous day. It helped to have a man on the inside even if it was only Civilai.

'Then I think you should go and talk to him,' Siri agreed. 'I'll wait here.'

Phoumi was incensed.

'I hadn't realised how much more complicated you'd make things for us. I wanted a medical opinion, not a stand-off,' he said. 'Couldn't you just take my word for it that your leader will ask us to take care of this? Do we really need to disturb him?'

'I think so,' Siri smiled.

Phoumi and the tall, lanky Major Dung hesitated, then walked off with great reluctance to their fictional meeting with the absent prime minister. Siri was left alone with the sentry. The soldier looked uncomfortable. Siri decided to take advantage of the fact nobody had introduced him and act like someone of importance. He walked to the edge of the carport where the rain fell in strings from the corrugated roof. He washed his hands under them.

'Been a long day, I imagine,' he said.

'Yes, sir.'

'Were you on the detail that discovered the body?'

'I was, sir.'

The boy hadn't looked once into Siri's frog-green eyes.

'Must have been a shock. Did you know her?'

'She's new. Didn't speak a lot of Vietnamese. Friendly enough though.'

'And nice looking.'

'Not bad, sir. Not really my type.'

'I gather your patrol was just strolling past and somebody smelt something odd. Is that right?'

'Not exactly, Comrade. There was no patrol scheduled. The major sent us out specially.'

'Major Dung?'

'Yes, sir. I gathered there'd been a report of something odd over in this sector. He sent half a dozen of us down to take a look.'

'That's a lot of men – I mean, just for taking a look.'

'Probably thought there was a security breach.'

'I imagine.'

'And we got down here and we could all smell it; sickly, sweet smell.'

'Who went in first?'

'None of us. We knew the stink only too well. One of the men went back to get the major. The rest of us hung around outside. When he arrived, he went to the door and took a look inside. I was standing behind him. I saw the girl. Shocking, it was.'

'When was this?'

'I don't know. About half an hour ago . . . an hour?'

'And Major Dung went straight over to the cinema to find security chief Phoumi?'

'So it seems. He sent the other men back to the barracks and left me here to watch the crime scene.'

'Good. Very good. And, apart from the major, nobody else went into the box?'

'No, sir.'

'Any idea who reported the "something odd"?'

'You'd have to ask the major that.'

'I'll do just that. I imagine he'll be back very soon. I just have to go and see someone for a minute. Tell him I'll be right back.'

'I will, sir.'

'By the way, was this overhead light on when you got here?'

'Yes, sir.'

Siri walked out into the drizzle and headed across Sixth Street. He had a cinematic urge to take out an umbrella and dance in the puddles but not the stomach for it. He also had a very strong feeling that he'd just been lied to.

They've transferred the manacle to my left hand and put a restraint around my ankles: two parallel metal bars with chains as heavy as doom that keep my feet forty centimetres apart. They came a few hours earlier, the boy guards, and nailed plywood across all the windows. Since then the fluorescents have been burning continuously and I have no idea of time. I'm covered in flea and mosquito bites and it's taking all my will power not to scratch myself raw. In fact I should have paid more attention at the temple when I was a novice. In a situation like this I really could use an off switch. This would be a good time to step outside my body.

The teenage guards bring me rice gruel that tastes of motor oil and vomit. But I have to eat. Bad nutrition is better than none at all. They bring a bucket too, as if I can perform here and now. The first time that happened, I started to explain the natural process of excretion, that the body needs seventy-five hours to process food. But one of the boys rammed the butt of his pistol into the side of my foolish head and I was suddenly flapping around inside an aviary of bats and black-birds. When I came round, the bucket and the unruly youth were gone. I can feel my head now. It's swollen to the size and shape of a pomelo. At first I thought I might be enjoying one of my fabulous nightmares. But the lump and the pain and the blood on my shoulder aren't imagined. Of course, that doesn't make this any less of a nightmare.

Behind me on a long, scratched and partially burned blackboard there are ten chalked sentences that I can't read. When my ex-roommate first arrived, they forced him to recite the sentences aloud. The man was barely able to see through his swollen black eyes. They kicked the words out of him. I closed my eyes and diverted my mind from the awful sounds by thinking about language. I'd always thought of it as a friend. It's guided me through life and shown me new directions. Each new language I learned added to me. I'd become richer. But a language you don't know, sir, that is one mean, unfriendly son-of-a-bitch. It's rude and secretive and it pushes you away, keeps you on the outside. And that's where I am now, on the outside. Not knowing what's going on makes my teeth curl in frustration. I've been grovelling for a quote about language to make myself feel more secure, but nothing comes to mind. It was true what the clerk said. I don't have any thoughts of my own.

At some time when I was asleep or unconscious, they took out the corpse. I'm alone now. I mean, in body. As you know, in spirit it's getting a bit crowded in here. Look at you; old, far too young, pregnant, bedraggled, innocent, pleading, but all of you unmistakably confused. You sit

33

cross-legged staring at me, you spirits of the dead, as if expecting me to entertain you, expecting me to have answers. But forgive me, I'm not on top of things enough to know what the questions are. I don't yet understand why I'm here or what's expected of me.

The smiley man came this afternoon ... or evening, whichever it was. He was so polite I was certain this was all some terrible mix-up.

'You must be in pain,' he said in basic high school French. 'Never mind. You'll feel better soon. I'm so sorry for all this inconvenience.'

The words dribbled with insincerity but that brief sharing of language buoyed me. It allowed me to step briefly back inside. He left me a pencil, not sharpened to a point, and a sheet of lined paper torn from a school exercise book. I fired questions at the man's back: his name, where he'd learned French, what he did, where we all were. But, once the smiley man had given his oh-so-polite speech, his duty was done and he clicked the door latch quietly behind him. I remember you smiled then, you spirits – ironic smiles, every one of you.

They're still here, the pencil and paper, untouched on the chequered tiles by my right hand.

'Your story,' the smiley man said. 'Just tell us your story and you'll be free to go.'

I sit with my back against the wall, staring at the door. I sigh. I reach for the pencil, angle the paper towards me and begin to write,

'Once upon a time there were three little pigs ...'

Dr Siri sat beneath the blazing white strip lights in the morgue at Mahosot. Soviet funding had led to the rewiring of a number of the old French buildings and the three technical advisors who'd come to install the lights insisted that it was vital in a hospital to have a minimum of 73 RNO or BZF, or some such twaddle, of visibility. He had no idea what that meant apart from the fact that if the Great Wall of China was visible from space in daylight, the Mahosot morgue would be a glittering beacon at night, visible from even the most distant solar system. He wore his old sunglasses to reduce the glare and decided that, on Monday, he'd borrow the hospital stepladder and remove two of the parallel tubes before everyone received third-degree burns.

Fortunately, he wasn't called upon that often to work at night. Even for the living, nothing was that urgent in Vientiane. The dead could always keep for another day. But this had been an exceptional day, and an exceptional case. The poor lady who lay on her side on the cutting table in front of him had been the centre of a political storm for much of the afternoon and evening. Siri had, of course, called Inspector Phosy from the nearest telephone he could find in K6. The inspector was the man responsible for all police matters concerning government officials. Phosy and two of his colleagues had jumped into the department jeep and sped to the scene of the crime.

There followed an unpleasant stand-off during which both the Vietnamese security personnel and the Lao National Police Force had stood toe to toe insisting that they had jurisdiction over the crime. Until it was sorted out, Siri wasn't allowed to remove the body to the morgue and the victim voiced her discontent by smelling violently. The Vietnamese called in reinforcements from their embassy. The police called in the military. It was starting to look as though 6th Street would be the scene of a new Indochinese war were it not for one simple fact. The movie ended and the polit-buro members, strolling off their stiff legs, came upon the stand-off.

'Don't be ridiculous,' they said. 'Of course this is a Lao matter. Enough of this nonsense.'

Broken Vietnamese faces notwithstanding, the matter was finally resolved. On their way back in the jeep, police inspector Phosy had appeared to be as annoyed with Siri as he was with the entire nation of Vietnam.

'Did I do something wrong?' Siri had asked.

'No.'

'Come on, Phosy. Something's eating you with a fork.'

'You didn't get my message last night?'

'The "need to see you urgently" message?'

'Yes, that one.'

'Not until early this morning. Madame Daeng saw it as an amber rather than a red alert.'

'Oh, did she? And this morning?'

'I had a swimming lesson.'

'Don't make fun of me.'

'I'm serious. The Seniors' Union has a class on Saturday mornings. They cleaned all the gunge out of the Lan Xang pool.'

'You're learning to swim, at your age?'

'I've found the god of drowning is particularly insensitive to the age of his victims. I've had one or two narrow escapes in water lately. I thought it was time to master the element. And if I suddenly have the urge to swim across to Thailand, I could—'

'And your swimming lesson took precedence over my request to see you?'

'Phosy, you have to admit you've become a little oversen-sitive since you became a father. You've had me drop everything and rush to the police dormitory for . . . for what? A little wind? A touch of diarrhoea? A small—'

'You can never be too careful.'

'Your wife's a nurse. And she's a very competent one. She can handle all these things.'

'Dr Siri, Dtui comes from a bloodline of disaster. Her mother lost ten children during or shortly after birth. Our country has a horrible record. Twenty per cent of kids don't make it to their first birthdays. Forty per cent don't reach eleven.'

'And I guarantee not one of them had a mother who was a qualified nurse and a father who could afford to put regular meals on the table. The only danger little Malee has, as far as I can see, is that her father's going to coddle her to death. Tell me, what was last night's emergency?'

'If you aren't going to take it seriously . . .'

'Come on. I'm listening.'

'She's yellow.'

'All over?'

'It's hepatitis.'

'What does Dtui say?'

'She doesn't know. She's got other things on her mind.'

'What does she say?'

'She said it's the light through the curtains.'

'What colour's the curtain?'

'White.'

'Phosy?'

'Creamy white.'

'It's yellow, Phosy. I've seen it. Yellow with cartoon dogs or some such.'

'The baby still looked yellow when I took her outside.'

'Then stop taking her outside. Goodness, man. It's the rainy season. She'll catch a real disease. Then you'll have something to complain about.'

Phosy hadn't appreciated the lecture. He'd sent two of his men with Siri to offload the corpse and retreated to his office to write his angry report. Madame Daeng had taken the motorcycle home from K6. Siri would be a little while settling poor Dew in at the morgue, then he'd walk back. He wished he could be home with his lovely new books but he needed time alone with the corpse to organise his thoughts. Dew still had a lot of talking to do, he decided. She knew her killer. That much was certain. Their midnight sauna pointed to the possibility that they were lovers. This rendezvous, he decided, was passion. The type of passion that makes you crazy enough to risk your career and your freedom for a few moments of pleasure. When he was young, Siri had known that passion himself.

He hadn't had time to search for a false compartment in which the killer might hide a sword. But he was convinced he wouldn't have found one. If you were planning to kill a lover, there were far more convenient – and much shorter – weapons that would have been easier to conceal. It was almost as if the épée was symbolic, perhaps even part of the ritual. He wondered if the épée was the message itself. What if it wasn't hidden at all? What if the girl knew she was about to die? Had she wanted to be killed? Had she brought it herself?

As often occurred in these confusing, ghost-ridden years of his life, Siri felt a familiar anger. He was the host, like it or not, of a thousand-year-old Hmong shaman by the name of Yeh Ming. It was like a gall-bladder infection, but of the soul. There was nothing tangible inside to operate on. He was stuck with this presence and still hadn't mastered the art of living with his ancestor. He'd wondered often whether the fault lay in his failure to grasp the true essence of religion. If he'd been a better Buddhist perhaps he could beat the eight-fold path to his spiritual back door, burst into the projection booth and catch old Yeh Ming tangled up in a thousand years of celluloid. Couldn't they then have sat down together, organised everything into reels, and canned and labelled them? Neither of them would have been confused. Then perhaps, just perhaps, he'd have some control over the spirits that flickered back and forth across his life. Perhaps Dew's soul could stroll up the central aisle and calmly explain why she was lying before him with a sword through her heart.

But, as it stood, Siri's connection to the afterlife was held together with old string. And, once again, he had to resort to the resources of his own mind, cover the dreams and premonitions in a blanket, and look at the facts. See what was right there in front of him. He used a pair of salad tongs to pick up the towel from its steel tray. That towel had worried him since he'd first seen it. What was it doing there on the floor covered in blood? No, not covered exactly. He laid it out across the second gurney and looked at the pattern. It was less saturated than he'd first thought. The blood had gathered at the centre like an ink blot test and all the corners but one were white. It didn't make sense to him. If it had been used to clean up after the murder, the stain would be patchier, streaked. This looked as if blood had merely seeped into it from one corner.

If he'd been in France or England he could have taken samples of the woman's blood, and samples from the towel, rushed them off to Serology and had a result – match or no match – before dinner. But he was in Laos and what Mahosot Hospital classified as a blood unit was old Mrs Bountien and an antique microscope. And she had a market garden of yams to look after so she only came in on Mondays, Wednesdays and Fridays.

Siri considered walking over to the dormitory and inviting Mr Geung to help him with the autopsy but he decided to let his assistant enjoy his leisure hours in peace. Siri turned on the noisy Russian air-conditioner, put on his attractive green Chinese overalls and his rubber gloves, and turned towards his corpse. Dew had the build of a short, 48-kilogram-class weightlifter. She was attractive but not classically pretty. She was strongly built, not unlike Siri's first wife. He got the impression she could have looked after herself in a struggle. He took hold of the handle of the sword and was beginning to wonder whether he'd have the strength to remove it.

'Y . . . you'll hurt your b . . . back.'

Siri turned and smiled. The Mr Geung radar never failed. Siri only had to stroll past the morgue on a weekend and Mr Geung would know. He'd be there like a shadow beside him. The morgue and the life and death it contained was Mr Geung's home.

'Mr Geung,' said Siri. 'Looks like we have a guest.'

'You didn't . . . didn't call me.'

'What for? You have the nose of a dog, my friend. I knew you'd be here.'

'Ha, I have a dog nose.' Geung sniffed like a bloodhound and walked to the storeroom to put on his apron. Canine sniffs and grunts and laughter emanated from behind the door. His condition was really only a problem to other people, those who felt uncomfortable around him, people like Judge Haeng. But Mr Geung pottered around inside his Down's Syndrome taking pleasure from simple things, enjoying the love he felt from his morgue family, doing his job. And his job was to assist Dr Comrade Siri. But the doctor couldn't help but notice there was something oddly different about Geung today. He decided he would bring it up once their work was done.

Siri held on to Dew's shoulders while Geung, in one glorious Excaliburic flourish, grabbed the handle bowl in both hands and yanked the épée from her chest. Siri looked at the congealed blood trail that led from her heart. He picked up the towel and spread it across her groin, lining up the stains like a piece of a large puzzle. It fitted but it didn't solve anything. He was almost convinced the blood on the towel had come from the deceased. It had clearly been on her lap at some stage. But, what he couldn't explain was why the towel was stained but had not been saturated by the considerable flow of blood that would have gushed from the wound. Nor could he imagine why it was on the floor when they discovered the body. There had been no blood on Dew's hands.

The autopsy took the standard two hours and produced no astounding revelations. She was fit, healthy, and had, at some stage, given birth. She had been killed almost immediately the sword pierced her heart and she had probably felt little pain. The murderer had either known exactly where to find the heart, and been skilful enough to impale it, or he had been very lucky. The shallow N or Z mark on her thigh was another matter. Siri knew it had not been inflicted by the sword as there had been very little bleeding, barely a trickle. The épée must have killed her first. But this meant the killer must have used a different weapon to sign his work. From the width of the cut and the condition of the skin, Siri assumed a small flat-bladed knife had been used, perhaps a sharp penknife. But it was a hurried, botched job. A last-minute thought perhaps? No. The killer had gone to the trouble of bringing the knife. Why hurry the final touch? Was he disturbed? Frightened? Disgusted at what he'd done? Siri hated autopsies that left more questions than answers.

For want of a police forensic investigation unit, Siri took the liberty of dusting (as they called it overseas) for fingerprints. He had a fine mixture of chalk and magnesium prepared for just such an eventuality. Despite the fact that he and Geung had been very careful not to touch the sword handle, it yielded no prints. Either it had been wiped clean or the killer had worn gloves. Perhaps a lesser investigator might have given up at that point, but Siri, guided by the guile of his hero Maigret of the Paris Sûreté, continued his curious dust down the shaft. And there he found it. One clear print at the top of the blade. He was proud of himself but had no idea what to do with his find. There may have been some simple way of recording the print but he hadn't yet learned that skill. So he put the épée on the top shelf in the storeroom and hoped the ceiling lizards wouldn't lick away his evidence.

Two tasks remained. Firstly, he would return to the scene of the crime and search for a hiding place for both a sword and a knife. Secondly, whilst there, he might even have another conversation with the Vietnamese guard who'd been given sentry duty in front of the K6 sauna. And then there was one more, very serious matter, not related to the murder. He walked to Geung who was scrubbing the overalls in the deep tub.

'Mr Geung,' he said.

'Yes, Comrade Doctor?'

'Your hair.'

Geung smiled. 'I . . . I'm very sexy.'

'Who did that to you?'

'It . . . it . . . it's a permanent wave. Nurse Dtui put it o . . . on my hair.'

'And you let her?'

'I'm very ss . . . sexy.'

'Irresistible.'

'Thank you.'

'I think we need to have a word with Nurse Dtui.'

3

GRUEL AND UNUSUAL

Not for any religious conviction, Sunday was a day of rest in Vientiane. It had certainly been the Sabbath when the French oppressors ruled the roost and it was a habit that carried forward even after the churches were closed and the preachers sent on their way. Although they would never admit it, there was a number of reasons for communist Vientiane to stick with old colonial trends. In fact, historically, had it not been for the French, there would have been no Vientiane in 1978.

In the sixteenth century the Lao king had moved the capital from Luang Prabang in the north to a run-down, almost indefensible ancient kingdom on the bank of the Mekhong. With all the advisors at his right hand, one might surely have mentioned the fact that on the far bank of that same river – a stretch of water sometimes so low and slow you can wade across it – lived the Thais: the mortal enemy of the Lao. To nobody's surprise, Vientiane was sacked on a number of occasions and finally left in ruins. Only its old stupas and one temple remained standing but even these had been tunnelled into and looted by scavenging Chinese bandits. And there the old city rotted, strangled by the encroaching jungle, ignored, until deep into the nineteenth century.

Enter the French. Following a treaty with the Siamese, the east bank of the Mekhong was ceded to the invaders from Europe. Vientiane was dug from the forest, replanned and rebuilt in French colonial style. Temples grew around the crippled stupas and That Luang, the soul of the Lao nation, was recreated from French missionary etchings of centuries past. The buildings were a confused mismatch of Asian frugality and modest European splendour. It was a typical South-east Asian city as conceived on a budget on a drawing board in Paris. Just as in Saigon and Phnom Penh, the colonists had always known what the locals wanted better than the natives knew themselves. And the children grew up believing that this was their style, their architecture, and they were annoyed that the hokey temples didn't make any attempt to fit it. But there it was, voilà, la nouvelle Vientiane, renamed to accommodate the French inability to pronounce the original name: Viang Chan.

And now, that same Vientiane which had once been consumed by jungle was being washed away by unseasonal and unceasing rains. Like ice-cubes in a sink, the buildings seemed to be melting away, first their mustard colours, then their shapes. The streets of brown mud melded into the shop fronts and invaded front yards. The heavy hibiscus bushes sagged and spread and blended together like slowly collapsing jellies. And, in their still-religious hearts, the Vientonians, who had prayed for rain for most of the previous year, were beginning to pray for it to stop.

Sunday was the day that Daeng shut her noodle shop and she and Siri would spend all their time together. Since the early rains had begun to thunder down on the city, just negotiating the motorcycle around town had become an adventure. There were potholes so deep it was believed they tunnelled all the way through to Melbourne, Australia. There were stretches of mud so slick it was like riding on hair oil, spots where you couldn't tell the road from the river. It made the city they lived in a wonderfully unpredictable place. On this particular Sunday their plan had been to have no plan. They might just slither around town or chance the northern road to Thangon and enjoy a fish lunch by the ferry crossing. Or they might hit a submerged rock and spend the day in a motorcycle repair shop. It didn't matter either way as long as they were together.

But Inspector Phosy had other plans for them. They were eating their pre-Sunday adventure breakfast behind the loosely pulled together shutters when they heard a thump against the metal.

'We're closed,' Daeng called.

'Siri, it's me,' came Phosy's voice.

The doctor thought he heard the splash of disappointment dropping into his belly. 'We're shut anyway,' he said. Then, under his breath he whispered to Daeng, 'A million *kip* says it's gripe.'

'Don't,' Daeng said. 'He's just a concerned father.'

'He's a . . . Ah! Phosy. Come in. Had breakfast yet?'

Daeng was already dishing out an extra bowl. Phosy had squeezed in between the shutters but paused there and gazed back towards the river bank.

'Did you know Crazy Rajid is camped opposite your shop?' he asked.

'Yes,' Siri nodded. 'He's been there on and off for a month.'

'We're assuming he's watching out for Siri,' Daeng added. 'Of course, it's hard to tell for certain.' She put the bowl of rice porridge on the table and poured a glass of fresh orange juice from the jug. 'We're guessing he thinks he owes us a debt of gratitude.'

'For saving his life? Well, he should,' Phosy said coldly. 'I can't think of anyone else who'd go to so much trouble to help a fool.'

Rajid was certainly crazy – mad as a lark – but he was no fool. He had migrated to the region from India with his father, mother and three siblings. The ship they travelled in went down in a heavy sea and only Rajid and his father, Bhiku, had been spared. The disaster had turned the young man's mind and he never again spoke to his father. The old man, who worked as an underpaid cook at the Happy Dine Indian restaurant, was still of the opinion that his son had been struck mute. But Siri and Phosy had heard Rajid speak, and the young man wrote weird but wonderful prose in Hindi. No, there was a good deal going on in the Indian's mind, not a fool at all. But, seeing Rajid camped out in the pouring rain beneath a beach umbrella night after night, a person would have to believe there were power lines down somewhere between his brain and his common sense.

Phosy paused and watched the Indian playing with a toad. To the policeman's mind, the two creatures were equally mindless. He shook his head and came to sit at the table. Once there, he said nothing and tucked into the meal as if he had a reservation. Daeng smiled at Siri.

'What brings you out on a drizzly Sunday morning, Inspector?' she asked.

'Bad news,' Phosy said. 'As if we haven't had enough. We've found another one.'

'Another what?' Siri asked.

'Another dead girl.'

'Lord help us,' said Daeng.

'Fully clothed, this time,' Phosy said between spoonfuls. 'Wearing a tracksuit. We found her in a school classroom. But it was a sword. Just the same as the girl yesterday. Through the heart.'

'When did you—' Siri began.

'Two hours ago. The head teacher at Sisangvone primary

school went in early to prepare for the Sunday Junior Youth Movement meeting and he found her in the room skewered to the blackboard.'

'Through the heart?' Siri considered the scene. 'So she was standing? Held up by the sword?'

Phosy nodded.

'That must have taken a lot of strength,' Daeng thought aloud.

'Is she still there?' Siri asked.

'No,' said Phosy. 'We took her over to the morgue. We got Director Suk out of bed and had him open up for us. Sorry. I know this is your family day . . .'

'I can't understand what's happening to this country,' Daeng sighed. She had already abandoned her breakfast, along with her hope for mankind. 'It's not even May and we've had seven murders in the country already this year. And all women. It's almost as if Laos is doing its utmost to keep up with North America. Vientiane is turning into New York City.'

'Madame Daeng,' Phosy said. 'Seven murders in New York would be one slack afternoon. We have a long way to go before things get that bad.'

'I'm sorry, Inspector,' she said. 'But seven murders is seven murders too many as far as I'm concerned. We've had our wars. We've killed our brothers because this or that politician or general told us to. But it's over. Can't we enjoy our peace yet? Can't we stop all this insanity?'

'I agree,' Phosy said, rising from his seat and wiping his mouth with a tissue. 'And there's no time like the present.' He drained his glass of juice and nodded. 'Thank you for breakfast. Doctor?'

Siri hurried upstairs to change and followed Phosy to the morgue on his Triumph. As Phosy's Intelligence Section had used up its petrol allowance for the month, Phosy was on the department's lilac Vespa. For once, Siri thought it wise not to make fun of the policeman about his effeminate mount. This was a different Phosy from the man he'd befriended two years earlier, from the cheerful policeman who'd married Siri's assistant, nurse Dtui. Something had happened. A peculiar intensity had landed on Phosy like an enormous blot and suffocated his sense of humour. Siri wondered whether it was the job, whether it had started to infect him. Confronting the face of evil in so many dark corners had to have an effect; dealing daily with the depraved. For a man who'd grown up believing that the Lao were inherently good and kind, it must come as a shock to learn that his fellow man and woman were just as capable of committing atrocities as the foreign devils.

When Siri arrived at the morgue, Mr Geung, Phosy's Sergeant Sihot, and nurse Dtui were there in the office waiting for him. Phosy followed the doctor inside and was obviously surprised to see his wife there.

'Where's the baby?' he asked Dtui accusingly.

Dtui smiled. It was a smile which usually made people feel at ease but it apparently had little effect on Phosy.

'She's at the Sunday crèche,' Dtui said.

Siri noticed Phosy jerk his head towards the door as if he wanted to talk to his wife out of earshot of the others. Everyone noticed the gesture, including Dtui who chose to ignore it. Phosy, obviously frustrated, was forced to resort to a strained laugh and a warning couched as a joke.

'You do know our daughter's only three months old?' he mumbled to the woven plastic rug.

'And what better time to start socialising?' Dtui said.

It was clear that if they'd been alone, a serious domestic dispute would have exploded at this point. Siri, it was, who snipped the red wire.

'We have a body in the cutting room,' he said. 'It's Sunday and everyone's irritable, especially me. The sooner we get this over with, the sooner we can return to our loved ones.'

It almost worked. Everyone snapped into action apart from Mr Geung who stood rocking in the corner by his desk. This was peculiar given that he usually led the charge into the examination room.

'Mr Geung?' said Siri.

'I . . .'

'Yes?'

'I . . . I don't have.'

'Have what, Geung?'

'A . . . a loved one.'

There was no sadness in his words. It was merely a statement like not having a bicycle or change for five hundred *kip*. He lived in a dormitory with three other male hospital employees and hadn't seen his distant family for a year. Siri could have ignored the comment and joked about it, but, were this a movie, it was the point when the audience would have broken into a spontaneous 'ahhh' and some old lady in the front row would cry loudly into her handkerchief. Although Siri was certain he felt much worse than Geung about this state of affairs, or lack of, he walked across the room and put his arm around his friend's shoulder.

'Little brother,' he said. 'There are forty nurses working at this hospital and I know for certain every one of them is in love with you.'

'It's d . . . different love,' Geung said immediately, as if he'd put many hours of thought into the mechanics of love.

'It's better love,' Siri stepped in. 'It's permanent. It has nothing to do with changing moods and passion.' As soon as the words left his mouth, Siri realised that passion was a concept that would take more years of understanding than the doctor had left on the earth. 'It's better.'

'It-it-it's better,' Geung repeated. But like a philosophical parrot he added a line of his own. 'Better than a real g . . . girlfriend.'

'Much better,' said Siri with little conviction. He walked them both into the next room but his mind lagged a few steps behind. Once again, increasingly happy to unload the weight of the world onto his own shoulders, Siri decided to see what he could do about finding Mr Geung a girlfriend . . . whether he wanted one or not. It couldn't be that difficult, he decided. As simple as pulling together the banks of the Mekhong to reunite the Lao and the North-eastern Thais.

Once again the autopsy was straightforward. Siri estimated the time of death to have been around nine p.m. the previous evening. The young woman was probably in her mid thirties, very attractive, in good physical shape but soft, not the same taut muscles of the previous victim. She had been killed by one single thrust of an épée that passed directly through the centre of her heart. As with the other girl, there were three lines etched onto the inside of her left thigh. This time the signature was more clearly a Z. The killer would have had to pull down the nylon tracksuit bottom to make his mark. He'd taken his time on this one and, as there was very little bleeding, it had obviously been cut there after the girl's death. Sergeant Sihot assured him the victim had been properly attired when she was discovered. The mark brought to Siri's mind the brand of Zorro, the masked swordsman, a part played so convincingly by Douglas Fairbanks.

Siri dusted the épée for prints but it yielded none. He had Geung put it on the shelf beside the first weapon and the body joined its predecessor in the morgue freezer. The bamboo tray Siri had built himself had been replaced by a Chinese stainless steel retractable shelf unit that could, at a pinch, accommodate three bodies in the single cooler.

Siri, Dtui, Civilai (who had been alerted to the new murder by Daeng when he stopped by the shop), and the two policemen sat in the morgue office drinking lethal Mahosot hospital coffee and eating Civilai's homemade brownies. The chocolate chips tasted a little like shotgun pellets but hospital coffee had a reputation for dissolving anything.

'So far,' Sergeant Sihot began, 'we haven't been able to identify this second victim. We're working on it. Nobody's reported a missing person as far as we know. But we have amassed a good deal of information about victim number one.'

He flipped open his notepad and all the pages fluttered onto the floor. The others helped him retrieve them but it took him a few minutes to put them in order.

'Sorry. Thank you,' he said at last. 'Have to get that fixed. All right. Victim number one is . . . was Hatavan Rattanasamay. Known by the nickname of Dew. She's twenty-nine years of age . . . I mean, she was.'

'Sihot, will you forget tenses and just give us the facts?' Phosy snapped.

'Yes, Inspector. Born in Bokeo. Married with two children. Her husband Chanti was . . . I mean, is chief engineer with Electricité du Lao. Dew returned from the Soviet Union in January this year. She'd just completed a four-year course in internal security in Moscow. Before she left she'd been a lieutenant in the People's Revolutionary Army. When she got back she'd done so well they promoted her to the rank of major and assigned her to the Prime Minister's security detail.'

'Any connections with fencing?' Civilai asked.

'We're waiting for the military to release her records,' Phosy answered. 'We do know that she took a number of physical fitness and self-defence courses. We just aren't sure which ones she enrolled in.'

'How did you get the personal information if the army hasn't released her file?' Siri asked.

'From the husband,' Sihot told him.

'Any emotions?' Dtui asked. 'Was he distraught? Bawling his eyes out?'

Sihot thought back to his interview.

'No,' he said. 'He seemed quite calm. Cheerful even.'

'His wife's just been killed and he was cheerful?' Dtui asked.

'The man just discovered his wife was with a strange man, naked in a . . . a steam room at two in the morning,' Phosy cut in. 'I can see a case for saving face during an interview, can't you?' Siri noticed a glare shared between the couple.

'Any views on who the lover might have been?' Civilai asked.

'I have to say the Vietnamese security people aren't the most forthcoming group,' Sihot confessed. 'In fact, they wouldn't speak to me. I got the odd brief grunt from the Lao security chief, Phoumi, but he wasn't very helpful. I got a feeling they're all holding something back. I did have more luck with the Lao counterparts on the bodyguard team. The Vietnamese didn't give them much of a direct role, it seems. There was a comment that our people are treated more like civilian security guards than trained soldiers. And language was a problem, too. Dew had Russian, as did a few of the Vietnamese, so she acted as a translator from time to time. Mostly the "Tell them to do this or that" kind of thing.'

'How many women are there on the Lao team?' Dtui asked.

'Two others beside Dew. One on the Vietnamese detail.'

'Any inappropriate advances from the men?' Siri asked.

'Not from the enlisted men,' Sihot recalled. 'I got the feeling they felt intimidated by Dew. Plus she was married.'

'Not the enlisted men?' Siri pushed. 'But something from the officers? Major Dung?'

During their brief encounter the previous day, Siri had gleaned the impression the Vietnamese was something of a playboy. He had that cinema idol sleaze to him. He was used to getting his way with women.

'He did try it on with one of the Lao girls,' Sihot said. 'She wasn't interested. Or so she told me.'

'And they didn't share a common language,' Civilai reminded them. 'He wouldn't have been able to pile on the charm. But with Dew he could communicate directly.'

'Do we know anything about Dew's marriage?' Dtui asked. 'Was it a happy one?'

Again Phosy jumped in. 'She'd left him with two kids for four years. A man might take objection to being treated like a babysitter while his wife went off to play in Europe. What do you—'

He was interrupted by a loud crunch. Sergeant Sihot had bitten into a chocolate chip and a corner of one tooth had snapped off. The policeman retrieved it from the debris and held it up proudly. His smile revealed that this wasn't the first time his teeth hadn't been up to a challenge.

'No worries,' he said. 'Happens all the time. Teeth like chalk, my wife says.'

'Sue the bastard, Sihot,' Siri laughed. 'Comrade Civilai shouldn't be allowed in a kitchen. His wife would be only too glad to get her oven back, isn't that right, old brother?'

Civilai blushed slightly but ignored the question and continued to gather the threads of the investigation.

'As I see it,' he said, 'we already have two suspects. Not bad after only one cup of coffee and one injury. We have the playboy Vietnamese major who sweeps Dew off her feet and causes her to risk her career for an hour or two of lust. And we have the husband, torn with jealousy, who watches his wife sneak off for her tryst and then, when she's alone, steals in to kill her.'

'I don't think we should narrow the field so soon,' Dtui decided. 'A smart young woman has lots of opportunities for an affair in this day and age.'

Only Siri caught Phosy's expression at that moment but it was one of unmistakable fury.

'You're right,' Civilai decided. 'I think we need to focus on the fencing connection. This is Laos. We are a small country at the edge of the world. Your average Lao wouldn't know an épée from an eggplant. I say we find anyone with a fencing background and we'll have our murderer. He can't be that hard to find.'

'I wouldn't rule out foreigners either,' said Siri. 'I noticed one or two fair heads strolling around K6 yesterday. We should find out which European advisors have permission to be out there.'

'Chief Phoumi has made interviewing at K6 very difficult,' Inspector Phosy conceded. 'They don't want us out there.'

'Hmm.' Civilai scratched his chin stubble. 'Now *that* I think I might be able to help with. I'm having dinner with the president this evening, just the two of us. And I'll be taking a couple of bottles of very good wine from my secret cache. I wouldn't be at all surprised if we could wrangle the security chief's full cooperation.'

Siri frowned. 'Brother, I've known the president for thirty

years. He's never once invited me for dinner. What's your secret?'

'I'm an agreeable person, Siri,' Civilai boasted. 'And I know when to keep my mouth shut.'

I emerge from a shallow sleep surrounded by the same type of inky darkness in which Daeng and I had awoken a few weeks earlier. A few weeks that have stretched into an infinite number of years. That night still full of hope and love. That night long before I arrived in hell. But, unlike that night with my wife's hand in mine, this dark surrounding me holds no promise. It's murky and hangs in the air with menace, like a vampire's cape. I've endured the endless hours of brightly burning strip lights and not known whether it was day or night. I've begun to babble to myself. To count seconds and minutes. To recite The Prisoner of Zenda *aloud in French, hoping it will all stave off the inevitable disorientation. It worked briefly. But now they're screwing with my confused mind by introducing a never-ending night. Cunning bastards. Or could it be a power failure? Have the captors' evil plans been thwarted by an unpaid electricity bill?*

'Keep it to yourself, Siri.'

They've already punished me for my flippancy. 'The Three Little Pigs' seems to have pushed them to their limits. They haven't beaten me or cut me with their thin bamboo canes. I have already endured those horrors alongside my unseen neighbours. It's as if I can feel as well as hear their punishment. But my minders are depriving me even of the sensation of pain. Instead they've removed gruel from the menu. And, as gruel was the only thing on that menu, I am now surviving on an occasional cup of water. And my sense of smell tells me what they've done to that water. But, didn't fakirs in India drink their own . . . ?

'Sustain, Siri. Take whatever they give you for sustenance.'

When the lights were still burning I was able to add the modest nutrition of cockroaches to my cocktail. Steve McQueen taught me that trick. Papillon.

'Your time will come soon enough, Siri,' Steve tells me. 'Your opportunity to die heroically. Take down six of the blackguards with you as you fight for your life.'

Perforated postage stamps with my face peering out. Primary school textbooks telling of the day Siri took down twelve, no, fifteen armed guards as he fought for his freedom. Siri the hero. A band around his head. 'Fifteen in one blow.' The year 2010. 'Yes, my grandfather knew Dr Siri Paiboun. He massacred entire armies with his bare hands. They finally finished him with a poisoned épée through the heart. It was the only way you could bring down a Siri.'

I have been catching myself more frequently engaged in such prattle, but I can only blame that Siri fellow. No self-control. Showing weakness. I'm open to attack. My protection against the phibob *is gone but they haven't yet come. They haven't begun to torment me into harming myself, or stopped my heart from beating as they do to the day labourers in their sleep. Busy, no doubt, troubling the souls of all those who are dying in this school building. This rotten school building.*

'A school? Surely a school is a place for growing . . . for acquiring. Surely a school should be a step forward, not a step back. A place for giving life a kick-start, a push, a roll. Surely a school shouldn't be the last place you see in your life?'

'I was a teacher,' the smiley man said in his neat but unexpressive French.

Surely not here. Surely not in this 'end of everything' high school.

'I learned more as a teacher than I ever did as a pupil,' he said. 'I learned that students need guidance and sometimes that guidance has to be cruel in order for it to be effective.'

'I'm not your student,' I told him. 'I'm your superior.'

Yes, I'm the grand emperor of knowing when to keep my independent mouth shut.

'If that's true,' said the man. 'Why are you in chains while I am free to walk out?'

'Because you're a despot,' I told him, 'and despots act out of panic. History shows us that a tyrant's reign is short because it's conducted in an atmosphere of fear. You'll always be looking over your shoulder. You'll always make mistakes. Despots invariably end up with a burning poker up their rear ends.'

The smile on the face of the smiling man sagged momentarily. Then, from the cloth bag over his shoulder he produced another sheet of paper and another pencil. He held them out to me.

'My student,' he said, 'you would be surprised how few people in here get a second chance. But I believe that even the most naive student wouldn't fail to learn from a mistake. And so I am giving you a second chance. If you get it right this time it will make your passage to freedom very simple. I can even give you the answers to your examination questions and you can walk from the room with a degree and honours.'

I had to laugh at that. I said, 'Great master, tell me the answers. Show me the light.'

The last of the unconvincing compassion drained from the man's eyes.

'You are a foreigner,' he said. 'And we don't want to involve you in our struggle. All you need to do is write what *my superiors want to read and you are free to return to your country.'*

I took the pencil and paper and sat poised to write.

'I'm ready, oh masterful one,' I said.

'All I expect is that you tell us your real name and describe in detail when the Vietnamese first recruited you as a spy. Tell us the name of your coordinator in Hanoi and what information he told you to gather. As simple as that. You write it. We file it. You go home.'

I did my best to match the man's smile tooth for tooth. And, yes, I did, I considered writing his confession. I wondered what the odds were of being released if I made up a story and names and places. But, deep in my soul, I knew there was no point. They could either execute me as a confessed spy or just shoot me or torture me to death as the fancy took them. I've heard and seen too much of what they're doing here. I will never see the outside of this school.

'Any chance of a bit of lunch before I start?' I asked. 'Writing fiction can really take it out of a person.'

The man sighed and carried his heavy smile to the door. He stood there and watched me tear off strips of paper and put them into my mouth.

'It has no nutritional value, of course,' I told him between mouthfuls. 'And all that glue and chemicals won't do me a lot of good. But it should quiet the grumbling in my gut for an hour or two. If I close my eyes it's just like eating noodles.'

The smiling man slammed the door behind him.

It's dark now and I feel an ache in my stomach. I wonder whether it's dark because I ate my homework and I'm being punished, or because the world has come to an end and there's nobody to turn on the power. And as I lie back contemplating being the last person on earth, starving to death in a classroom, something moves in the darkness and takes hold of my hand.

'. . . and he was dead.'

'He was dead?'

'Completely.'

'He was dead?'

'Is your needle stuck?'

'What happened to the Hollywood ending?'

Siri and Daeng lay on their mattress. It was one a.m. Whatever bribes needed to be paid to whomever on the Thai side of the river had been paid and the street lamps burned yellow there. The glow shimmied across the Mekhong and crawled up the Lao bank. Despite the drizzly clouds that masked the starry sky, there were no longer any completely black nights. Even by the dim light that filtered through the rose-patterned cotton curtains Siri could see his wife clearly and she could see him. There would be no mistaken identity on that bed.

'It wasn't a Hollywood film, dear husband,' she reminded him. 'It was pure Chinese propaganda and Wei Loo was dead as a beefsteak by the end of it.'

'But Ming Zi had spent two hours looking for him.'

'Tough! It epitomised the futility of false hope.'

Siri sat up on his elbows and was starting to wish he hadn't chosen this time to have Daeng tell him the story of the movie he'd missed, *The Train from the Xiang Wu Irrigation Plant*. He couldn't hide his devastation.

'But what's the message?' he asked. 'Struggle, struggle, struggle and you'll end up with a dead boyfriend?'

'All right. I'm not quite at the end of the film yet. Wei Loo had died constructing a dam. We get this in flashback through sepia lenses. There'd been a freak flash flood and he'd rushed to the site, rescued all his colleagues, and sacrificed his own life to prevent the dam being washed away. Once she'd recovered from the shock, Ming Zi understood there was more to life than personal relationships. She realised that love for a mega-project and the development of the country was more satisfying than mere love for another human being.'

'Rot.'

'She found solace. As, coincidentally, she was also a qualified hydroelectric engineer, she applied for the position of project coordinator on her fiancé's dam. Of course she didn't play the sympathy card. She didn't tell anyone who she was. She was appointed purely on her qualifications and experience. She was a conscientious worker, very popular with the men and women under her. But on the eve of the grand opening of the new dam . . .'

'Oh, don't tell me.'

'. . . there's another storm and another unprecedented flash flood.'

'Which had been precedented.'

'Exactly.'

'And Ming Zi saves the planet.'

'Just the dam and twenty comrades.'

'Of course she dies?'

'Penultimate scene.'

'Holding a red flag?'

'She was underwater but she held on to it.'

'And the closing scene?'

'The grand opening of the Xiang Wu Irrigation Plant with the lovers' photographs displayed on easels on either side of the starter button.'

'Reunited in death. Oh, I wish I'd seen it.'

'Everyone was in tears.'

'I bet.'

'Even the Chinese ambassador and he'd seen it twice.'

Siri sighed and rolled off the bed.

'If only life were a film,' he said. 'Birth, life, love, adventure and death in under two hours. Nothing superfluous. Succinct, simple dialogue. Nothing boring. No roles for characters outside the main plot.'

The window was open and rain dribbled down from the top awning in strings of pearl droplets. Through them he could see Rajid sitting on a stool under the umbrella on the river bank.

'He still there?' Daeng asked.

'At least he's under the umbrella now.'

'Did he eat his supper?'

'I can't see the plate. Do you think he ever sleeps?'

'What's he doing?'

'It's dark but if he's doing what I think he's doing, I don't think you'd want to know.'

'Virile young man, isn't he?'

'Very.'

He was about to make a comment like, 'Perhaps we should find him a girlfriend,' but it occurred to him he was slowly sliding into the role of auntie to the masses since he'd married Daeng. He wanted to help everyone; Mr Geung, Phosy and Dtui, the Hmong, the starving people in Bangladesh, whales, and now here he was fretting over a street Indian. How would he ever find a mate for a non-speaking, self-abusing flasher from Delhi? Not even beautiful Ming Zi with her perfect skin could find true love. Siri started to wonder whether he was the only lucky romantic on the planet. No, he couldn't find romance for Rajid but he could attempt to replace the blown fuse in the relationship with his father. A young man shouldn't go through life hating someone who loves him. Siri had attempted to talk to Rajid before but not with any great belief in his own ability. Now, after several evenings with Sartre he was beginning to believe anything was possible, or at least, that if he didn't solve problems himself, nobody else was going to solve them for him.

'Won't be a minute,' he said, heading for the door.

'Take an umbrella.'

Daeng was always one step ahead of her husband.

Siri joined Rajid under the beach umbrella. They were sharing a small rainless cylinder of space and the little man was unpredictable. Sometimes he'd sit with you. Others he'd run and hide like a street cat. This was a sitting night.

'OK, Rajid,' said Siri, sinking down to squat on the back of his heels. 'Let's assume you understand everything I'm saying because I think you do. I know you can write because your father translated your poems for me. And if you can write, you can think, *ergo*, you can understand.'

Rajid's concentration was already flagging. He seemed to be looking around for some other place to be.

'And, let's assume,' Siri continued, 'that you're here watching over me because you're grateful that I saved your life. By the way, I'm glad I did save your life because I think it's a life worth saving. We'd all be sorry not to have you around. But you're right. You owe me. A life is a big debt to owe so I'm asking you to repay that debt. I want you to talk to—'

Rajid sprang from his seat as suddenly as a cricket, but Siri had been expecting it and his reflexes were still sharp. He caught hold of the Indian's wrist and held it tightly. Rajid squirmed and growled like a trapped animal but Siri wasn't about to let him go until he was finished with his speech. He anchored his free arm around the umbrella stem and focused on his breathing until the wild man calmed down. It took some while.

At last, Siri continued, 'I want you to talk to your father. I know you can speak. I've heard you. Your father didn't kill your family, Rajid.'

The man shook violently but couldn't break the doctor's grip.

'The ocean killed them,' said Siri. 'The unsafe, unregistered boat killed them. Fate killed them. Hate all of those if you like, but not your father. He suffered even more than you when it happened. But every day he sees you like this he has to relive your family tragedy. I know you see it too. I know you have that same nightmare. I know what you saw disconnected some mechanism in your head and I'd bet you're as confused as anyone can be. But your father loves you and you're breaking his heart by punish—'

Rajid wrenched his arm from Siri's grasp and twisted his lithe body. He crashed into the umbrella and sent it tumbling into the damp undergrowth. His body fell sprawling onto the mud but he recovered before the doctor could get his bearings and scurried down the river bank and vanished in the darkness. Siri sighed, righted the umbrella and collected the plate of half-eaten dinner. He trudged back towards the shop and looked up to see Daeng enjoying the show from the upstairs window.

'Nicely done,' she called.

4

BILLBOARD TOP TEN

The rain had let up briefly sometime on the Monday morning and the toads and frogs were yelling their delight like an orchestra of bedsprings and didgeridoos. All along the river bank young children in their school shirts were scooping the happy beasts into cardboard boxes and cement sacks and escorting them home to the larder. With so little to be had at the fresh market, families grew whatever they could around their homes, raised chickens and improvised. A lot of the stomach-turning but nutritious fare once considered the mainstay of the ignorant country folks had made a comeback on the kitchen tables of the city.

Toads, if one remembered to remove the poisonous skin and eggs, tasted vaguely of duck. *Pa dtaek,* fermented fish sauce, was so pungent it had to be stored in earthenware jars as far from the house as possible. Snakes made an interesting stew. Then there were the little creepy critters; fat white grubs that smelt bad but tasted fabulous, scorpion claws, fried termites, beetles, grasshoppers, and the absolutely delicious – Michelin five star – red-ants eggs: squishy heaven in every bite.

As Siri walked along that oh-so-noisy river bank on his way to work, he saw a pelican gliding above the surface of the water. It was a marvellous bird, proud and resourceful, and he imagined how it would taste with a little chilli

paste and fresh yams. Hungry people made poor environ-
mentalists.

Before reaching the hospital he passed two of the new billboards. If 1977 had been the year of the drought, 1978 had
to be the year of the government billboard. They'd sprung up
everywhere urging the population to work harder, be honest,
love the nation, and grow bananas. A kind critic might have
called the artwork naive. Siri had three or four adjectives of
his own to describe it. He believed if some archaeologist four
hundred years from now were to uncover only billboards as
evidence of an ancient civilisation, they would be forced to
assume the Lao had been a wooden, asymmetrical, poorly
proportioned race with no necks. Their schoolchildren, even
at seven or eight years of age, had the traumatised expressions of forty-year-old addicts. And there was no way to
distinguish between male and female adults apart from hair-
styles or hats. Short-haired, hatless beings were asexual.

If there had been a department of billboards somewhere,
it was very likely vying for the role of ministry because it was
frighteningly prolific and without shame. At the entrance to
the lane leading to Vientiane's largest mosque was a board
encouraging everyone to breed pigs. Not twenty metres from
the Lao Patriotic Women's Association was another board
proudly boasting 'WOMEN – DEVELOPING OUR
COUNTRY AS MOTHERS AND LABOURERS'. Siri had
hoped the rains would erase all the silly propaganda and let
the population think for itself. But they were standing up to
the weather better than the leaning front fences and posts.

Inspector Phosy and Sergeant Sihot were waiting for Siri
beneath the arch at the mouth of the lane that led into the
hospital. The water was ten centimetres deep there and both
men had their shoes in their hands and their trouser cuffs
rolled up.

'Couldn't you have found a drier place to wait?' Siri asked.

'Your hospital's under water,' Phosy complained. 'Anywhere else and we'd need oxygen tanks. Are you ready?'

'Ready for what?' Siri asked.

'We thought you'd like to come out with us to visit the crime scenes,' Sihot said.

'You have permission from K6?' Siri asked.

'Must have been good wine,' Phosy said.

It was fortunate that the Intelligence Section's Willy's jeep had a high wheelbase and four-wheel drive because the road out to K6 was porridge. Phosy drove slowly and Siri sat in the rear seat with Sihot, catching up on the news of victim number two. Sihot was a solid, military type, more chipped out of rock than created. You wouldn't want to hit him on the head with a mallet for fear of damaging the mallet. He lost one page of his notebook in a stormy gust of wind but he assured Siri it contained nothing of any importance.

'Victim number two,' he read, shouting above the roar of the troubled engine, 'named Khantaly Sisamouth, nickname, Kiang. Age thirty-two. Single. Born in Xieng Khaw, way up north. Taught primary school in the liberated zone for ten years then was sent to Bulgaria to study library science.'

'Who did she offend to get that assignment?' Siri asked.

'It sounded like hell to me, too, Doctor.'

'Library science in Bulgarian. Poor thing.'

'She was there for two years and came back with what they call a certificate in information technology.'

'And how did you identify her?'

'Her mother, Doctor. Said her girl hadn't come home on Saturday night. She filed a missing person report at the local political office and they contacted us. She identified her daughter from our Polaroids.'

67

'Did she know where Kiang went to on Saturday night?'

'She had no idea, Comrade. Told the mother she was off for some exercise in the evening. She was all dressed up in her tracksuit. Mother's just recovering from hepatitis so she went to bed early. When she woke up the daughter's bed hadn't been slept in.'

'Any connections between the two victims?'

'None that we've found apart from them both studying in the eastern bloc.'

'Lovers? Friends? Fencing connections?'

'We're looking into it. Right now, that's all we've got.'

As if to emphasise the point, the next half-empty page flipped from his notebook and curled away in the slipstream of the jeep.

At K6, a very reluctant Comrade Phoumi was there to meet them. The rain had started again, a depressing northern European sprinkling. The guards from the PM's protection team were lined up in front of the sauna. But, with so much military testosterone on display, there wasn't one umbrella between them. Dr Siri, who had fewer problems displaying his feminine side, emerged from the jeep hoisting a bright yellow umbrella with orange toadstools and lime-green goblins. No words were spoken.

Phoumi and Major Dung led the way to the door of the bungalow in whose yard sat the carport and the sauna. The windows were all open to ventilate a house that had obviously not been occupied for some time. Phosy and Sihot sat at the kitchen table with their notepads and it was agreed the security personnel would come to be interviewed one by one. As had been hastily arranged, Comrade Viset, a Vietnamese-speaking Lao attached to military intelligence, was to act as translator. As the first two interviewees were

Phoumi and Dung, an atmosphere of belligerence and non-cooperation was established early on.

Siri was not privy to the events in the front kitchen. He had been encouraged by Phosy to 'float around' and pick up information outside. The unguarded sauna structure was his first stop. Somebody had replaced the burnt-out bulb, probably the investigators. He turned on the light and sat on the lower bench. As he studied the simple packing-case structure he became more and more convinced that neither of the weapons, the knife nor the épée, could have been concealed. For confirmation, he prodded and poked every wooden slat, every roof tile, every floorboard. It was what it appeared to be, a wooden box with a gas tank and a pile of stones. No secret compartments. No trickery. But, just as the burning light in the carport had worried him two days earlier, the light inside the sauna now gave him the same troubled feeling. The light had been switched on and had burnt out. It seemed very likely that once he had done the job, the killer had turned on both lights to . . . what? To attract attention? Had he wanted the body to be found quickly?

Siri went outside and located the Vietnamese sentry he'd spoken to on Saturday. He was standing towards the rear of the interview queue and Siri pulled him to one side. The doctor had a theory and he was about to test it with a blatant lie.

'We have a problem,' Siri said to the young man after a few niceties. 'I believe you know what that problem is.'

The soldier looked at Siri and hesitated before he spoke.

'I don't understand, sir.'

'You told me you'd stood behind your major and seen the state of the girl inside.'

'So?'

'There was no light inside. From a metre beyond the

doorway you couldn't have seen anything but her feet. Everything was in shadow. No windows.'

'I saw her.'

'I believe you did, but not then. Once he'd witnessed what was inside that room, the major closed the door and came looking for the head of security. He left you there and told you not to let anyone in the sauna.'

'That's right, he did.'

'And everyone left, apart from you.'

'What are you trying to say?'

'That you were curious, so you went in and took a peek for yourself.'

'That's a lie. No, sir. I would never do that.'

'Is that so?'

'It is.'

'Then, you see that up there?' Siri pointed to a box attached to one of the posts that carried the power cables.

'Yes.'

'You know what that is?'

'It's a junction box.' The soldier was sweating.

'Is it? You forget where you are. You've heard of the CIA, I assume?'

'Of course.'

'Then you know what they're capable of. They're fanatical about surveillance. Every house in this compound has a camera and microphone trained on it. You see that lump at the bottom?'

'It . . . it's a nut.'

'Of course it's supposed to look like a nut. It's a closed-circuit camera lens. The images are all fed back to a central console behind the scout hut. You're a TV star, my boy.'

Siri was holding his poker hand – six high – and he was calling. There followed a tense moment of silence.

'I just wanted a quick look,' the soldier confessed. Siri sighed but kept quiet. 'I wanted to . . . you know? I was curious. I didn't . . . I didn't do anything.'

'But you removed the towel from her lap.'

'I just slid it down a little bit, that's all. And it slipped between her legs. I was about to put it back but I heard you all coming along the street. I barely made it out in time.'

'It was on her lap when you went in?'

'Yeah, covering her . . . you know.'

'Yes, I know. Thank you.'

Siri sent the man back to the queue. He'd heard exactly what he was hoping for. If the towel had been on her lap when she was killed it would have been as bloody as hell. It would have soaked up several litres of blood. But it hadn't. The only explanation was that the killer had placed the towel across her lap after he'd killed her, for modesty. It was a polite, very Lao gesture at the end of an horrific, very un-Lao murder. And it left Siri with no idea of what kind of killer he should be looking for.

The doctor returned to the sauna and processed this new information as he sat on the wooden bench. He felt a presence in the little room, not vivid enough to be described as a visitation and several layers away from communication as if it stood behind five plates of opaque glass. But he was sure Dew's spirit was there. The girl who had died with a smile on her face and a question mark above her head was trying to get in touch but neither he nor she knew how to go about it.

'If you have anything to tell me,' he said quietly, 'now would be a really good time.'

But, if she did, she kept it to herself and Siri, as frustrated by the spirit world as ever, walked out of the sauna and into a deluge of rain that darted accusingly like index fingers out of the black clouds. He could have taken shelter beneath the carport but it was full of soldiers so he jogged with blind conviction out of the gate and into the street. By the time he reached the house opposite he was already two kilograms heavier from the water soaked into his clothes. Beneath the porch roof a man in his early fifties sat on a breeze block with a broom leaning against the front door of the house beside him. Siri joined him and they both laughed.

'Looks like it might rain,' the man said. He was slight but muscular, with skin as brown as lacquered teak. A weather-beaten Vietnamese peasant hat sat on the balcony in front of him.

'Rain? Feels more like ball bearings,' Siri corrected him. They laughed again. Siri sat on the front step beside the man and squirmed in his wet underwear. 'Been busy?'

'Can't get much done in this weather,' the man said. 'The radio seems to think there are monsoons queued up like bicycle taxis just over the border.'

Despite his appearance, the man spoke with a certain refinement and an almost unperceivable tinge of an accent. Siri recalled a conversation he'd had with the king before he was sent north. This man had a similar way about him, a modest class.

'Is this your house?' Siri asked. It was an unnecessary question because the extended buttocks bushes were overgrown and knocking at the windows and the lawn grass was taller than the average goat. The man laughed.

'No, sir,' he said. 'I work here at K6. I'm Miht. I look after the verges and the trees. Cut the odd lawn every now and then. I'd need a chainsaw for this one, mind.'

To Siri's ear, the word 'sir' had come reluctantly from the man's lips.

'Been working here long?' he asked.

'More than ten years now.'

'That long? So, you'd remember the good old American days.'

'That I would.'

'I thought that generation of Lao servants had all left along with the USAID people.'

'And you'd be right. The cooks, the housekeepers and drivers, most of them fled. But, to tell the truth, I didn't have anywhere to go. I was just a handyman around the place. I didn't work specifically for any family. I imagine the Pathet Lao didn't see me as a threat. There are half a dozen of us old-timers still working here.'

'They pay you?'

'Rice ration, sir. Free room to sleep in. Can't complain.'

They chewed on sweet stems of grass and watched the restless Vietnamese soldiers opposite.

'What a performance, eh?' Siri said.

'You're with the police?'

'No, brother.'

'Really? I thought I saw you arrive with the police.'

'And so you did. I'm the coroner, Siri Paiboun. They had me look at the body.'

'I see.'

'Did you know the people who lived in that house?' Siri asked.

'A few passed through in my time.'

'Do you recall who it was that put up the sauna?'

'Of course, the last couple, the Jansens. I was the one who found the wood for them.'

'What were they like?'

'Nice enough. Husband was very keen. He was working on education projects, I seem to recall. She was just a house-wife but she was kind, you know? Some of the wives of the experts got stuck into the gin but Mrs Jansen got involved with projects too. She helped out with scholarships, that kind of thing.'

'You seem to know a lot about them.'

'I got most of it from their house staff. I'm not much of a one for English language. I'd be out front trimming the trees and the houseboys and maids would come trotting down the driveways with all the latest gossip. I wasn't that interested but it passed the time.'

'How many staff did they have?'

'They had a fellow that cooked for them. His wife would come in three days a week to clean. And there was a gardener who doubled as their night watchman.'

'Why do you suppose they built a sauna in the middle of the tropics?'

'Mr Jansen was from Sweden or Iceland. Somewhere like that. He believed you couldn't get all the poison out of your system unless you had a good steam.'

'And everyone knew it was here?'

'In those days they did. You couldn't keep a secret then. They tried to get the Lao staff to sample it but nobody was game. It seemed like a silly idea if you ask me. I can't imagine what a Lao girl was doing in there in the middle of the night.'

'Do you know if anyone else has used it since the Americans left?'

'I can't remember seeing anyone over here at all. They didn't put any of their people in these houses by the external wall. They were afraid it'd be too easy to lob a hand grenade over. Not safe, they said. So they let all these places turn to jungle. As far as I know, none of the new regime people had any idea what it was. Just thought it was a box, probably.'

'Is there any way in and out of the compound apart from through the main gate?'

'There used to be, brother. Just before the Americans left there were more holes than a mesh stocking. The staff used them to smuggle out equipment and furniture; parting gifts from the Americans before they were kicked out. But when the Pathet Lao boys moved in they patched up most of them.'

'Most of them?'

'The old hands know of one or two places you could still get under the wall.'

'So it would be possible for someone without a pass to get into the compound.'

'Technically. You'd have to be careful to avoid the security patrols. Trigger-happy bunch. They'd probably shoot you before they asked who you were.'

5

HALF A DOZEN MEN IN
SEARCH OF A SMELL

The interviews hadn't taken as long as Sihot and Phosy had imagined. The answers had all been so pat it was as if everyone had memorised them from an official circular. 'I barely knew the girl.' 'Didn't talk to her.' 'I have no idea about her personal life.' 'She seemed like a good soldier.' Phosy had noticed the bandage on Security Chief Phoumi's wrist and enquired about it. He was told it was a torn ligament from a motorcycle accident. The rest of his answers were brief and unhelpful. Only Major Dung, in that cocky style of his, had strayed from the script. Even the interpreter was annoyed by his responses to the questions.

'Do you have any knowledge of the victim having an extra-marital affair?'

'It wouldn't surprise me,' Dung had said with a grin. 'She put out enough signals.'

'Meaning?'

'A lot of your Lao girls in uniform start to think like men. They like to put themselves around. Gather feathers for their caps.'

'Are you saying this from personal experience?'

'I might have taken her up on it if I were younger . . . less fastidious.'

'She approached you?'

Dung grinned and raised his eyebrow for the nth time. Phosy wanted to reach over and knock that eyebrow clean off his face.

'She made it quite obvious she wanted me, yes.'

The Intelligence Department jeep drove into the Electricité du Lao compound on Samsenthai and, after a brief chat with the guard at the gate, pulled up in front of the office of the chief engineer. As they drove, Siri had passed on his findings from K6 and listened intently to the results of the interviews. Before they climbed down into the deep puddles, he asked,

'Did you find out why our playboy major sent soldiers over to Sixth Street in the first place?'

'He said he got a call from the wife of one of the residents complaining about a strange smell,' Sihot told him.

'Did he say who?'

'Said she didn't leave her name.'

'Convenient. So he sent half a dozen men in search of a smell?'

'Does seem a bit much, doesn't it, Doctor.'

'And another thing. If you're called to a murder scene, your first reaction would be to go inside the room and confirm that the girl is, in fact, dead. According to the guard, Dung just took a look from the doorway, shut the door, and went in search of his boss.'

'It's possible the Vietnamese wasn't authorised to make that determination,' Phosy suggested. 'There might be some protocol involved.'

'Be worth checking on that, though,' Siri nodded. 'Then there was the peculiar incident of dragging me out of a perfectly good film and getting me to examine the body. And, once I'd confirmed she was dead, they decided they could handle the case and they couldn't wait to get rid of me.

It could have been just them covering their rear ends when it came to filing the report. Or, there might be something more sinister going on.'

'I wasn't much taken with the security chief myself,' said Sihot. 'Now, there was a man with a secret if ever I saw one.'

They were disturbed by a tall man with greased-back hair who came down the front steps to greet them. He wore a spotless white shirt with sleeves folded to his elbows and a tight patent leather belt that seemed to divide him into segments like an ant.

'Can I help you, Comrades?' he said.

'Comrade Chanti,' said Sihot, stepping down from the jeep and into a pool of water. He shook the man's hand and indicated to his colleagues. 'This is Inspector Phosy of police intelligence and Dr Siri attached to the Ministry of Justice.'

They passed on their condolences to the husband of Dew and he suggested they go inside and out of the damned rain. Despite mumbling that he had a lot of work on his plate, he led them to the canteen where they ordered a thermos of tea and a plate of two-day-old Chinese doughnuts.

Phosy took up the questioning where Sihot had left off. They had their tactics worked out.

'Comrade Chanti,' he said. 'This morning we received transcripts of your wife's courses in the USSR. It appears she learned to fence while she was there.'

'She what?'

'She learned to use a sword.'

Chanti looked surprised.

'You didn't know?' Siri asked.

'No.' The man sipped at his tea.

'She didn't tell you about her courses?' Phosy asked.

'Not a lot,' he replied.

'You don't see her for four years and you aren't interested in what she studied?' Siri pushed.

'I'm interested. Of course, I'm interested . . .'

'But?'

'She didn't get around to mentioning it.'

'How would you describe your marriage, Comrade?' Phosy asked.

'If this is an interrogation I should be read my rights or something, shouldn't I?' Chanti said coldly.

'I'm afraid the legislators haven't got around to giving you any rights just yet,' Phosy countered. 'So perhaps you could just answer the question.'

'No need to get defensive,' added Sihot.

'I'm not. I'm not being defensive. I'm just . . . I'm just upset.'

'Of course, you've just lost your wife,' Siri sympathised. 'It's only natural for you to be irritable.'

'I am not . . . All right. Yes. I suppose I am. I'm sorry. My marriage was . . . was a typical Lao marriage.'

'Really?' Phosy asked. 'I thought in typical Lao marriages the husband goes out to work and the wife stays at home and looks after the children. The wife certainly doesn't run off for four years and leave her husband to look after two little ones.'

'I . . .'

'How old are your children, Comrade Chanti?' Siri asked.

'What? How old?'

'Yes.'

'Five and . . . seven?'

'You don't sound too sure,' Phosy observed.

'I'm certain.'

Sihot produced his notebook from his top pocket. It was bound in a large rubber band that he had trouble removing.

'According to our files,' he said. 'Your children are six and eight.'

'What? Well, yes. That could be right.'

'You don't spend much time with your children, do you, Comrade?' Phosy said.

'I see them.'

'But you don't live with them.'

'Her mother looks after them.'

'*Her*?'

'Dew's. They stay there. I work long hours. I can't . . .'

'You shouldn't have to,' Phosy agreed. 'It's a woman's job.'

'She had no right to abandon you with them,' Siri put in. 'How old was the youngest when she left? Two? My word. You must have had a lot of serious discussions about the implications before she left.'

'She didn't consult with me. Just announced she was going,' Chanti said.

'You know, I'd be really pissed if my wife pulled a trick like that on me,' Sihot grumbled, half to himself.

'It was demeaning,' Chanti confessed.

'I bet it was,' Phosy agreed. 'And finally she comes back and you think it might be all right. Everything might get back to the way it was. You could be together as a family again.'

'And then she moves in with her mother and the children and tells you she wants a divorce,' said Siri.

'You can't . . .' Chanti began. 'Did her mother tell you that?'

'Yes.'

'Well, it's not true. She didn't want a divorce. Just some time to think. We could have sorted it out.'

'So you thought,' Siri said. 'But then you find out she has a lover. After all that waiting, supporting her children . . .'

'I . . . I didn't know.'

'Of course, you couldn't have been certain,' Phosy kept up the attack, 'but when she's been back only two months and tells you she has an assignment at K6 and she'll be working nights, staying out there . . . All those soldiers . . .'

'How must you feel?' Sihot tutted and shook his head.

'I wanted . . .'

'Yes?'

'I wanted it all to be over.'

'Well, it certainly is now, ' Phosy reminded him.

'Not like that.'

'But, "like that" is how it ended. A sword through the heart.'

'Look, you can't do this to me.' There was a fire burning in Chanti's eyes. 'It's not fair. Just leave me alone.'

'One final question, if I may, Comrade,' Sihot asked. 'Do you happen to know of a woman called Khantaly Sisamouth? Or you might know her better by her nickname – Kiang.'

'No,' said Chanti.

The three investigators looked at one another. When working for long enough in crime prevention, a policeman, even an amateur medical sleuth, learns to recognise the 'paradoxical no'. The paradoxical no is a cunning little beast because it has the appearance of a 'no', but it is clearly a 'yes' in costume. Comrade Chanti was lying to them.

What they all believed would be the final stop of the day was at the Sisangvone primary school. Although Monday classes hadn't been interrupted, the classroom which had been the scene of the previous day's murder had been sealed off and its children distributed to other rooms. The head teacher unlocked the door and stood back to let them in.

'Do you always keep this locked when there's no class?' Phosy asked.

The tall but undernourished teacher shook his head and a pencil fell out from behind his ear.

'No,' he said, bending to retrieve it. 'Usually not. I put a padlock on it when the sergeant here told me to keep the children out.' He started to unfasten the wooden shutters.

'You aren't afraid of things being stolen?' Phosy asked.

The head teacher laughed. 'What's to steal? We've just the one set of books for the teachers, none for the children. We buy our own chalk and keep it with us.' He fished out two sticks from his top pocket as evidence. 'And the desks and chairs are so old they have French chewing gum stuck to the bottom of them.'

Siri smiled and shook the teacher's hand as he walked into the classroom. The lack of books evidently extended to a lack of paper and paint. The few pictures on the walls were drawn in pencil on flaps torn from cardboard boxes. The desks and chairs had been pushed against the walls leaving an empty space in the centre of the room. Once varnished, the wooden floor had now been buffed grey by generations of feet and scratched to high heaven by the shifting of furniture. This was a classroom with a history.

'Comrade, could you tell the doctor what you told us?' Sihot asked of the teacher.

'All right,' he said. 'I came in on Sunday morning at about seven. My wife and I live in a shared house down the street so I can walk here. The local youth movement conducts a political pathfinders session on Sunday mornings for the older children. We use this room 'cause it's the biggest. Sometimes they like to do activities where the kids have to move around. When I got in, I was surprised to see all this furniture moved back. But I assumed the youth cadres had come early to set things up. I started to open the shutters. That's when I noticed the young lady.'

Siri walked to the blackboard. It was made of *sao* wood, a type of oak, hard enough to make boats out of. The point of the sword had entered the board at a height almost level with his own heart. The thrust must have been terribly powerful. Powerful enough to keep the victim on her feet. The blood had formed a figure-of-eight stain where she'd been standing.

'Our last class was on Saturday morning,' the teacher was saying in the background. 'After that, I went from room to room making sure nobody had left anything behind. Forgetful bunch, these children. I shut all the doors. I had a regional educational administrators' meeting in the afternoon and went straight home after that.'

'So nobody was here in the afternoon or evening' Siri asked.

'Sometimes the children like to come and sit and play. I don't begrudge them that. This isn't much on atmosphere but it's better than the crowded conditions some of them have to put up with at home. But the weather's been shocking lately. You saw the football field, or rather, you didn't. It looks like a paddy field. Not many people want to leave their homes in weather like this.'

'We had a couple of our men talk to the kids, Doctor,' Sihot said. 'None of them were here Saturday afternoon or evening. Nobody saw anything.'

Siri stopped suddenly and stared at the wall beside the door, then up at the ceiling.

'Head teacher, you don't have electricity.'

'No, Comrade,' replied the teacher. 'Education keeps telling us they'll have us connected up by the end of the year. They've been saying that for two years.'

Siri was confused. Even if he was two hours out with his estimation of the time of death, which he doubted, it would still have been dark in this classroom. Too dark to spear somebody accurately in the heart. Either the perpetrator was carrying a torch, or . . .

Siri walked around the room with Sihot close behind, his notepad at the ready. The doctor found what he was looking for on a desk at the front near the wall. It was just a small heap of wax moulded around an empty circle of space.

'Do you use candles often, Comrade?' he asked the teacher.

'No, Comrade. Beyond our budget, I'm afraid,' he replied.

'Then it would appear our killer brought them with him and took them home when he was through.'

They found similar deposits of wax on six of the desks. There might have been more, removed along with the candles.

'Not exactly floodlighting,' Siri said, 'but enough to light up their duelling arena.'

'You think they were swordfighting in here?' Phosy asked.

'They cleared a space, lit up the room. Our victim was dressed for sport. It's as good a guess as any, I'd say.'

'And you,' Phosy looked at Sihot. 'What's wrong with you, man? Do you have pebbles there for eyes? I send you here to investigate and you can't even see great lumps of wax?'

Sihot bunched up the corners of his mouth. Not a sulk exactly, more an attempt not to burst into tears. It saddened Siri to see a strong man embarrassed and he was surprised. He'd never known Phosy to rebuke his men in public. In fact, the inspector wasn't given to outbursts. He would normally shake his head and privately bemoan the lack of grey matter in the police force. This was particularly out of character. Something was wrong.

'Any chance she died by accident?' Phosy asked Siri, still staring at Sihot.

'I doubt that,' Siri said. 'If it's just a sparring match they'd have some cork thingamabobs on the ends of their weapons. At the very least they'd be fighting with blunt swords. The épée we pulled out of the victim was sharpened to a fine edge. The killer knew exactly what he was doing.'

The jeep went by Police Headquarters with the intention of dropping off Sihot. There was a lot of paperwork that hadn't been started. The plan from there was for Phosy to drive Siri to the morgue, return the Willy's jeep to the garage, and go through the data they'd collected on the two victims, looking for connections. But, as Civilai often said, 'Intentions can be as flimsy as toilet paper in a cheap bar.'

As they pulled into the compound, a police boy dressed in a shirt so big it made him look as if he'd shrunk overnight leapt from the guard booth and waved his arms.

'Should I drive over him?' Sihot asked.

'Better stop, I suppose,' Phosy told him.

The boy ran around to the inspector in the passenger seat.

'Sir, you have to go to K6,' he said. 'There's been a murder.'

Given the pace of communication in the republic, it wasn't unthinkable for this to have been the message from two days hence just reached the guard post. But Phosy had a bad feeling that wasn't the case.

'Who told you?' he asked.

'Vietnamese security guy on a motorcycle, about an hour ago,' said the boy.

6

THE CASE OF THE THREE ÉPÉES

In the ever-flowing words of ex-politburo member Civilai, before the épée murders time in the People's Democratic Republic of Laos had been speeding by like a thirty-year-old Peugeot on blocks. The country had been stone-cold frozen to the edge of its seats waiting for news of the two major initiatives of 1978. After three years of planning, the cooperative movement was finally launched as outlined in the order No. 97: Regulation of Cooperative Farming. Under this accelerated programme the government was certain it would be self-sufficient in food grains by 1981. The economy would be revived and the purest tenet of communism would be realised at the rice roots level.

But the leaders very quickly realised that, like communism, collectivism worked much better on paper than on dirt. The five cooperative principles as per order No. 98d had been sound enough: 1. Volunteerism. 2. Mutual benefit. 3. Democratic management. 4. Planned production. 5. Distribution of produce and profit according to labour performed with the right attitude. Thirty to forty families would be gathered together in one collective and all their resources pooled. Each man and woman would receive work points based on an eight-hour day. Technically, the families would be able to join and leave at will.

But villages in Laos had traditionally been self-sufficient.

They hadn't given anything to the government and the government hadn't given them anything back. So questions were asked such as, 'Why should we start sharing now?'

Siri explained the problem to Dtui like this: 'Farmer A. has two buffalos and a hectare of land. Farmer B. has one buffalo and half a hectare. A smiling cadre arrives at the village one day and congratulates them on their acceptance into the greater cooperative network. He informs them that, as from today, they have one-and-a-half buffalos each and three-quarters of a hectare of rice field to tend. Farmer B. runs off to tell his wife of their good fortune while farmer A. sits on a rock wondering where he went wrong.'

In fact, if the system had operated truly on a voluntary basis, everyone would have volunteered themselves out. As a result, they were strongly urged – often by the toothless smile of an AK47 – to give it a go for three years. Of the five principles of cooperative farming it was soon clear that only those who had nothing to begin with would progress with any joy past the first. Yet the leaders not only believed the system would be successful, they also held that the agronomic revolution would miraculously transform Laos from an agricultural economy to a technologically advanced socialist state. Naturally, in order to get there, they had to do a little work on the raw material: the Lao themselves.

The second initiative, a big public relations push for 1978, planned to coincide with the billboard invasion, was the creation of Socialist Man. A sort of poor relative of Super-, Bat-, and Spiderman, Socialist Man was the ideological Frankenstein of the Party. He was the embodiment of everything perfect in a good socialist. He was steadfast, had a spirit of solidarity, was a good father and respected the laws. One evening, Siri, Daeng and Civilai had even gone so far as to design him a costume; a green leotard to represent the

young rice shoots, rubber boots to keep his feet dry, naturally, a red cape adorned with a hammer and sickle, and a
scabbard for his hoe. Daeng had been insistent there should
be a New Socialist Woman to keep him company. If any of
them had had even the remotest skills as artists they would
have produced an entire comic book, perhaps even
submitted it to a publisher in New York and – ignoring the
irony completely – become wealthy capitalists.

So, given the lack of other stimulating news, it was
evident why the deaths of three apparently unrelated women
– all skewered with a weapon 99.9 (recurring) per cent of the
population had never heard of – was the talk of the markets
and the Lao Patriotic Women's Association tea rooms.

When Siri and the two detectives had arrived back at K6
on that painfully long and wet Monday, Security Chief
Phoumi was at the gate to meet them and he was looking
far more ruffled than he had been during the investigation
of the first murder. He sat in the back of the jeep and
directed Sihot to the auditorium. Siri knew it well. It was
the same hall in which he had watched ten minutes of *The
Train From the Xiang Wu Irrigation Plant* not two days
earlier. During the American days it had been an open-air
gymnasium, basically a roof on posts with a stage for
dramas. Not given to openness or drama, the Pathet Lao
had bricked it up, attached air-conditioners, and had been
using it as a meeting hall.

The jeep splashed to a halt at the foot of the steps and
they hurried up to the auditorium doors and pushed through
a gaggle of onlookers and into the hall. The chairs had been
stacked neatly to one side and there was a pile of tumbling
mats and gym equipment at the rear of the room, presumably left over from the high-school days. Whereas the
previous two murder scenes had been comparatively neat,

almost serene, the auditorium was a bloody mess. A crimson trail of drag marks and splashes began at the mats and snaked across the concrete floor in the direction of the stage where the victim lay in a crumpled heap. She was face down on the handle of the sword with the blade sticking out of her side like a toothpick in a cocktail sausage. Siri and Phosy exchanged glances.

'This one put up a fight,' said Siri.

With Major Dung and half-a-dozen Vietnamese soldiers standing in the doorway watching, Siri and Sihot eased the victim onto her side. She was about thirty, short and muscular like victim one. The sword pierced her left breast, entering her chest between the fifth and sixth ribs. Not a frontal hit on the heart like the others but a hit nevertheless. Her face might once have been attractive but it now wore a death mask of horror. She had been in torment when the life left her, of that there was no doubt. She wore a thick denim jacket and, incongruously, culottes and running shoes. It appeared a mark had been cut rudely into her thigh but it was impossible to read as the area was awash with blood. It would need to be cleaned to see whether it was the same Zorro brand as appeared on the two previous victims.

'That's one a day,' Phosy said, looking back at the trail of blood. 'How many damned more are there going to be?'

'He got sloppy,' Siri said. 'If we're going to find evidence, this is where it'll be. This is where he made his mistake. If you can get those sightseers out of here and give me half an hour, I'll see what I can come up with.'

Phosy yelled 'Out!' and, to Siri's surprise, the Vietnamese entourage left without a fight. The policeman followed them outside. The double doors slammed and the silence of the auditorium made Siri feel uneasy. Again he had the sense he was close to a spirit but it was holding back. He wondered if it knew it was on the other side. Some ghosts took a lot of convincing they were dead. He called out, 'I know you're here,' and his words seemed to cause some consternation in the afterlife. He caught the briefest of glimpses, no more than a flash, like two people on trains going in opposite directions. And the glimpse he'd been afforded was frightening enough. The spirit was incensed, its face contorted, its middle finger raised. He was mystified.

It took him a few moments to catch his breath but no interpretation of the vision came to him. He walked unsteadily to the point where the blood trail began. The tumbling mats were leaning against the rear wall, six deep. At the level of his heart there was a puncture mark in the front mat. A narrow trail of blood trickled down from it to join a veritable atlas of spots and splotches about twenty centimetres from the ground. Thence a cascade to the concrete where a deep pool of blood congealed.

Siri shuffled through the mats but the sword had only penetrated the one at the front. There were splatters on the mats and the wall. Beside the stack was a scratched wooden beam with two bolts at waist height. For some reason an inordinate amount of blood had spurted in its direction. Siri assumed it was at the level of the exit wound. It might have been an irrelevance but he was prone to remember even the smallest detail. There were bloody footprints leading to and from the mats. At first glance they appeared to have been made by the same shoes but Sihot would have to confirm that assumption. The footsteps leading towards the stage told a miserable story. They were meandering and interspersed with puddles of blood becoming more desperate as they reached the body of the victim. A body drained white as cigarette paper.

He knelt beside her and turned over her bloody hand. There were deep scratches on her palms that he took to be defence wounds. What must she have gone through? She was a fighter, there was no doubt about it. Although the original colour of her shoes was unrecognisable, the tread seemed to match the footprints all around. The doctor was certain she'd have a lot more to tell him when they got her back to the morgue but he wanted to be certain he hadn't overlooked anything in the auditorium. He made one more slow circuit. He retraced the blood trail, taking note of footprints which could have been those of another person or merely skid-marks and distortions. He returned to the mats, imagined her leaning back against them, skewered with a sword but not dead. How could she have gone so far once her heart had been pierced? What was the murderer doing as she staggered around? Did he watch her? Had he already fled, assuming she was dead?

Siri would leave Sergeant Sihot to photograph the scene but the pictures would never capture the menace that lurked there in this musty room. Nor could they recall the scents of sweat and blood and fear. He walked to the door and, like a painter stepping back to admire his work, he turned around to take in the scene one last time. And that was when he saw it, a small white speck on the window ledge above the mats. He hurried back and dragged a balance bench over to them. He angled it against the window ledge, being careful not to disturb the mats or the pool of blood, and shimmied up it. As he neared the top he could see that the object was a small brown medicine bottle with a white label. He pulled a tissue from his pocket, took hold of the bottle by its cap and read the handwritten lettering: 'vitamins'.

In front of the auditorium, under the porch roof, Sihot

and Phosy were questioning the woman who'd found the body. Her face was still blanched from the awful discovery. The Vietnamese were nowhere to be seen but on the far side of the street, beneath a small shelter, sat the gardener with his chin perched on the handle of his broom. He raised his hand when he saw Siri but the doctor felt oddly uncomfortable returning the wave. Siri approached the policemen and raised his brow to Sihot who broke away and went into the building to take his photographs. Phosy thanked the woman and she headed off into the rain on wobbly legs.

'Anything?' Siri asked.

'The witness is a cleaner here,' Phosy said. 'She recognised the victim. Says she's a medic, based out at the old Settha Hospital at Silver City. But she comes here to K6 three times a week to man a clinic they opened for the staff. She has a little office at the old youth club. Yesterday was one of her regular days. The cleaner unlocked the hall at eleven to get it ready for tonight's lecture. Any idea how long the medic's been dead?'

'I'd say sometime last night. Around ten?'

'Damn.' He looked at the bottle in Siri's hand. 'Find something?'

'It might not be connected. I found it on the window sill above the sports equipment. The label says it's vitamins but labels have been known to tell fibs.'

'You haven't opened it?'

'Not yet. I want to take it back to the morgue . . .'

'And perform more of your fingerprint magic?'

'Don't mock. One day, that magic will solve one of your cases, Inspector.'

'I'll believe that when I see it. So, is she ready to go?'

'As ready as she'll ever be.'

'I'll go and take a look around. Did you find anything unusual in there?'

'It's all unusual, Phosy. All of it.'

Nurse Dtui and Mr Geung were still waiting in the morgue office when Siri and the third victim arrived. They'd been waiting all day, not knowing where their boss was. Waiting and bailing. There were steps leading to the front door of the morgue, which was just as well because the building was surrounded by sixty centimetres of water. Most of the lower buildings were barricaded with sandbags and Mahosot was taking on the appearance of a hospital deep in the heart of Venice. X-ray had already brought in a rowing boat to ferry patients back to the ward. The morgue would have held up to the flood but for a slight crack in the back wall which allowed water to seep into the cutting room. Dtui and Geung had failed to patch it up with adhesive bandage so they resorted to surrounding it with a semi-circular orchestra pit of sandbags. It refilled every half hour and looked like a small ornamental pond.

They walked into the vestibule to watch the arrival of the new body.

'My adoring husband isn't with you?' Dtui asked Siri.

'He had to go straight to police HQ with Sihot,' Siri replied.

'I'm sure he did.'

On any other day, Siri would have followed up on Dtui's comment, but this was far from any other day. Two orderlies carried the corpse past the office door and into the autopsy area. The body was wrapped in a tarpaulin in an attempt to preserve the blood trails.

'Ano . . . another guest f . . . for room one,' smiled Geung. He liked to keep busy. He followed the orderlies and barked at them to be careful.

'Oh, Doc. That isn't—' Dtui began.

'It's another one. Yes, Dtui.'

'The same MO?'

'I get the feeling it would have been. Except this one fought back. She refused to go quietly.'

'I like her already.'

They removed the épée and placed it with the other two. There was something different about it, lighter or . . . But Siri would get to that later. They undressed the young woman as Dtui made notes about the bloodstains on her skin and clothing. The victim was physically fit, with a well defined musculature. Unusual for a Lao woman. Probably an athlete. They took their allotted three photographs. They washed the corpse and noticed immediately that the Zorro brand on her thigh was deep, much deeper than those of her predecessors'.

'In fact,' Dtui said, looking closely at the wound, 'I'd say one of these cuts is deep enough to have sliced an artery. What do you think, Doctor?'

When Dtui wasn't breastfeeding or burping or lulling Malee to sleep, Siri liked to have her comment during autopsies. He still had hope she'd secure a scholarship in the Soviet bloc and study to take over from him at the morgue. She already showed more enthusiasm and acumen than Siri himself.

'Let's have a look,' Siri said, and leaned over the body.

He cut gently at the flesh around the Z and worked his way inward towards the slashes. The cuts were wild, almost fanatical. Completely different from the carefully carved thigh of the second victim, Kiang. It was the cross cut, the axis of the Z, that had dug deepest and had, in fact, nicked the femoral artery.

'Hmm. Now that's interesting,' he said.

'This is where all the blood came from,' Dtui decided.

'And, if that's the case . . .'

'The Z had to have been cut before she was killed with the sword.'

'Otherwise?'

'Otherwise the wound wouldn't have bled like the Nam Pou fountain. How did he keep her still enough to sign her thigh? It must have hurt like hell.'

Siri thought about the bottle of medicine. If it had contained some kind of sedative, that might have been enough. The killer drugged the woman and was signing her thigh when she came round. All possible. Once they were done with the autopsy Siri would spend time with the bottle and its contents.

'She might have been drugged,' he said. 'In fact they all might have been drugged. Teacher Oum's off at a mini re-education seminar and she's the only one with the chemicals to find out what our three ladies had in their stomachs. We won't know for sure until she gets back tomorrow. So, let's keep delving.'

The medic had been a well-endowed young lady and the sword had entered her left breast from the south-west. After his Y incision, Siri and Dtui set about tracing the path of the blade. They arrived at the point where it had passed through the rib cage. The bones were unmarked so they had to assume the sword passed between the ribs without touching them. Enter Mr Geung. He wielded his rib-cutters like a ferocious Greek warrior. If one were to ignore his perm he might have been taken for a middle-aged Achilles. Siri and Dtui stood back to admire his work.

'You really have to stop treating our Mr Geung like a poodle, nurse,' whispered Siri.

'I really don't know what you mean,' she replied.

'I think you do. And I'm serious. Enough's enough.'

Dtui adopted a Lao band-aid smile to cover her embarrassment. Within minutes, Geung's work was done and they had access to the inner sanctum of organs. Siri stepped forward and began to probe. Then stood back in surprise.

'Well, I'll be . . .' he said.

'What is it?' Dtui asked, and stepped up to the table. Her face dropped in astonishment. 'She . . .'

'I know,' Siri smiled. 'Fascinating, isn't it?'

'I don't know.' Dtui shook her head and began to fumble around in the victim's chest cavity. 'Does the word "fascinating" describe something that's physically impossible? She hasn't got a heart.'

The lung was clearly visible but there was no heart nestled against it.

'Nurse Dtui, surely your medical training would have told you we all have to have a heart in order to function. So, as we know this young lady was walking around just twenty-four hours ago, logic would dictate that she must have a heart. We just have to go looking for it.'

He pulled back the flap of skin to the left of his incision and smiled.

'There you are, you sneaky devil,' he smiled. The heart smiled back at him from beneath the medic's right breast.

'It's on the wrong side, Doc,' Dtui said.

'It certainly is.'

'You seen this before?'

'Seen? No. Not with my own eyes. But I have heard of it. The most famous example of it was in the 007 film, *Dr. No*. They thought they had dispatched the villain with a bullet through the heart. But it wasn't there.'

'That's a movie. They make those things up.'

'In this case, no. It's a real condition called dextrocardia

96

and we have a perfect example of it right here. Mr Geung, the camera please. I think this deserves a photograph. We may never see anything like this again.'

Geung took one photo in close-up of the victim's chest and one of Siri and Dtui crouching by the misplaced organ. Naturally, Mr Geung wanted to have his photo taken too with the right-sided heart but they were able to convince him not to make a V sign. All three apologised to the corpse but they felt she wouldn't have objected.

'Do you think she knew?' Dtui asked.

'Hard to tell. It doesn't look as if she's had any major surgery. They might have mentioned it to her during medicals but, given the overall standard of nursing skills here it's quite possible nobody noticed. Present company excepted, of course. It probably didn't affect her physically, in fact she looks in very good shape. Less inconvenient than being born with two thumbs on the one hand, I'd guess. But one thing's for certain, the perpetrator certainly couldn't have known. And that could explain why she didn't die immediately.'

'You mean, the sword didn't kill her?'

'Let's take a look. If it didn't puncture the lung she might have survived the wound.'

Siri was right. There was no puncturing of the lung, not so much as a nick. The sword had passed behind the ribs and through the no-man's-land where her heart should have been. There was damage to muscle and tissue but nothing life-threatening. The blade had slid in front of the lung and out the side of her body. Hard as it may have been to believe, the sword through her chest looked much worse than it was. It hadn't killed her. The Z signature on her thigh had.

'It must have confused the heck out of the killer,' Dtui said as they washed up. 'He pins her through the heart and starts to cut her thigh and there she is wandering around like the living dead. He probably had to chase after her to finish it. No wonder it was messy. Doctor?'

Siri was deep in thought, going back over the crime scene in his mind, the bloodstains, the footprints.

'Doc?'

'Yes, sorry. I was just trying to organise a few things in my head.'

'It's all explained, isn't it?'

'What? Yes. All explained.'

'Good, so I can go? I have a daughter who thinks the crèche worker's her mother.'

'Yes, of course. Get out of here. I don't want to be the . . .'

He was going to say, 'the cause of a family break-up.' It was supposed to be a joke but something about the past few days made him think it wouldn't have been all that funny.

'Be the what, Dr Siri?'

'Be the evil employer who forces his staff to work all night.'

'Oh, I don't mind. And . . . I'll apologise to Geung on my way out. I understand. I'm stuck in mothering mode, venting my frustrations on the poor dear.'

'Thank you. I—'

'OK, I'm gone.' And she was. Their serious talk would have to wait.

7

BLACKBOARD SINGEING IN
THE DEAD OF NIGHT

Siri sat on a bench in front of the office of Judge Haeng at the Ministry of Justice. From his seat, if he leaned forward, he could see the windows of the office of the new minister, a man who'd spent his entire life fighting for the socialist cause. So occupied had he been with this struggle that a law degree – or even a college education – had been out of reach. This was a fact that Judge Haeng, the possessor of an authentic, if abridged, law degree from the Soviet Union, never failed to point out. While the figurehead sat in his air-conditioned office, Judge Haeng performed all the active duties of the ministry. All right, perhaps he passed most of them on to his assistant Manivone and her staff, but at least he spoke to people, he delegated, he diligently signed whatever Manivone put in front of him. At least he was still alive. He had no idea what was happening in the newly furbished upstairs room. He often got his new clerk to pass along the corridor once a day to see if he detected a pungent smell of decay coming from the room.

Judge Haeng was a bitter man. The only good news in his book of torment was the fact that Comrade Phat, the Vietnamese advisor, had moved upstairs also. Haeng had shaken off his albatross and was free to make wrong decisions and screw up projects without assistance. His paperwork had to pass 'upstairs' but as Manivone did most of it, he didn't have to worry.

'Call him in,' Siri heard from inside the room and the door to the office opened and a young man with a cherry tomato nose stepped out. His eyes watered and his expression was strained as if he had several sliced onions concealed in his undershirt.

'Dr Siri?' the boy said, looking left and right, although there was only one potential Dr Siri sitting directly in front of him.

'That would be me,' Siri said.

'The judge will see you now.'

'You work here?'

'Just started.'

'Do you have a cold?'

'Sinuses,' said the boy.

'I could give you something for it. I work at the morgue—'

'You think it's that serious?'

'No. I'm a doctor. The morgue is irrelevant. I was just telling you where to find me.'

'Thanks.'

'Not a problem.'

It always helped to have an ally in the enemy camp. Since his arrival from Moscow, Judge Haeng had been a concrete block set around the doctor's ankles. He'd barely spoken one civil word to Siri in all that time, which was why his reaction on this occasion came as something of a surprise. The spotty-faced judge rose from his desk with his hand extended. So unexpected was this gesture that Siri instinctively looked across the room to see what the man was pointing at. When he turned back the hand was still there so he shook it limply. It was as damp as he'd always imagined it to be.

'Siri, Siri, Siri, my old friend,' said the judge.

Siri quickly scanned the judge's head for lumps or other evidence that he'd suffered an injury.

'You want something?' Siri asked.

Haeng laughed. He reached beside him for his walking stick and hobbled around to the other side of his desk. Siri still marvelled at how quickly the infection had spread from the judge's imagination to his perfectly healthy leg.

'Don't be silly, Siri,' he said. 'Two old comrades getting together for a chat. Why do we need a reason?' He cast a sideways glance at the young clerk now ensconced at the advisor's old desk. Siri was about to take his place on the wonky interrogation seat but Haeng waved him away.

'Let's get comfortable,' he said.

He gestured to the vinyl couch and the uneven tin coffee table where a bottle of Cola and two glasses sat in expectation. Siri, more nervous with every revelation, edged to the sofa and sat. The springs played a short tune of welcome. They played a different tune entirely when the judge joined him and he poured them both a drink. Siri hated Cola. Even when it became a luxury item the taste didn't improve. It was still heavily sugared engine oil to Dr Siri.

He was closer to Haeng now but still couldn't see the wound on his head that had caused this sudden change in personality. Perhaps it was his thyroid. Glands had been known to bring about mood swings. Haeng raised his glass and expected Siri to do the same. It was too creepy, even for a man who spoke to ghosts.

'All right, I give up,' Siri said. 'What's happened?'

'Siri, Siri. You! You've happened. You don't suppose that little bit of news wouldn't somehow find its way to my office, do you? I can't begin to tell you how proud we are.'

At last, Siri understood. 'The hero shortlist.'

'I can't tell you what a boon it would be for the Justice Department if one of its own was selected,' said Haeng.

'How could it have any effect on the credibility of a ministry?' Siri asked, bemused.

'Do you need to ask?'

Siri was distracted momentarily by an old lady who had come to sit at the judge's desk. She had a face that defied guesswork as to her age and wore the traditional clothing of a country woman. Her mouth was a splatter of betel nut. He knew the old lady well even though he didn't recall meeting her when she was still alive. She'd been with him from time to time, just sitting, just there, never speaking. A monk had once hinted she might have been Siri's birth mother, but there was no way of confirming or denying it. He called her his 'mother angel' anyway, just in case. Of all the visitations he experienced from day to day, his mother angel was the one he most felt a need to communicate with. He had a lot of gaps in his early memories. But she sat and chewed and made no effort at all to answer his questions.

Judge Haeng was babbling on about something in the background. Siri interrupted him.

'If you were a bank I'd understand,' he said. 'You could use me on advertising hoardings. "Dr Siri is proud to be a director of the such and such bank." That type of thing. Or a farm implement manufacturer. "Dr Siri drives a Kwailek tractor. Why don't you?" But you're a ministry.'

'And a fledgling ministry in a fledgling democracy, Siri. We need the farmers to trust us.'

'Then stop making them join collectives.'

Haeng ignored the comment.

'We need the common people on our side,' he said. 'The simple man is a moth drawn to the bright light of a halo around the head of a great leader. We need their support and they need a hero.'

Siri saw himself in his green leotard, flying down from the ministry turrets to aid the commoners, fix that dam, shift that bale. He laughed and shrugged in the direction of his dead mother. He felt a 'but' coming.

'We're almost there,' Haeng said. 'There's just one small area that needs addressing.'

'I'm not giving up on the Hmong,' Siri told him.

'The . . . ? Oh, no problem. We're a multi-ethnic society, Siri. Compassion for our ethnic brothers and sisters can do you no harm at the polls. It won't get you anywhere, but it won't hurt.'

'So, what's my "small area"?'

'Siri, there are rumours about you . . . and ghosts.'

Siri's mother was dribbling betel juice all over the judge's reports. Siri smiled and she might have smiled back. It was hard to tell.

'What type of rumours?' Siri asked.

'Siri, I'm going to ask you bluntly and I expect a blunt answer. Are you a shaman?'

'Absolutely not.'

He hosted a shaman, but that was hardly the same thing. He had conducted a séance and travelled to the other world, and confronted demons, but that wasn't the question. Haeng leaned back and sighed as if a javelin had been removed from his foot.

'Excellent,' he said, 'because I have heard second-hand reports that you are . . . apparently, that you dabble in spirit worship.'

'Judge Haeng,' Siri said earnestly. 'I can honestly say that the only spirit I worship is fermented from rice and left to stand for a month.'

'That's what I thought. Good. I can forward my report tomorrow with a clear conscience. Glad we cleared that up. Good luck.'

Haeng lifted his Cola and Siri raised his and heard the clink as the two glasses met. He sipped the bubbleless, luke-warm sugar-oil without tasting it. He was surprised at how effortlessly he had skirted around the judge's accusations. His normal self would have left doubts and messed with the judge's mind. But Siri knew what was at stake here; hero status. And, if he were honest with himself he would have to admit, yes, he wanted to be a hero. He'd earned it. It wasn't the glory and adulation he desired. It was simply that he'd been a fair, honest and hard-working man all his life. Assuming the DHC didn't turn him into some Asian Errol Flynn, there were far worse role models out there for young Lao to follow. He was proud of the decisions he'd made and the direction he'd taken. Damn it. Yes. He would be a hero even if it killed him.

He looked at his mother who was sitting on the desk ripping up reports. She nodded. Yes there were character flaws; he was disrespectful, and given to grumpiness, he talked to dead people and he drank too much, but, as everyone knew, time had a way of smudging over a hero's personality faults.

The electricity is back on and the eternal day has returned to my classroom. My tough Lao belly has been invaded by foreign devils – bacteria whose names should not be spoken aloud. I am suffering from cramps and chronic diarrhoea. As I have no control over my bowels I have removed all my clothes and piled them at one extreme of the length of my chains. Soiled clothing is a breeding ground for more diseases than I care to tell you. At the other extreme of my shackles is my toilet. I use half the water they give me to keep myself clean as best I can. It's as sanitary as I am able to manage given the conditions. I'm a doctor. I balance the risks.

The monk is asleep, chained not a leg's length away. There's a smile on his face. His subconscious is apparently unaware of the terror that surrounds him. I don't know when they carried him in. He arrived like a demon in the night and took hold of my hand, frightened the living daylights out of me.

'You are the one who speak French?' he asked in a poor version of the language.

'Oui,' I said.

'Have they tortured you yet?'

'They're saving me for the dinner show.'

The monk managed a laugh that quickly dilapidated into a dry cough.

'It will not be long, brother,' he said. 'It will not be long.'

'Thanks for the encouragement. What are you in for?'

The conversation elated me after so long without warmth, only inhuman contact, only the smiley man and you ghosts. No offence.

'They found me,' the monk said. 'I am a monk. I was the last in the temple. I was responsible to protect the palm leaf scrolls. We have thousand, priceless, cannot be replace. I was in the vault under the hall of prayer. It was impossible to find it if you don't know where was it. I have the dry food, the running water that I can boil it. I could stay there for ever. I go out at night if I want the fresh food, fruit, the animal. But everyone was starve. Not much the food. Then they come, these rains. These miserable rains. And the flood make me to find a dry place for the scrolls.'

'And they caught you.'

'All monks are dead, brother. All. All die because they don't worship Brother Number One.'

The monk was still holding my hand as he spoke. His soft voice was calming.

'Why didn't they kill you?' I asked.

'They will. They kill everyone here. They will kill you. Nobody come out of this place, S21, alive. But they think we know something. If we speak they kill us fast. Don't speak, they kill us slow.'

'And do you know something?'

There was a silence that seemed to stretch out into the darkness.

'No,' he said.

'Where did you learn your French?'

'Marseille. I was on the scholarship. Four year, but poor French even so, no?'

'You're an unusual monk.'

The monk laughed and as he did so the lights came on. They blinded me. I threw my hands in front of my eyes to cut out the dazzle. I remember I opened my fingers slowly until I could focus in the glare. The monk slowly appeared to me. Dark veins stood out on his shaven head. He was solid, almost without a neck, the type of man you could tell had heavy bones even without weighing him. He wasn't dressed in saffron but wore black pyjamas like the guards, like the military, like everybody in the damned country. They were too small on him. The shirt pulled tight across his chest.

'Where are your robes, comrade?' I asked.

'They stripped me and burned them. Burned them in the same fire as the books, same fire as all the palm leaf manu-script.'

There was no expression on the monk's face but I knew what he felt. I have . . . had my own cache of valuable old *books and the thought of watching them burn fills me with sadness. The monk reached for the shackles at his ankle. He pulled at them angrily like a wild chained dog.*

'I tried that,' I told him. 'No hope unless you've got an oxyacetylene torch there under your shirt.'

'I would like to have met you under better circumstances,' said the big monk. 'What's your name, brother?'

'Siri.'

'I'm Yin Keo.'

We talked for an hour and the guards had come. They brought gruel for the monk and fetid water for me.

'This is all they give you?' Yin Keo asked when the guards left.

'I'm watching my weight.'

'No, then take this,' the big monk held out his bowl.

'I can't.'

'Serious. Look at me. I have some layers of muscle to burn before I am hungry.'

I took the bowl and handed Yin Keo the water.

'I won't say no, then. I'm a little short of nutrients. I'll pay this back in a future life, assuming we both make it through Nirvana.'

But now the monk sleeps and I wish I'd stuck with the water. I chip another corner off the charred blackboard and chew on it. I wonder how it got burnt. I imagine the pupils sneaking into their school in the dead of night and setting fire to it. I imagine how my teeth look. I imagine them to be as black as a cave in an impoverished limestone monument. See how poetic I'm becoming? Give me another month of this and I shall be a posthumous poet laureate. Then they'll honour me. Nothing like death for elevating a man to fame.

8

PERFUME? LIPSTICK STAINS?

They sat in Madame Daeng's noodle shop like ragtag generals in a sweet-smelling war room. Not many of the shops in Vientiane had electricity, even though the hydro-electric dam just sixty kilometres away was pumping out six megawatts of the stuff every day. Most stores and restaurants closed before nightfall so they hadn't bothered to petition their local cadres. But Daeng's noodle establishment was on the same grid as the Banque Pour le Commerce Exterior Lao as well as the Women's Association, so burning brightly above the generals was one very new strip light, not at all dissimilar to the two in Siri's cutting room at the morgue.

Around the table were Siri and Daeng, Sergeant Sihot, Civilai, and Phosy who sat opposite Dtui and the baby. In many ways this group *was* a small army. They'd fought battles, defeated guileful enemies and suffered wounds. It was Tuesday evening and each of the generals had been too busy in one way or another to get together before this. Spread across the table was a large sheet of sugar paper upon which the names of the three victims had been written like locations on a map. They were labelled with their nicknames and the order in which they'd been dispatched; Dew 1, Kiang 2, Jim, 3. The generals had all sent a discrete and silent prayer to Buddha for not sending them a number four or five over the past two days. The State frowned on soliciting favours from heaven but it seemed to have worked.

Supper over, it was Sihot with his famous frittering notepad who was the first to speak. He had three loose pages laid side by side in front of him on the table.

'Victim number three,' he said, flipping up the third sheet. 'Sunisa Simmarit, nickname, Jim. Twenty-four. Single. Was trained as a medic in Laos by the Americans. End of seventy-five she was sent to East Germany with the intention of being there six years to be trained as a doctor. Apparently didn't pass her second-year exams and was sent home. Still a medic.'

'But a German-speaking medic with two years of medical training,' said Civilai.

'More like *one*, comrade,' Sihot corrected him. 'First year was mostly language training. Came back in March this year. Was assigned to Settha Hospital, basic nursing duties plus translating for the East German personnel. Three half-days out at K6 looking after the minor ailments of the domestic staff.'

'And how did she get that posting?' Siri asked.

Sihot flipped over two of his note sheets like a shell-game hustler looking for the pea. He found the answer under the third sheet.

'Here,' he said. 'Jim was a Vietnamese speaker. Father Lao. Mother Vietnamese. The old medic broke her leg and they needed someone to fill in for her. With all the Vietnamese out at K6 these days she was the obvious choice.'

'So she was a second woman who could communicate with the bodyguards,' Phosy reminded them.

'Specifically Major Dung,' said Siri who had selected his favourite suspect. 'Single woman. Not bad looking. Lao. Just his type.'

'And a fencer, to boot,' said Phosy.

Somebody let forth a long whistle.

'You don't say?' said Siri.

'And a very good one by all accounts,' Sihot went on. 'So good, in fact, she won a couple of local competitions in Germany. There was talk of her going on to bigger tournaments.'

'All right,' said Daeng. She stood up and refilled everyone's after-supper teacups. 'We're getting close. We have two fencers and three women in Europe. We have almost enough connections. There's only one that doesn't fit. Any more news about Kiang?'

'Right. That's where the connection gets disconnected,' said Sihot. 'Kiang was something of a non-sporting type. She didn't take any physical education classes in Bulgaria at all. No self-defence. Nothing.'

'That surprises me,' said Civilai, 'considering the number of life-threatening situations librarians find themselves in. (Daeng crinkled her brow but he pretended not to see.) I mean, overdue book, customer reaches for a machete in her handbag, quick karate chop to the solar plexus, thwack, down goes the rule-breaker, money retrieved. One more victory for Library Woman. Potential rendezvous with Socialist Man. I think I need a drink.'

'We get the point, old brother,' said Siri. 'She does run against the rhythm. Three fencers and the case would be solved. Midnight duels. To the victor, the spoils.'

Everyone looked at the two old men as if they were speaking a foreign language. They occasionally forgot where they were and brought one too many European delicacy to the noodle table.

'Odd, though,' Dtui said, back at the noodles of the matter. 'Two fit girls, both fencers, and one dorky but good-looking librarian.' Malee munched obliviously on her mother's nipple and had nothing to add.

'And even more curious, that the only victim wearing sports clothes, heading off to exercise on a Saturday night, was the librarian,' Siri pointed out.

'Is there anything to tie them together socially?' Daeng asked. 'Any possibility they met up somewhere? Some orientation before they headed off to Eastern Europe?'

Sihot reshuffled his pages.

'Unlikely,' he said. 'They all left at different times.'

Daeng persevered, 'Some Eastern European reunion club when they got back? Communist college alumni association? Debriefing seminar?'

'Daeng, my old friend,' Civilai chuckled. 'Do you honestly believe we're that organised? We can barely keep track of who's off where. It's every ministry for himself. When their people come back they want them out in the field as quickly as possible, frustrated and frustrating because there are no words to describe all the bewildering concepts they've learned in all those exotic languages that they really didn't quite understand themselves. It's chaos. Life back here is far too complicated to sit down and draw up a programme for an "I survived the Soviet Bloc Club". And don't forget you need signatures and stamps from seven thousand middle-ranking bureaucrats just to get permission for a meeting with your own relatives to discuss who gets to use the bathroom first in the morning.'

Daeng laughed.

'So, we'll forget the possibility they met up socially?' she asked.

'We should technically have a permit to be sitting here,' he replied. 'Did I mention I needed a drink?'

Siri slipped his arm around his friend's shoulder.

'You can all see why he was such a hit up at the parliament building, can't you?' he said. 'A born diplomat. I'm surprised they found such a sweet man expendable.'

'All right,' said Phosy. 'We have more important things to discuss, if you don't mind.' He ran his finger over the victim map and allowed it to spiral to a central point. He picked up the crayon and wrote a 'Z' at the centroid of the triangle. 'What if the perpetrator is a sword coach? He takes students, advanced and beginner. He offers classes, seduces his students and then impales them through the heart. Victim one is at intermediate level. Victim two is a beginner. Perhaps she was stimulated by watching competitions in Bulgaria but was too embarrassed to take classes there. But victim three is a champion and he gets into the type of fight he hadn't expected. She matches him. He thinks he's killed her but he doesn't know about her weird heart and she's still kicking. The shock gets to him, or maybe he's injured, so he stops his killing spree.'

There was a moment of quiet as they all digested this possibility. At last, Siri spoke up.

'Brilliant,' he said.

'It makes sense to me,' Civilai agreed.

Phosy allowed himself a modest smile.

'And how would anyone go about finding themselves a fencing coach in Laos?' Dtui asked. 'We don't actually have notice boards or newspaper advertisements. This isn't Thailand, you know.'

'Word of mouth,' he said, staring blackly back at her.

'Well, so far, we haven't found any connection between the three women,' Dtui continued. 'Whose mouth did this magic word come from?'

'You begin with a theory and you work back from there,' Phosy said, calmly.

'Oh, thanks for the lesson in police procedure,' Dtui mocked.

The generals had been watching the exchange like the front row at the French Open. The couple felt the silence and looked down at the table with embarrassment.

'I could use a drink,' Civilai said.

Daeng raised the teapot.

'I was thinking more of sugar-cane juice, Madame Daeng. The fermented kind.' Civilai had successfully distracted everyone's attention by playing the rather rude guest. Civilai was, luckily for them, Civilai. Daeng laughed and went to the rear of the kitchen where she produced a bottle of Thai rum from a cupboard. Both Siri and Civilai watched with amazement as she walked back to the table.

'Have you found a cure for rheumatism?' Civilai asked. 'You're trotting around like a young calf.'

'It comes and goes,' she said, returning to the table with the bottle.

'As do hangovers,' said Sihot.

Siri said nothing. He knew that rheumatoid arthritis didn't come and go at all, especially not at his wife's advanced stage. Just that afternoon she'd been limping painfully, never complaining but certainly in discomfort. Now, here she was being brave so as not to embarrass her guests. She was some woman. The rum helped gather together the loose ends of the atmosphere and for reasons he couldn't work out, the kick of the alcohol reminded Siri about old Mrs Bountien's blood analysis findings.

'There are those of us at Mahosot,' he began, 'who believe she merely matches the colour, like on a paint chart; dark red, light red. But it was her considered opinion that the blood on the sauna towel belonged to Dew. She said there was only the one blood type.'

'So, your modesty theory still holds,' Civilai said. 'She was covered with a towel out of propriety.'

'It's the only possibility that makes sense,' Siri continued. 'Which would suggest the killer had some fondness for his victim. At least he showed some respect to the body. They appreciate that.'

'Who do?' Sihot asked.

'The bodies,' said Dtui. Sihot was about to inquire further but Siri had the floor.

'Then, next on my list is fingerprints . . .'

He was interrupted by hoots of derision. Thus far, he had failed to convince anyone of his qualifications to extract or compare fingerprints. Despite the fact that the western world had been using the system for hundreds of years, communist Laos was not yet ready for such an innovation. Siri remained firm that he would have the last laugh in this matter. He ignored the laughter and forged ahead.

'I have compared the prints I found on the first and third épées,' he said, 'with those of the victims. Although it's extremely difficult to tell (another hoot) . . . to tell without projecting the prints on some sort of screen—'

'. . . or buying a decent pair of glasses,' Civilai laughed.

'. . . or comparing them under a microscope,' Siri continued. 'Sadly, Mrs Bountien did not allow me to use hers and the only other one I know of is at Dong Dok college, locked up. But, from the evidence of my naked eye I am convinced that the print on blade one does not belong to the victim, whereas the two prints I found on sword three, did.'

Everybody applauded.

'And this tells us . . . ?' Phosy asked.

'I'm not sure (he rode out the final jeers), apart from the fact that the print on sword one is likely that of the perpetrator.'

'Who we don't have with us to compare it with,' Dtui nodded.

'But we will. Trust me. Then you'll all thank me for having concrete evidence. And while I have the floor, the épées themselves are interesting. They aren't all the same.'

Sihot found an empty page in his notepad and prepared to take notes.

'The first two,' Siri said, 'were very similar. About ninety centimetres long with a traditional triangular shaft. But somebody had gone to the trouble to hone the angles of the triangle into three very dangerous, almost razor-sharp rims. The third was quite unusual in that the blade was almost round. The angles had been filed smooth. It was more like the shaft of an arrow. You could hardly inflict damage with it. But the tip had been sharpened to a point like a needle. Just touching it would be sufficient to draw blood.'

'So, do you suppose they're different types of blades for different competitions?' Phosy asked.

'It's possible, I suppose. I don't know enough about the sport. It's likely the killer collected whatever type of weapon he could find wherever he happened to be, and brought them back to Laos. But there was something about all three of them that looked . . . I don't know, as if they'd been re-engineered. As if they were designed for a specific purpose.'

'We need to find a fencing expert,' Daeng decided.

'Apart from our assassin I doubt you'd find anyone in the country who could tell you which end to hold,' Civilai suggested.

'That doesn't include the embassies,' she told him. 'I bet we'd find someone there with fencing experience. Someone who wasn't thrown out of fencing class after two weeks.'

She smiled at her husband.

'Good point,' Phosy decided. 'Sihot, I want you to go to the European embassies tomorrow and hunt us out a fencer.'

'The embassies?' Sihot said with a look of distress on his face.

'Don't worry, Sergeant Sihot,' Daeng smiled. 'They'll all have someone to interpret.'

'And, Inspector Phosy,' Civilai said with the early signs of a slur. 'I'm sure you've thought of this already, but I think now would be as good a time as any to get to know the three girls more intimately. Talk to their families and friends. Trace their movements since they returned from—'

'As you say, Comrade,' Phosy growled, 'we're already on it.'

'Excellent,' Civilai beamed.

'And I think the fencing coach theory as a starting point is a very solid one,' Siri decided. 'In fact it's the only theory we have.'

With a few more comments and suggestions which led nowhere, the meeting broke up, and then into small fragments. Phosy and Sihot went over their notes at the noodle table. Daeng invited Dtui and Malee to the upstairs junk room to engage in a little 'girl stuff'. Siri and Civilai took their drinks and two chairs and the remainder of the bottle out to the front of the shop where they sat beneath the narrow green awning. It had been raining so long the air was wet; not moist but sodden like a slop rag. A person might have expected the rain to wash away the mugginess, to rinse the humidity clean out of the air, but it didn't go away. It loitered under cover, inside houses, beneath temple eaves. It sapped your energy and made you want to go outside and stand in the rain.

The road sloped away from the shop, more from subsidence than design. It was perhaps the only reason why they hadn't been flooded like most of the other businesses. The river was higher than anyone remembered seeing it in April but it was the incessant rain that filled the unguttered streets, not the loping Mekhong. That beast wouldn't flood for another four or five months.

'Too wet for our little Indian friend,' said Civilai, noticing that Rajid's umbrella stood unoccupied.

'We haven't seen him since my attempted man-to-man,' Siri replied. 'If he has any sense he'll be under cover somewhere with a bottle of Johnny Walker and three *sao rumwong* dancers to keep him warm.'

'If he had any sense he wouldn't be who he is.'

'Granted.'

'How's his dad, Bhiku?'

'Still churning out curry. Still without a hundred *kip* to his name.'

'See what I mean?' said Civilai. 'No matter how bad things get, there's always somebody worse off than you.'

'And life is so hard on an old politburo member, isn't it, brother? How *was* dinner with the president by the way?'

'Nice young fellow. I don't get to see him as much as I used to.'

'Did you give him your "I don't know who the real enemies are any more" speech?' said Siri.

'For some reason he tends to steer our conversations around to food and literature. He did hint that he thought the revolution had come five years too soon.'

'Huh, he really thinks five more years would have made us better prepared?'

'No, his point was that in five years time people like Dr Siri and me wouldn't be around to complain about everything.'

'He mentioned me? I'm touched. Did he have too much to drink and drop any top secret information? Plans to invade China? Racing tips?'

'In fact, he asked me a favour. That was the subterfuge behind the candlelit dinner. He wants me to go to Kampuchea.'

'Permanently?'

'Four or five days. They're on some public relations kick. Having a reception of some kind.'

'Really? I haven't been there since the forties. It was still Cambodia in those days. Boua and I had just been recruited by the French to set up a youth camp in the south. They sent us to Phnom Penh for orientation. One of the prettiest cities in Asia. Marvellous time. I'll never forget it. Me and Boua walking hand-in-hand along the Boulevard Noradom.'

'A story I'm sure Madame Daeng would love to hear.'

'No secrets between us, old brother. Although it might be true there are times I paint the truth with slightly less bushy brushes than it warrants. You know? I can't say I've heard much news from our southern neighbours since the Reds took over.'

'Nobody has. Not even the president really knows what they're doing. He was there on an official visit not so long ago, but they didn't let him out of his box. This trip would be a chance to chat socially with the people in charge, visit some of the collectives, you know the thing.'

'And you said yes?'

'Of course I did. Free trip overseas, all expenses paid, luxury accommodation, the best food and wine in Indochina. Who wouldn't?'

'But – and there's no offence intended here – why you?'

'Because I'm witty and charming . . .'

'I know. I know. But this sounds like something the PM or one of the politburo boys would jump at.'

'I did ask that, trying very hard not to make myself sound unworthy, and he suggested there might be just a tad of political tension between the Khmer Rouge and Hanoi. Since I dropped off the edge of the Central Committee, they stopped showing me the high-end communiqués. I have no more idea what's going on over there than you do. But I do know the KR haven't been sucking up to their old colleagues the way Hanoi would have liked. I imagine we're under pressure from Vietnam not to send a top-level delegation. I'm the B team.'

'They will brief you on all this before they put you on the plane?'

'No doubt they'll brief both of us.'

'Us being . . . ?'

'He asked me to nominate a travelling companion. I nominated you.'

'You what? Are you mad? No, of course you are. And he agreed?'

'Without hesitation.'

'Just how many bottles did you two get through?'

Malee slept on the cot in the spare room while her mother and Daeng unpacked books from hemp gunny sacks.

'Are you sure you're supposed to have these?' Dtui asked.

'Absolutely not,' Daeng replied with gay candour.

'Then you might get in trouble.'

'I'm sure there's a hit squad at the Ministry of Culture loading their weapons as we speak.'

'What are you going to do with them all?'

'Make shelves.'

'Madame Daeng, you really can't be planning to put them on display?'

'Siri's afraid they'll get rain-damaged in the attic. Some of them are quite valuable. The doctor believes there'll come a day when the paranoia dies down and owning foreign language books won't guarantee you a four-year trip to a seminar camp. Oh, don't look so worried. We aren't planning to put them down in the shop. This door's usually kept locked. Siri can come here after work and sit on the cot and indulge himself in one of his many vices in peace.'

'Where did they all come from?'

'It's a long story.'

'I'm not really in a hurry to go home.'

Daeng smiled drily and filed that comment under D in her mind. 'They're from a temple,' she said.

'A French temple?'

'No. A good old-fashioned Lao temple that just happened to have a French language library. Some of the oldest were donated by missionaries many years ago. The novices studying at the temple were taught general subjects through the medium of French. The brighter ones were allowed to borrow books from the library. Siri went to that temple school before they accepted him into the southern lycée.'

'Really? It must be ancient.'

'I'll tell him you said so.' Waking briefly, Malee gurgled and smiled before closing her eyes again. 'I see she has her mother's sense of humour.'

'She's already a lot funnier than me, Madame Daeng.'

And, with perfect comic timing, Malee let out a little fart in her sleep. The two women broke up like giggly schoolgirls.

'See what I mean?' said Dtui. 'OK, tell me about the books from the temple.'

'All right. In a nutshell, Siri was a very keen student. He'd been sponsored by a wealthy French spinster who paid for his further study in Paris. Once he arrived, he discovered they didn't accept his lycée qualifications from Laos so they made him repeat high school there before he could go on to study medicine. Not difficult for Siri but a terrible waste of time. In the interim, his benefactor passed away so Siri was forced to work for a few years to save up the money for his studies. He went to university, married his lovely Boua, graduated and spent some time as an intern. None of which is relevant to the books other than to show you that it was a very long time before he could return to Laos.

'He and Boua were working in the south and Siri returned to his temple school library often. The collection had expanded significantly since he'd been away. He borrowed books and taught the odd classes to the novices. The monks liked him. Respected him for what he'd achieved. The revolution came and was won and the monks in Savanakhet were worried. They loved their books and, although not with the rabid fervour of Marxist regimes in other parts of the world, the Pathet Lao were symbolically destroying foreign-language books in Vientiane and Luang Prabang. So the southern monks closed the library and hid the books. They were afraid the stash would be discovered some day and that they'd be punished.

'Last week, a rice truck arrived from the south. It stopped just there outside the shop. It was piled high with rice sacks. I tried to explain to the driver and his assistant that I hadn't ordered any rice. In fact mine is a noodle shop and I don't even sell the stuff. But they said Dr Siri had ordered it himself "for a special project". When he came home for lunch and saw our new wall of rice sacks he was as bemused as me. He opened one. It was padded with hay and inside that were these. The whole library. The monks had decided to make Siri the custodian.'

'Ignoring the fact they could get him and you arrested.'

'I suppose they trusted his resourcefulness.'

'And his master plan is to build shelves?'

Daeng laughed. 'Well, they do say if you want to hide something you should make it so obvious nobody notices it. He's been as happy as a whistling duck since they arrived. His precious Voltaire has been lurking in the bottom of his cloth bag for a fortnight.'

'Can you read them?'

'My French was barely good enough to convince the colonists I wasn't a threat ... appropriate for my lowly standing in society. "*Oui, Monsieur. Non, Madame.*" Poor enough that they'd happily leave top-secret information lying open on the desks I swept around. But not good enough for Voltaire. There is a small set of French primers I've been working through. I'm not sure why. I'm not expecting the French to invade us again any time soon.'

They worked silently for a few minutes removing the books from their sacks, unwrapping the hay, sniffing the old bindings. Daeng was about to set off along a subtle chain of questions to discover the reason for the unpleasantness in her friend's marriage. But Dtui saved her the trouble.

'Phosy has another woman,' she said, not looking up from the books.

Daeng coughed her surprise.

'Don't be ridiculous,' she said. She expected Dtui to put up a fight but the nurse merely pursed her lips and her eyes swelled with tears. 'Dtui?' Daeng slid across the wooden floorboards to sit beside her friend. Malee stirred and twisted before settling down. 'Dtui?'

'I'm sorry,' Dtui smiled. 'I promised I wouldn't cry when this happened.'

'What? What's happened?'

'Like I said. I'm in the wife bank. Safe. He's free to go off and make deposits in other accounts.'

'You didn't just make that up on the spur of the moment.'

'My ma used to say it all the time.'

'That was your ma, and those were different times.'

'Men haven't become different creatures.'

'That's true, but I still don't believe it.'

'It's a fact.'

'You have proof?'

'I don't need any, auntie. A wife knows. I see all the signs. It was my own fault. He didn't tell me . . . hasn't ever told me he loves me. In fact, dumb old me, he'd come right out with it, hadn't he? Said he didn't love me but he'd do the right thing. Said he liked me. Liked me and respected me. And what does desperate fat Dtui do?'

'I don't—'

'She says, "Oh, OK. *Like* is good. I'll take that. I have all the love we'll ever need. Maybe, with a little patience, your *like* will grow a few more leaves over the years, a blossom or two. That's plenty. Once Malee came along I thought she'd bind us together but she didn't. Even the *like*'s started to wilt.'

'Dtui, you can't—'

'First he became this super-vigilant father: "Don't talk to her like that. Don't give her too much of this." Then he started with the one-word answers to long questions, the grunts, the late nights, the working weekends.'

'I—'

'The, "I'm really tired, I can't."'

'Perfume? Lipstick stains?' asked Madame Daeng.

'Who can afford perfume and lipstick in this day and age? And you don't need forensic evidence, Madame Daeng. You know when your man's drifting away.'

Later that night, once Siri had slammed the door of Civilai's cream Citroën, reminded him to turn on the headlights, and sent him floating off home, he showered, cleaned his teeth and joined Daeng in their room. She was sitting on the foot of the bed brushing her hair without a recognisable aim or outcome.

'How did it go?' he asked.

Daeng was silent. 'The talk?' he reminded her.

She turned her head towards him and stared into his river-frog green eyes.

'He's having an affair, Siri.'

Siri laughed.

'He is not,' he said.

'Either that or he's having a mental breakdown, because only a man out of his mind would exhibit all the signs of having an affair if he wasn't actually having one.'

'Daeng, you were supposed to put her mind at ease. Not join her.'

'I'm not sure any more.'

'Why not? You know Phosy. He's married to Dtui and to his job. How on earth is he going to find any extramarital time between those two?'

'You have to ask him, Siri.'

'Ask him if he's fooling around?'

'Ask him straight out. You'd recognise if he was lying.'

'It's ridiculous.'

'Please.'

He sighed. 'All right.'

She sniffed at the fine hair on his cheek.

'Thank you,' she said. 'It's the penalty you pay for having a perfect partner who causes you no strife. You have to do all your suffering through other people's relationships.'

'I suppose.'

'Any gossip from increasingly cantankerous Civilai?'

'Ah, right.'

'What is it?'

'I might be popping over to Cambodia for a day or two.'

9

BULGARIAN 101

The shackles have chafed my skin. I am certain an infection is bubbling beneath the metal ankle bracelet. One problem with being a doctor is that you're instinctively obliged to analyse the roots of every ailment. You can't merely sit back and enjoy the misery, ignorant of what's happening to you. Not surprisingly, understanding my medical conditions has never made me feel any better.

For some never-to-be-explained reason, my mother angel has joined the audience. She must have smuggled herself in the luggage. She's sitting cross-legged at the far left side of the classroom by the door, gnawing on her betel. I'd introduce her to you but you probably don't speak Lao. She's just one of your number, twenty or so spaced-out spirits watching the show. I try to imagine the scene from your point of view. Siri, naked, chafed, incontinent. Heavy monk, tears in his eyes. Could this be a climax at the end of a very dull play? An operatic final scene. If nothing comes of this I warrant you'll expect your money back. Am I right? But wait, the heavy monk begins to speak.

'What's that you're eating, brother?'

'Burnt wood,' I tell him. 'It appears the kids set fire to the blackboard before they graduated. I took the liberty of breaking off the corner of the frame. I hope these fellows don't withhold my security deposit. They look like a tough bunch.'

I can feel myself weakening. I can feel the energy and will sapping from my old body. But it isn't hunger that drives me to eat the blackboard. It is a hope that the charcoal at the core of the charred wood might act to remove the toxins from my body and stop these runs. It's unlikely, but worth the try.

'I admire your spirit,' says the heavy monk. 'I used to have a sense of humour. They took that from me as well.' He looks at me with a dramatic sincerity. 'Old doctor, I feel my days are numbered. Do you mind if I unburden myself before they take me?'

I decide to play him along.

'You mean like a confessional?'

'Is it exclusively for Catholics?'

'They do have a better accounting system. I wouldn't know how many self-flagellations or press-ups to impose on you.'

'It doesn't matter. The very act of talking to someone who doesn't judge should be enough. I . . . I did all the things they're accusing me of. I was a spy for the Vietnamese. I've been sending messages to—'

'Oh, do shut up,' I tell him.

'What?'

I've taken as much as I can. The thought of one more gruel donation has kept me silent, biting my tongue until now. But I'm damned if I'll allow myself to be subjected to any more of this.

'Well,' I say, 'I suppose I could listen to you as you list your sins and you tell me how good it feels to get it out of your system. And then you'll say something like, "Is there anything you'd like to confess, brother?" And I take this heaven-sent opportunity to spew forth the locations of all the top-secret Vietnamese missile silos and the names of all my spy schoolteachers and their hat sizes. Spare me.'

'I don't know what you're talking about.'

'Don't you? That's a shame.'

'What are you trying to say, old man?'

'That you're a poor excuse for a human being. That's what. You're no more a monk than I'm a malt grinder. The old, "get into his heart and drain him of information" routine. It's been done to death. My word, if this is the best your founding fathers can come up with, I'd give your ugly regime six weeks before it vanishes up its own backside.'

'You can't t—'

'Has this ruse ever worked? I don't believe anyone conscious would ever fall for it. Go on, get out. Call your cronies and tell them you've failed.'

The kind eyes of the heavy, and now defrocked, monk cloud over. The smile curls into a smirk. He glares at me. He glares needles into my eyes. Then he shouts for the guards and, as they unlock his chains, the man has the audacity to ask, 'What was it that gave me away?'

I'm flabbergasted. Astounded. Does he really believe I'll point out his errors so he'll be able to get it right on the next poor soul? Instead, I give him a gesture I've seen work effectively in some Hollywood films. I've found very little opportunity to use it myself. It involves the unfurling of the digitus medius. The monk has obviously seen the same movies. He stretches, walks back to me and slaps me with the back of his hand across the cheek. He turns and walks out of the room. I know that whatever cruelty awaits me beyond that door has just increased ten-fold, but I don't care.

And what is this, my hard-to-please poltergeists? You haven't been lifted by this display? Inspired? You sit with no noticeable emotion on your faces. Ah, but there she smiles, my mother, a very broad smile that drools with bloody red *betel. A mother's pride for her clever son. So clever he's doomed himself.*

Word had come back from teacher Oum at the Lycée Vientiane that the tests on victims one and two had proven negative for sedatives. Siri was now more certain than ever that both women knew and trusted their killer. He hadn't found it necessary to render them unconscious before impaling them with ninety centimetres of steel. But the contents of the vitamin bottle he'd found at the auditorium had been more difficult to analyse. The results showed a strong possibility, although not conclusive, that it had contained morphine elixir. If it was indeed connected to the case it added to the questions rather than answered them. What was it for? It had to be assumed that either the killer or the victim had consumed the elixir to deaden pain. As there was no evidence of previous injuries on Jim's body, and no indication of illness or disease, the likelihood was that the killer had been suffering in some way. Perhaps from an injury sustained in one of his attacks. Teacher Oum had only just got round to looking at the samples from the third victim and was in the process of testing them for morphine. There was a good deal to discuss.

Phosy's Intelligence Section at Police HQ had, in its heyday, enjoyed a staff of five. Then, some genius at the Ministry of Interior had decided Vientiane was under control and three of Phosy's men had been dispatched to the provinces. Despite their own comparative inexperience, they had been sent to train ex-foot soldiers in the art of policing; a thankless and hopeless operation. So Phosy and Sihot were it as far as detecting was concerned. As they had three victims, and as Siri had done all he could in the morgue,

Phosy recruited him unofficially to help out. He was given the task of looking into the life of Kiang, the second victim. For a closet detective like Siri, this was not unlike winning a Nobel prize. He took Nurse Dtui with him as back-up and left Geung to guard the morgue.

Apart from Ministry of Education copies of Kiang's academic records obtained from Bulgaria, the only source of information they had for Kiang was her mother. So, that's where they began. The house was in That Luang district on a hill which was unlikely to experience the floods. Two ancient flamboyant trees stood guard outside the front fence which itself had taken root and sprouted leaves. A straw and bamboo gazebo sagged in front of the house. It stood beside an enormous grey water jar that spilled over with run-off from the roof. Dtui and the doctor climbed down from the Triumph wearing their huge blue plastic ponchos. They looked like giant morning glory. Siri was from the old 'wear little, get soaked, dry off' school of surviving the monsoons but Dtui had insisted he try one of the new Soviet ponchos. It kept off the rain sure enough, but in Laos whose humidity reached a factor of eighty-two, it merely acted like a portable steam room and rendered them both soaked beneath the plastic.

'Who's there?' came a woman's voice from inside the house.

'Dr Siri and Nurse Dtui from Mahosot hospital,' Dtui called.

A woman appeared in the open doorway wiping her hands on a cloth. She was tall with greasy cheeks and hair pulled back in a bun so severe her ears were almost behind her.

'Mahosot?' she said, alarmed. 'What's happened now?'

'We're from the morgue,' Siri told her. 'We're very sorry about your loss.'

'The . . . ? Oh, of course.' Her sadness overwhelmed the visitors.

'We're helping the police put together a file on the victims,' Siri continued. 'If it isn't too painful, I was hoping we . . .'

The woman seemed to awaken with a start.

'Oh, my. I'm sorry. Where are my manners? Come in, please.'

They drank tea and ate excellent homemade *kanom krok* sweet patties at the kitchen table. The inside of the house spoke of more affluent times. Happier days. Now it seemed to be draped in the same shroud as its owner. Kiang's mother told them of her husband's death to malaria in 1968. How he had been the dean of education in the liberated zone. How his eldest girl had trained with him and become a teacher, a brilliant, well-liked teacher. How she had been in love with a soldier who was killed in a battle in Xiang Khouang. How the mother's second child had contracted dengue and been taken from them two years earlier, now Kiang. How their youngest son, Ming, wanted to mourn for them but didn't know how because the schools didn't teach you how to pray any more.

By the time the mother had finished the litany, Dtui and Siri would have gladly committed suicide right there at the kitchen table. But the woman hadn't cried or used her voice to elicit sympathy. She'd smiled as she recalled her loved ones. She seemed to enjoy the reminiscences. Yet she wore her sadness like a bright blouse and it was impossible not to notice it.

'Did she tell you anything about her time in Bulgaria?' Dtui asked with a catch in her throat.

'It was hard,' she replied. 'I know it was hard but she never complained. She sent me a small share of her per diem every month just to help out, and a letter. She always tried to be cheerful but I know it was a difficult time for her. The language. Heavens above. How did she ever learn it?'

'Did she have any friends over there?' Siri asked. 'Other Lao?'

'There were five girls all selected by their district education offices. The Bulgarian embassy offered a scholarship to teachers but they insisted they study in different cities. So Kiang didn't have anyone close she could share her feelings with.'

'Did she have a boyfriend back here she could write to?'

'No, nurse. She'd been so in love with Soop, her soldier, that nobody else could match up. She had more offers of marriage than I can count, suitors coming by the house all the time, but she turned them all down.'

'Do you know if she met anyone while she was away?'

'In Bulgaria?' She let out a little laugh. 'I have to confess my girl was a little afraid of western men. No, that's not true. I'd say it bordered on being petrified. She was scared to death of them.'

'Any reason why?' Siri asked.

'The smell, Doctor,' she said. 'You know, that odour they have, as if they're a different species? Really, most of them are animals. Oversexed, loud. I feared for her safety every day. She was a beautiful girl, Doctor.'

'You must have been relieved when she came back,' said Dtui.

'She was so happy. She wasn't a racist but she was pleased to be back amongst her own kind. They put her to work straight away out at the library at Dong Dok. She was supposed to be cataloguing their books except they didn't have anything to catalogue. They'd thrown out all the American and French language materials and what little there was in Lao was Roneoed and poor quality. All the new books were Vietnamese, Russian and Chinese and she couldn't read any of them. You'd have thought they'd send her somewhere with a language that might be useful to learn, wouldn't you?'

'How long had she been back?' Dtui asked.

'She came back in January.'

'And since then, no new friendships? No boyfriends?

'Doctor, I know she was only thirty-two but I really think the idea of having a boyfriend didn't appeal to her any more. She loved being here at home. They don't pay very much at Dong Dok, sometimes they don't pay at all. But she got rice and tinned foods from the co-op and she was happy to know that she could provide for me and her brother, Ming.'

'It sounds like you two were close,' Dtui said.

'I know we were mother and daughter but in fact we were more like sisters. There were no secrets between us.'

The mother smiled that incongruous sweet and sour smile again that had the visitors reaching for the razor blades. She poured them all more tea. Siri didn't want to worm his way into any more bitter apples but the question had to be asked.

'On the night she died,' he began, 'she told you she was going to exercise?'

Kiang's mother nodded and her eyes became moist opals of despair. 'Yes, I have to say I was a little surprised. Shocked, even. She'd found her old high school tracksuit somewhere deep in the closet and she marched in and announced she was going to get fit. She'd never shown any interest in sports at school. In fact, I think the tracksuit was still in its original plastic. She had a nice figure. She didn't eat sweet food. I don't know what had entered her mind.'

'You don't know who she went with?'

'I forgot to ask. I was so surprised. I laughed. I asked her what had brought on this sudden urge to get fit. She said something that sounded very Party to me. Oh! Sorry.'

'No offence taken,' Siri said.

'She said, "The body's a machine and if you don't oil a machine it dries up and shuts down and it's no use to anyone." It didn't sound like the kind of thing she'd make up herself. And that was the last . . .'

The opals cracked and tears rolled and the woman's greasy cheeks put up no resistance and sadness dripped into the teacup she held in her hand.

Siri and Dtui rode from the house on the hill with lumps in their throats. They weren't really in a mood to socialise but before returning to the morgue, they made a brief detour to the Lao Patriotic Women's Association. There, they met up with their old friend Dr Pornsawan. They were only in the office for half an hour but they made a deal that – if the spirits were feeling particularly benevolent – might change one or two lives for the better. Goodness knew, after a visit with Kiang's mother, they needed to spread some cheer.

10

THE DR SIRI MEMORIAL LIBRARY

The announcement of the results from the three investigations was scheduled to take place at Police HQ. Dtui had found several excuses not to attend so Siri arrived by himself. There was no evidence that the departed officers had ever existed. Their typewriters and pens, even their desks and chairs had been pilfered by other departments. You couldn't leave belongings unattended for too long in a Lao police station. All that remained in the large airy room were the tables of Phosy and Sihot and ten metal filing cabinets. They pushed the tables together, ordered coffee from the food stall opposite and sat around the victim chart.

'Who's first?' Siri asked.

They deferred to age and Siri described in detail what he and Dtui had learned that afternoon. Despite Phosy's encouragement for Siri to take notes, he'd assured the young man that there was absolutely nothing wrong with his memory. This he proved by reciting verbatim all of the facts and figures from his visit to Kiang's house. He was followed by Sergeant Sihot whose memory existed between two thick *bureau de poste* rubber bands in an untidy wad of paper. This he thumbed through until he arrived at his interview with Mrs Bop, the mother of victim number one, Dew.

'I have to begin by saying,' he began by saying, 'that Comrade Dew's mother was not all that helpful when it came to her daughter's activities in Russia. Nor did she have much to offer in regards to her daughter's actions since her return to Laos. Nor did she have any idea why her daughter was sitting naked in a steam room on the night of her death. One of the neighbours suggested to me the girl had just dumped the kids on her mother's lap and washed her hands of them four years earlier. The neighbour didn't see Dew or the husband come to visit that often. On the positive side, Dew's mother and her husband, aged sixty-three and sixty-five respectively, gave me the impression they had a genuine affection for their grandchildren. I couldn't say the same for their relationship with Comrade Dew.'

'Which begs the question,' Siri said, 'what were Dew and her husband doing together in the first place?'

'My question exactly, Doctor,' Sihot agreed. 'They didn't appear to invest a lot of time and effort in their children's upbringing. The grandparents got some money every month from the father but that was all.'

The wooden shutters on either side of the large room were open and a sudden gust passed through taking two of Sihot's sheets with it. He was about to run after them then realised what the wind had taken.

'No problem,' he said. 'Old case. I still have Comrade Dew here.'

'We're relieved to hear it,' Phosy grumbled.

'I went to see the clerk who registered the marriage back in 1973 when the couple moved to Vientiane. I discovered that both husband and wife had been in the military at the time of their marriage. They came from Phongsali which is where the original certificate was issued. I have the name of the military witness who co-signed the certificate and I'm attempting to get in touch with him.'

'Good job, Sihot,' said Siri.

'Thank you, Comrade.'

'Any background information on our prowling wolf Vietnamese major?' Siri asked.

'Getting military information from the Vietnamese is like getting blood from a crab,' Phosy told him. 'There are channels. But the wheels are in motion. We'll have to be patient.'

'Did anyone ask him at the interview . . . ?'

'If he was a fencer? Yes. He said no. He said no to most of the questions. But we found out he was in Czechoslovakia for eighteen months of military training. He forgot to mention that as well. We're chasing that up with the Czech embassy. They owe us a favour.'

'All right, Phosy,' said Siri, leaning back on his chair. 'That just leaves you.'

'And our real fencer, Jim,' Phosy said. 'All I got from the files was that her parents were "casual staff". It's the catchall phrase for everything from day labourers to hotel bellboys. The records didn't say where they'd worked. In the old days, everyone not in government service who could write, put "casual staff" on their documents. Her mother was Vietnamese and probably didn't have any official status here, so I doubt there's anything on record anywhere. We only know she was Vietnamese because Jim wrote it on her application for the eastern bloc. No permanent address. No personal details about the parents.

'We do know Jim enrolled aged sixteen as a trainee medic with the American refugee hospital in Nam Tha. She was one of the star pupils by all accounts. When the Yanks fled, our people found Jim running one of the clinics without any supervision. They all called her "doctor" up there. Our own medical officials were so impressed with her skills and her dedication that they overlooked the fact she'd been selected and trained by Americans and made a scholarship available to her in the Soviet Union. They wanted her to qualify as a real doctor. There was an awful shortage. But she refused that and two other scholarship placements. Cited pressure of work. Not ready to leave. But then a scholarship post came up in East Germany and she finally agreed. She spent a year studying German, picked it up without effort, then launched on the first year of pre-med. It was one of those accelerated courses the Europeans put on for third-world countries. They assume we don't have the brains to attend regular medical schools and that our people don't get as sick as theirs so we don't need seven years of study.'

Phosy looked up from his notes to find both Siri and Sihot smiling at him.

'What? It's true. It is. Anyway, Jim sailed through her language classes and the first two semesters of medicine. Top of her class in everything. Then something went wrong. She failed her first year final exams. Not just failed but bombed completely. They let her do a supplementary exam and she failed that as well. Under the terms of her scholarship they had no choice but to send her home.'

'That's weird,' said Siri. 'And nobody knows what happened?'

'No.'

'Anything from her classmates?'

'There might be, but don't forget they're all still over there studying. I've written to the Lao student union representative in Berlin. But even with express delivery it could be two or three weeks before we hear back from them. I don't have an international telephone budget.'

'Any chance of finding her parents, Inspector?' Sihot asked.

'I'm on it, Sergeant. But I get the feeling they're old regime. Just the fact their daughter got work on a US medical mission makes me think they had some American connections.'

'And that could bring us back to K6,' Siri said. 'I think the locations of the killings are important. It can't be a coincidence that two of the girls were murdered right there under the noses of the Vietnamese and Lao security services. The killing at Sisangvone primary school doesn't fit in any respect so I think we should put that on the back shelf and focus on K6. I'm wondering whether Jim's parents might have been on the staff there before seventy-five.'

'And jumped ship with all the others,' Sihot agreed. 'It might explain why Jim didn't want to go into too much detail about what her parents did. It might have affected her application to study.'

'I met a fellow who tends the grounds out there,' Siri recalled. 'His name's Miht. He's one of the overlappers. He'd probably remember a Vietnamese/Lao couple with a smart daughter from the American days. In fact, you might want to check him out as a suspect as well. I can't give you a good reason why. It's just a feeling I have in my gut that he's connected in some way. He seemed to be . . . observing. I know observing's a Lao hobby but he was making an art out of it.'

'I'll look into it, Doctor,' said Sihot.

'Let's not forget, whoever killed the two women at K6 had a right to be there,' Phosy added. 'We should consider all the staff suspects. With the cabinet members living out there, it isn't the easiest place to get in to. How many people are we talking about, Sihot?'

A stony-faced girl in a faded uniform came trotting in dripping water all over the place from her umbrella. She handed Phosy a sheet of paper, giving Sihot time to reshuffle his pack.

'Including domestic staff,' Sihot read, 'labourers, soldiers, security personnel, and all the politicians and their families . . . just over five hundred, Inspector.'

'Better odds than having the entire country to search through,' Siri reminded them.

'And the odds might have improved even more,' Phosy said, reading the sheet.

'What's that?' Siri asked.

'It's the Electricité du Lao work roster for rewiring the east side of the compound. The names of the workers with security clearance. And whose name do we see right here at the top?'

'I only know one person who works for Electricité du Lao,' Siri said. 'The husband of Dew.'

'No?' said Sihot. 'Comrade Chanti? I don't believe it. Twice we talked to him and not once did he mention he was working out at K6.'

'Perhaps we didn't ask the right questions,' Phosy growled.

Once the meeting was over and the next round of interviews scheduled, Siri asked Phosy if he could walk him to his motorcycle. The rain hadn't stopped. There were those beginning to believe it never would. It was falling wheezily now, catching its breath before the next major expectoration.

'What is it, Doctor?' Phosy asked with an almost irritated tone.

'There doesn't always need to be something, son,' Siri smiled. 'With all the nastiness we've been dealing with, we sometimes forget to find a minute or two to pass the time of day, take an interest in each other.'

Phosy stopped. 'What do you want, Siri?'

'Ah, well. If you insist. Are you having an affair behind Dtui's back, Phosy?'

Phosy's smile was as drab as the day.

'Anything else?' he asked.

'That's all.'

'Then I'll see you tomorrow.'

Phosy turned and started to walk away.

'Are you just going to leave me standing here in the rain without an answer?'

Phosy ran up the wooden steps and into his office, swerving to avoid a jet of water arcing from the broken roof tiles.

'It certainly would seem so,' Siri answered himself.

'So, what do you think it meant?' Madame Daeng asked later that evening. She and Siri were putting up shelves in the room they were now whimsically calling The Dr Siri Memorial Library. Daeng was the carpenter in the family. Siri just handed her nails when told to. He was impressed at how well her late-afternoon sawing was fitting neatly together.

'I thought perhaps you'd know,' he replied.

'I wasn't there, was I? Nail! I'd need to have been there. Was it an embarrassed smile? A "don't be ridiculous" smile? An ironic "wouldn't you like to know?" smile? Nail!'

'It was just a . . . you know? A smile.'

'Then you have to ask him again. And next time, read the smile.'

'Why doesn't Dtui ask him herself?'

'She's already made her mind up. Nail!'

'I don't—'

'Siri, concentrate. That was a toothpick.'

'Sorry. I don't feel comfortable interfering. They haven't exactly asked for our help, you know.'

'Neither did any of the strays and orphans you're putting up at your house free of charge. Neither did Mr Geung or Crazy Rajid who you've probably frightened clear across the river. These are our friends. Nail! They don't always have to ask for help.'

'You're right,' he said. 'I'll invite him out for a few drinks, loosen him up, tell him about the myriad extramarital affairs I'm involved in and he'll feel an instant camaraderie and come out with his story all by himself.'

'Now you're thinking. Nail!'

It was mid-morning and Siri was in the morgue office sitting at his desk with a magnifying glass trying to match the fingerprints on Jim's épée with the very smudged print he'd found on the bottom of the vitamin bottle. All three swords lay parked across his desk. Nurse Dtui was at her own desk studying Russian. She hadn't entirely given up hope that, one day in the future, she might continue her studies overseas. This épée case – three women given scholarships – had caused her to wonder how her own course in the Soviet Union might have been progressing if only . . .

She'd been on her way, tickets booked, woollen hats crocheted, when, 'wham', hit head-on by events. A little bit of lust induced by a powerful but foolish crush, a deter-mined sperm, rampant biology, and there she was: with child but without mate. Her sperm donor had felt obliged to do the right thing and she'd said 'Yes'. Clearly her mistake. Beautiful baby, womanising husband. One out of two wasn't bad. She was feeling resentment towards the three women who'd studied overseas. It was as if they'd taken her place but not taken full advantage of their good fortune. Wrong and irrational, Dtui, but better to channel your disappointment into three dead people than one live one who, let's be honest, hadn't really promised her that much.

'What are you doing, Dtui?'

'Trying to understand the instructions on all this equipment the Soviets keep throwing at us. The freezer's been here since last year and we still don't know how to turn it down.'

'Good. That can wait. Come and take a look at this.'

She walked across to his desk and leaned over the magnifying glass Siri held over the vitamin bottle.

'In your opinion,' he asked, 'is this a thumb-print or a smudged fingerprint?'

'It looks a little . . .'

'Yes?'

'A little bit like the face of Ho Chi Minh.'

'Dtui, I'm being serious.'

'It's a miracle. Uncle Ho has returned—'

She was interrupted by the sound of the door banging against the filing cabinet. Mr Geung walked into the office drenched as a water rat, obviously in a poor mood.

'What's wrong, hon?' Dtui asked.

'Nothing,' he replied, and slumped down at his little desk in the corner. He shook the rain from his head. His perm looked like a crêpe.

'If nothing's wrong,' Dtui said, 'where are the two cups of coffee you went to the canteen to buy?'

Geung looked at his hands to confirm they weren't holding a tray.

'Oh,' he said. He stood, started for the door, then had second thoughts and returned to his seat. He was obviously being pulled in two different directions by the oxen of conscience.

'Mr Geung, did something happen?' Siri asked.

'No!'

'Geung?' Dtui pushed.

'A . . . a . . . a . . . a woman,' he said, agitated and animated.

'Yes?'

'In the can, the can . . . the canteen. She . . . she . . .'

'She what, hon?'

'She . . . she's feeble-minded like me.'

'Mr Geung, how many times do we have to tell you? There's nothing feeble about your mind. You have—'

'A condition,' Geung cut in. 'Called Down's Syndrome. And . . . and . . . and she does, too.'

'Really?' said Siri. 'I wonder what she's doing here.'

'Probably a patient,' Dtui suggested.

'No, no, no,' said Geung. He was rocking so drastically back and forth in his seat he was making the room feel like an ocean liner in a squall. 'She's . . . she's in . . . in a uniform.'

'Well, that explains it,' Siri nodded. 'She's come to work here.'

'I . . . I . . . no, no good.'

'What are you so mad about, Geung?' Dtui asked.

'It's my hospital,' he said. He stood, tapped the desktop four times, and headed off out the door.

Dtui looked at Siri. 'He seems upset.'

'Who'd have thought Down's Syndrome sufferers could be territorial? You know, it is really condescending of us to think he'd get along with a girl just because she has the same condition.'

'Dr Pornsawan said she's got a lovely personality.'

'Even so . . .'

'Doc, we aren't locking them in a room together. It's a big

144

hospital. They don't have to talk. We just arranged a part-time job for a girl, that's all.'

'All right, but I don't want you pushing him.'

'I wouldn't dream—'

'Who aren't we pushing?' came a voice.

They looked up to see Civilai in the doorway fanning himself with several loose sheets of damp paper.

'Hello, brother,' Siri smiled. 'What did you bring me?'

'Travel documents.'

'Travel . . . ? Oh, shit. Cambodia. I'd forgotten completely.'

'It's all official. We leave on Friday.'

'This Friday? Oh, look. I'm not sure I can. We're in the middle of this case, and—'

'Afraid you have no choice, old man.' He turned back to shake his umbrella in the vestibule and left it standing open there before walking into the office.

Civilai put the papers on Siri's desk. The doctor detected a faint odour of neglect about his friend.

'What do you mean I have no choice?' Siri asked.

'Your boss, Judge Haeng, got wind of our little trip. He was delighted. Said a high-profile visit like this would do wonders for your chances for you-know-what. He's given you four days off.'

'I don't want four days off. Not now. Surely, solving this case should take priority.'

'He did mention that your role in the épée murder investigation was over, that you are merely a coroner, and that it's all in the hands of the police now.'

'He did, did he?'

'We're just humble servants, Siri. Bite the bullet. We pop over for the May Day reception, tour a couple of farms, eat and drink ourselves silly and we're back before anyone's noticed we've gone. I doubt Phosy will close the case in the interim. It'll still be there for us to solve when we come back.'

'I thought you said they only had one flight in and out a fortnight?'

'Normally, yes. But this is a special occasion. They've laid on an extra flight from Peking. We'll be going with the Chinese delegation.'

'Really? That should be fun,' said Siri. 'You'll have a chance to tell them what you think of them. When's the orientation?'

'Nothing scheduled yet. Why the panic on getting briefed?'

'I haven't been out of the country for seven years. I'm interested to know what's happening out there in the real world.'

Despite my obstinacy, they continue to bring me my fetid water every couple of hours. Somebody wants to keep me alive – barely. The lights burn on. Time's dragging like a heavy body over rocks. The whole story is crawling along too slowly to be film. In the cinema I would have made my daring escape hours ago. Certainly, for my sanity it helps to see it all as theatre; the screams broadcast from a tape recorder in the wings. The insect bites merely carefully applied stage make-up. A theatrical slap to the face. It's only acting. Don't hide your eyes, son.

The charcoal has helped. I am back in control, if not of the consistency, at least of the timing. I can now wait for the bucket they bring. The boys. The boys with three watches rattling around their wrists like bracelets. The boys not old enough to shave. The clone boys, identical to the one in my dark dream. Playing soldier with live ammunition. A real gun pointed at my forehead. Night after night. That finger, twitching, deciding whether to squeeze the trigger and take this old man out. And some nights he doesn't. And some nights he does. And on those nights when the gun blasts, I find myself walking through what's left of my nightmare with nothing above my frayed neck. But, even on those head-less nights I can hear the eerily beautiful singing. It's a dream. Who needs ears? All right. All right. Perhaps I sense the sounds. Would that work? The honeydew voice of a man. The words mean nothing to me but I can tell he's singing to his lover. And each night I wake in a humid inside-the-house sweat and I tell my wife, 'Something bad is going to happen.' And Madame Daeng brushes back my hair and says, 'It's only a dream.'

But it isn't.

The key clicks in the lock of the unpainted door. Why lock the door? I'm not going anywhere chained by the ankle to eight metres of lead pipe, am I now? And sure as hell there wouldn't be a queue to get in. Why lock the door? Why lock the door? And they don't need to worry about you folks any more: you dead ones, you ghosties. You can come and go as you like, lock or no lock. And you came, didn't you? But you stayed. And you sit, bored out of your minds. Dr Siri on the stage, forgetting his lines, forgetting his mind, edging on delirium, bordering on insanity. And I understand. Really I do. You aren't just watching. You're waiting, aren't you? Waiting like vultures for me to leave my body and join you on your quest to find a better place. Oh, that's easy. Anywhere is a better place than this.

The smiley man is in the doorway. A silent 'boo' and 'hiss' from the stalls. The boys unfasten me, force me to get dressed. Wrap a scarf around my eyes. Poke me with their bamboo canes. Whip my legs. It's only acting, son. You can open your eyes. *But then it comes to me, when I should be concentrating on the pain, when I should be fearing what torture I am being led to, it is now I solve the mystery of the three épées. And I know that a man will walk into a concrete yard somewhere, a yard stained with the blood of others, and be shot for something he didn't do. Riddled with mistaken bullets. Perhaps it has already happened. How long have I been here? The future and the past all hang here in the glow of the overhead lamps, hypnotised by the light, not knowing where to fly.*

Only I can save him, this wrongly convicted man. The proof has been there all the time and I've ignored it. 'Stop the torture. Somebody hand me a phone. Hey, boy, run this note across the street to Vientiane. Here's fifty kip. Lassie, girl, go find Judge Haeng. Tell him he's got the wrong man. I'm sorry, I'm a little tied up or I'd go myself. Tied up, whipped, burnt, electrocuted . . . bits removed and mutilated.'

I let out a manic laugh in the face of death.

'I see you're in good spirits still,' the smiley man says as I'm dragged out like the garbage – stage right. 'We'll see what we can do about that.'

'Boo' and 'hiss,' cries the silent audience.

There was no sound of footsteps, only the hushed click of the latch and the door opened.

'You should be a spy,' Siri said.

'Can't sleep?' Daeng asked.

Siri was sitting cross-legged on the floor of the home library, a desk lamp leaning over his shoulder like a curious, light-headed stork. Sunrise wasn't that far off. A book, heavy as a temple lintel, pinned the old doctor to the ground.

'Camus,' he said.

'The soap people?'

'Distant relative.'

'Does he have a cure for insomnia?'

'Who has insomnia? Just a peculiar dream. I wasn't in a hurry to get back into it.'

She sat on the cot.

'Do you want to tell me about it?'

'It involved children and guns.'

'Then, perhaps you shouldn't . . .'

'I've had a thought.'

'Good. Then all this was worthwhile.'

'Your question about eastern European alumni and clubs and reunions.'

'Civilai squashed me flat as a postage stamp on that one.'

'He did, but he shouldn't have. There is something. Imagine you've spent four years in Bulgaria and you've just come back to Laos. What is it you need?'

'Food that isn't dripping with fat?'

'No! I mean, yes. But something else. You've spent four years learning and speaking a foreign language. You have knowledge. Skills that you learned in that language. Do you just switch that all off when you come home?'

'You find someone who speaks the same language to keep your hand in.'

'You could do, but I can't imagine a day when we Lao would sit down and speak to each other in Bulgarian just to maintain a language. It isn't natural. And it's far too active for us. There's a less stressful, passive outlet.'

'Books.'

'Exactly. And where would Russian, German and Bulgarian speakers go to keep up with the news and the latest technical advances in their adopted countries?'

Daeng clicked her fingers.

'The government bookshop on Sethathirat.'

'It's the only place. Lao translations of Marx, Lenin, and Engels. Socialist newsletters and magazines in foreign languages. Poster-sized photographs of politburo members. All those perfect gifts for birthdays and weddings.'

'The victims could have met there, browsing, shared their experiences and become friends. And . . .'

'And that's where they met him.'

'The sword coach. Bravo. At three a.m. it all sounds perfectly plausible. But now you have to put in some sleeping hours so you're alive enough to follow up on this train of thought in the morning.' She stood up and stretched her aching legs. 'Does your author have a parting comment for us before we retire?'

'You know, I think he does,' Siri said. He heaved back the pages to a strip of paper that poked forlornly upwards and ran his finger down the page until he found the quotation he'd discovered earlier.

'*I know of only one duty*,' he read. '*And that is to love.*'

'I think I'm going to like Mr Camay,' Daeng smiled.

11

THE PATRON SAINT OF
FRENCH FIREMEN

The male clerk at the government bookshop was ugly enough to draw tears from a lime. It was as if he had breathed in too heavily one day, perhaps in shock, and his skin and all his features had been sucked inward, stopping only when they hit solid bone. But his teeth, the only camel teeth in the whole of the PDR Laos, stood out proudly from his jaw like a prehistoric jetty. He was tall and gaunt and ungainly, and more than a few prospective customers had taken one step into the store, seen him standing there behind the counter like Hell's own gatekeeper, and withdrawn in terror. Even Siri baulked momentarily when he saw him through the window. When the doctor pushed open the door, a brass bell tinkled above his head like a small idea.

'Comrade,' the clerk sang. 'Welcome.'

It was a peculiar bookshop, dark, in spite of the large windows, and unfriendly. There weren't walls of book spines to walk along and browse. What scant reading material they had was displayed flat on boards like beef or fish at a country market. One or two selected tomes were held captive in glass cabinets. In two minutes a customer could perform one perfunctory circuit of the room – feigning interest in this or that – then be on his way. But Siri had cause to stay longer after his circuit, during which he

identified Russian, German and – although he wasn't certain
– what looked like Bulgarian magazines. The clerk, with
nothing else to do, had observed Siri's every move.

'We have the latest *Your Country – Your Livestock* from
Romania just in,' he said with an imperfectly straight face.
'Hot off the press.'

'I think I'll wait for the translation,' Siri decided.

'Very well,' said the clerk. He was either smiling or
suffering some inward agony.

'Have you worked here long?' Siri asked.

'Worked and managed since we opened,' the clerk said
proudly. 'I do all the bookwork and conceive of and execute
the displays. Every month or so, as new books arrive, I
change the theme to stimulate consumer interest. It's one of
the skills I learned overseas.'

Siri looked around in search of a theme.

'This month is . . . ?' he asked.

'Red,' said the man, without a hint of sarcasm.

'Red?'

'Naturally, there aren't always enough pure red covers to
do the display justice. But, as you can see, there's pink and
mauve and purple, all within the same segment of the spec-
trum, to accentuate the mood. Last month was—'

'No, don't tell me. Blue?'

The clerk laughed. It was a horrid sight.

'Good guess,' he said. 'But that was February. March was
black and white. As you can imagine, we don't have too
many covers in black and white in this modern age, but, by
opening each book at its title page . . .'

'It must have been a sight to see. I wish I'd been here.'
Siri shook his head in amazement as he looked around. It
was true, the red book covers were inside the display
cabinet like gallery exhibits. 'Tell me, Comrade, do you

have many returnees from the eastern bloc coming to use your service?'

'Returnees are our burgeoning target market, Comrade. As the number of returnees swells, I imagine in ten years we'll have to move to larger premises.'

'But, right now?'

'You have to understand,' said the clerk, pointing a spindly ginseng finger at the doctor. 'Not many of our brothers and sisters have returned to Laos this soon.'

'I do understand that. I'm just interested. How many returnees do you have subscribing to say . . . Russian journals?'

The clerk reached below the counter for a ledger thick as a door step. He opened the cover and flipped two or three pages. He laboured over the list for longer than necessary.

'Four,' he said.

'Hmm. Then I imagine the odds of two customers actually bumping into each other are quite remote.'

'Unless they're in the reading room at the same time.'

'You have a reading room?'

'A small one. But I encourage customers to use it when they're here. I have tea in there. On occasions the odd sesame biscuit.'

'Could I see it?'

'Certainly.'

The clerk walked around the counter on his long uncoordinated legs. Siri's chin came to his solar plexus. He led the doctor to a door at the rear of the store and opened it to reveal a small windowless room which could have been the parlour of an elderly royalist. Two comfortable sofas scattered liberally with unmatching cushions bordered a large teak coffee table with a cotton doily at its centre. Resting upon that was a basket of colourful but unconvincing plastic flowers. Around the walls were large tourist posters of Moscow, Berlin, Belgrade and Prague, a handwritten sign saying 'WELCOME TO OUR READING ROOM' in eight languages, and butterflies, a lot of three-dimensional butterflies cut out of coloured paper. To one side a taller table held a tin tray with upturned cups, a sugar dish in a moat of water to discourage ants, and a large pink flowery thermos.

Ignoring the absence of natural light and the leaning towards kitsch it was a pleasant room. Some love had gone into it, some appreciation that customers might lack a convivial place to read in their crowded dormitories. And if two customers should be here at the same time with common experiences from Europe, otherwise incompatible people might become friends. And what better place for a killer to stalk his victims?

'Comrade,' Siri turned to the clerk who was standing uncomfortably close, 'do the names Hatavan Rattanasamay, Khantaly Sisamouth, or Sunisa Simmarit mean anything to you?'

Siri bunched his fists in hope as the man considered his question.

'Yes,' said the clerk.

'Which one?'

'All of them.'

Madame Daeng's noodle shop was fast becoming the surrogate after-hours police briefing room. While he waited for the actual police officers to arrive, Civilai stood beneath the altar Daeng had lovingly built and decorated. It was a two-storey affair attached to the main pillar of the building. It was traditional to have a spirit house outside as a boarding inn for the displaced spirits of the land, but the authorities were being finicky about residents displaying their animism blatantly in public. So Daeng had flown in the face of tradition and brought them inside. She had even dared to house them under the same roof as the ancestral shrine.

The ancestors lived upstairs in a thirty-centimetre-square box behind a barricade of Buddhas, incense sticks, wooden elephants, Chinese and Indian deities, a half bottle of red Fanta, and Sainte-Barbe, the patron saint of firemen whom Daeng had rescued from the bin of one of the French oppressors back in the fifties. Downstairs lived the re-housed *phaphoom*. These spirits of the earth were unashamed capitalists. Like the poor Lao who lusted after the consumer items they heard about on Thai radio, the *phaphoom* were far more cooperative when bribed. A free lodging wasn't always enough. Madame Daeng's spirit house was straight from the high society catalogues. Inside was all the doll's furniture she could cram into the space; a refrigerator, TV, bathtub, wardrobe, and shoe rack. Parked on a ledge in front were a toy school bus and a Mercedes Benz with diplomatic plates just in case they felt like an excursion.

Civilai chuckled to himself. Daeng was married to a man who lived amongst spirits. Surely, with such personal contact, she could dispense with all this mumbo jumbo. Why would a woman so worldly, so astute, put so much effort into superstition? He was reaching for the patron saint of French firemen when Madame Daeng came down the stairs.

'Don't you dare,' she called.

'I was just—'

'Then don't. A woman's spirit house is her soul. Leave it alone.'

'You're an enigma, Madame Daeng.'

'And plan to stay that way.'

A lilac Vespa stopped directly beneath the shop awning and a rain-sodden Phosy climbed from its seat.

'Will it ever stop raining?' he asked nobody in particular. He kicked off his sandals and shook himself like a dog before entering. He carried a wad of papers wrapped in several plastic bags. They were obviously more important than himself in shorts and a T-shirt. At the sound of the bike, Siri had shelved his book and come downstairs.

'No Sihot?' he asked.

'Family crisis,' Phosy told him. 'Seems the more relatives you have to live with the more crises you have to endure.'

'And where's Dtui?' Daeng asked.

Phosy hesitated.

'She's not here? I came straight from the ministry,' he said. 'Haven't had a chance to go home.'

'You were at the ministry dressed like that?' she asked.

'Er, no. I have . . . I have spare clothes at the office.'

On their way to the meeting table, Siri and Daeng exchanged one of their now customary glances. Once they were seated, Civilai, oblivious to any domestic drama, opened the proceedings. Siri noticed that his friend was wearing the same clothes he'd worn the last time they'd seen him.

'As instructed,' Civilai began, 'I performed my under-hand duties at K6. Being a resident there and having no known police background, I was able to do my spying with relative ease. As you know, in my dotage I have become something of an Adonis in the kitchen. So, on Thursday I took a tray of sweet, freshly baked macaroons to the old stable building which the Vietnamese use as their centre of operations. As I am a frail and harmless pensioner, but fluent in Vietnamese, the guards quickly opened up to me and started to share secrets. My macaroons have that effect on people. The soldiers made no secret of the fact that they dislike their commander, Major Dung. They don't like his womanising ways or his personality, but they all agreed he is a man with many skills. Most pertinent of these is that the major is an expert in, amongst other things, a Vietnamese martial art called *quoc ngu*. It is, basically, the use of a double-edged sword. And he brought at least one with him.'

'I knew it,' Siri said.

'One of the men had seen him practising with it in the clearing behind the stables,' Civilai added.

'What about fencing swords?' Phosy asked.

'Nobody I spoke to there knew what fencing was so I can't answer that. The macaroons ran out before I could get any more information about Dung. But, as an aside, I enquired about the project being undertaken by Electricité du Lao. It appears that both the auditorium and the houses around the garden sauna are included in the rewiring schedule. Your Comrade Chanti would surely have been at both locations, at least during the planning stage.'

'Sihot went to talk to him today,' Phosy told them. 'We'll see what he had to say for himself tomorrow.'

Civilai accepted a glass of rum and soda from Madame Daeng with an overly polite nod. No Thai hooch this but genuine Bacardi he'd brought along himself, courtesy of the president. He sipped at his drink, smacked his lips and said,

'Which brings me finally to the groundsman, Miht. I'd seen him around often but never had cause to talk to him. He turned out to be a very knowledgeable fellow. But he couldn't come up with a memory of a Lao/Vietnamese couple with a daughter who trained with the American doctors. He was, without a shadow of a doubt, lying to me.'

'What makes you think that?' Phosy asked.

'Well, he isn't the only survivor from the old to the new regime. There are two or three more who stayed on to ring in the new. One of them is called Comrade Tip, the washing lady. She maintains the small laundry at K6. My wife used to take our bedding there because our line isn't strong enough to hold up all those wet sheets and covers. Comrade Tip knew exactly who I was talking about. She couldn't remember the mother's name but the father was a cook/handyman called Rote. Their daughter was a precocious girl called Jim. She'd done really well in school, charmed the Americans, and ended up in a mission hospital in Nam Tha.'

'And did she recall where this couple worked?' Siri asked.

'As clear as day.' Civilai smiled and sipped his drink. 'At the Jansen house. The house with the sauna.'

This revelation led to a frenzy of questions and qualifications and hypotheses. But mainly it caused a single headache that throbbed in the temples of everyone present. What did it mean? The parents of victim number three, Jim, had worked at the house where victim number one was killed. Siri tipped onto the back legs of his chair and let the spirit beam arrest his fall. He'd imagined the case in more simple terms; the victims met a bad man who had clearance at K6 and he killed them. Now it seemed the crime had a history. It was like planning a red theme and having delivery after delivery of drastically yellow books.

'Damn,' he said. 'Phosy, are your findings going to make this any more complicated?'

The inspector hadn't accepted a drink. Recently he'd become Phosy the temperate. Siri wondered how he would ever elicit secrets from a sober man.

'I looked down the list of bookshop patrons you gave me,' Phosy said. 'All three victims had subscribed to receive journals in their respective fields, paid for by the embassies that sponsored them. I showed the clerk Polaroids of the victims and he was certain he'd seen all three utilising the reading room. He said that Saturday afternoon was the most popular as Saturday was a half-day for most workers. There might be seven or eight customers in there at a time. People even sitting on cushions on the ground. I doubt they were all engrossed in the malt yield of the Ukraine. It was a sort of informal reading club. Of course, there's no guarantee our killer put his name down to subscribe to anything, but we're working our way down the list. It's the best lead so far.'

After the meeting, Siri wasn't of a mood to sit and drink with Civilai. He had a room full of books and a limited number of years to get through them. But Civilai had insisted in that belligerent way of men who are starting to lean too heavily on the bottle. He seemed more out of control than usual. He didn't even know he was putting on old clothes to go visiting. Only a man living by himself would be allowed to make such a mistake.

'Where's Mrs Nong?' Siri asked.

'Surely you mean, how's Mrs Nong?' Civilai said. They were sitting at the gingham Formica tabletop. Madame Daeng had gone upstairs. Phosy had left, presumably to pursue his nefarious late-night habits. A large purple gecko hung boldly from the far wall like an ornament. It had interrupted the conversation several times with its rude burps.

'No, I mean "where",' Siri confirmed. 'She wouldn't have let you out in this state.'

Civilai laughed.

'Am I in a state, Siri?'

The doctor remained silent and stared at his friend. Even the gecko held its breath.

'She's visiting her sister,' Civilai said at last.

'Her sister lives in Khouvieng,' Siri reminded him. 'That's a twenty-minute trip from your house.'

'I mean she's staying there for a few days. She's not well. The sister. The sister's not well.'

Siri continued to stare. Rain dripped and splashed from the rear window shutter.

'She likes to stay there sometimes,' Civilai added.

Stare.

'Quite a lot of times lately, in fact. She's been gone a couple of weeks now. I'm starting to wonder, you know, wonder if she's planning to come back at all.'

He delivered it like a joke but neither of them laughed.

Stare.

'I do wonder, since that little bit of political hoo-hah we went through last year, I mean, since the . . . since my retirement, I do wonder whether I've been even more difficult to live with than usual. All this baking. Goodness, she's barely been able to get into her own kitchen. I'd snap at her if she tried. She probably goes to her sister's just for the opportunity to cook something. I wonder if I've been awful about a lot of things.'

Stare.

'I'm planning to get my act together. And you don't have to tell me this stuff doesn't help.' He symbolically pushed the glass away. 'Alcohol is an ally to the contented but a foe to those with heavy hearts. Not sure who said that. I probably made it up myself. Damned good, I think. I still have flashes of the old genius every now and then. Moments of lucid thought. Increasingly cantankerous though. I imagine she'd say that.'

He ran his finger across the cool plastic table top tracing the squares.

'I'm going to see her, of course.'

The gecko clicked like a clock.

'Tomorrow seems as good a day as any. Don't you think?'
Stare.

'Hmm, well, you've certainly put a damper on this party,
Dr Siri Paiboun.' He lifted his wrist to look at a watch he'd
forgotten to put on. 'And just look at the time. I have shirts
to wash.' He scraped back his chair, abandoned his drink,
blew his young brother a kiss and meandered unsteadily
between the tables to the open shutters.

'Don't forget to put your lights on,' Siri shouted as his
friend slipped behind a curtain of rain. He sighed. Was it the
weather? Did the constant grey turn everything negative?
Why was everybody having so much trouble getting along?
Half the world not finding love at all, the other half not
knowing how to hold on to it. Or had it always been like
this?

'Things have to be sorted out before it's too late,' he told
the gecko.

Siri read until one a.m. The second Soviet strip light, newly
installed in the second-floor library, had illuminated his
book with such enthusiasm that he could see the flecks of
wood fibre in the paper. His mind could have stayed up all
night but his body craved sleep. He apologised to Monsieur
Sartre and went to bed. For once, Madame Daeng didn't stir
when he joined her and, as soon as the ghost of his missing
left earlobe hit the pillow, he was thrown into that nightmare. The same boy, wearing Siri's talisman around his
neck. The same moment of indecision. Would he laugh and
walk away or would he pull the trigger? The moment
dragged through time, allowing the panic to take hold. Will
he blow off the doctor's head tonight, or not? The finger
twitches, then relaxes. The boy smiles and walks on. A sigh.
Head *on* night. And in the distance he hears the voice. The

melodic voice of love and promise. A sound so enchanting Siri is drawn to it like a night moth to the bright fire trail of a jet engine. No good can come of it. He reaches into his own dream and grabs for his stupid music-following self. 'Don't do it,' he calls, and he finds himself just in time and throws his arms around himself and drags himself out of his nightmare.

And his pillow was wet with sweat because he knew that if he were to ever find the singer, all hope for mankind would be lost.

'Bad dream again?' Daeng asked.

'Something bad is going to happen,' he told her.

She brushed back his hair and said, 'It's only a dream.'

But it wasn't.

12

FOUR MONKS AT A FUNERAL

Sometimes, torture can be just the threat of torture, the promise of misery. The imagination can scroll through a menu of horrors more awful than anything a half-witted interrogator might come up with. There are those so petrified by what their own minds have envisaged that they're shouting their confessions even before the torturer comes for them. It's only just occurred to me what a weapon my own mind can be against me. My own gun pointed at my own temple. I am light-headed and weak already, certainly not thinking clearly. I can see, but cannot feel the bruises nor taste the blood but I know my right wrist is broken.

They took me to a room and removed my blindfold. The smiley man and the heavy monk were there. There was a pervading stench of bitter blood and disinfectant. They chained me to an armchair without a cushion, sat me on the bare springs that cut into the backs of my thighs. It's comical to think about it but those damned springs could nip like angry crabs. The torturers ignored me. They left me sitting and went about their business. Their business was a young girl, no older than fifteen. What kind of subversive could she have been? When they'd finished with her she was as good as dead. I had my eyes closed for the whole ordeal but my ears told me everything.

Then it was quiet and the heavy monk pulled up a school

seat and sat on it. He looked ridiculous, like an elephant in a baby's chair. He was wearing black pyjamas that fitted him now. The charade was over. He flipped down the wooden writing arm that rested on his fat thigh.

'This,' he said, 'is your life. After you hear, you will indicate that you understand what it say and you will sign. You will sign today, or you will sign after the bones in your foot are broke one after one. Or you will sign the next day after we take out your eye. But some time you will sign. Better for us all to sign now.'

My only thought then was that if this man were truly to put on saffron robes, they would sizzle against his skin and catch fire. I grew up with monks. I know there's more to being a monk than cutting off your hair and eyebrows. There's deportment, manners, and a way of speaking that come from truly understanding the dharma. They're not learned but acquired and the heavy monk had none of these traits. But I'd tested him anyway, just to be certain. I told him a story about the seven monks who chanted in front of my mother's funeral pyre. He saw nothing wrong with the tale even though I pushed him on it. Any true monk would know that four monks have to chant in front of the pyre. I hadn't bothered with any other tests.

'My name is Siri Paiboun,' the fake monk read aloud. 'I am an agent for the Vietnamese Liberation Army. I am Lao but I went to school in Hanoi where I was trained in espionage by the Vietnamese secret service. My cover is that I am a Lao medical doctor on a state mission. My objective for coming to Democratic Kamphuchea in May 1978 was to collect data for my comrades in Hanoi and to commit acts of sabotage against my enemies, the Khmer. I am ashamed of my actions and accept the punishment of death.'

The heavy monk twirled the paper around on the writing

arm and put one more blunt pencil on top of it. The poor man must have really been under pressure from somewhere to get my signature before he ripped off my head. But I was getting bored with all those pencils.

'We find some interesting reading material in your hotel room,' he said. 'This is enough evidence of your treachery. So we borrow your documents. Your travel paper do not have your signature. If it do, we can sign your name ourself. We want only your signature, now. Simple. Not to eat the pencil or the paper. If you do this again I will cut off your nose here and now. You understand?'

I nodded.

'If I open the cuff, you will sign?'

I nodded again and remained passive as the man reached over and slipped the hex key into the manacle slot. I was tired; physically tired and tired of all this. Tired of suffering and tired of the performance of these ignorant men . . . and tired of living. Yes, I was finally tired of the effort of staying alive. But I had one last burst of energy to share. I'd been a wrestler and boxer at university, the lightest weight class but I pack a good right. I just needed a clear target. Once my hand was free, I reached for the pencil but my unsteady fingers sent it tumbling to the floor. The heavy monk glared at me.

'Sorry,' I said. When the man leaned down to pick it up I sent a mighty haymaker into that chubby cheek of his. Oh, it was a delight. There was a crack and a streak of pain shot down my arm. But I felt the cheekbone snap beneath my knuckle and the heavy monk fell across the floor like a collapsing stack of firewood. The man was stunned at first, not knowing where he was, then he looked up and focused on me. There was hatred in him. It shrouded him like a cloud of soot. He staggered to his feet and lammed into me, sending wild punches to my face and body. I had just the one arm free to fend off the blows and put in some more of my own. But I had no strength. If the smiley man hadn't pulled the heavy monk off, there was little doubt I would have been beaten to death. The boy guards carried what was left of my resolve back to the classroom and dumped me here by the blackboard.

And here I lay, too tender to move. I doubt the little guard creatures understood why my blood-bloated lips were smiling. It was because I had just seen the light. At last I understood. I'd been waiting for the phibob, baffled as to why they hadn't come for me. But it's obvious, isn't it? What worse could they do to me? Even if they gave me their best shot, they couldn't top any of this. You know it all, don't you, my spirits? Yes, that's right. Nod those heads. You know it all. I've had time to regret that I am still alive. But I want to go with a flourish. One last heroic act. I'll be joining you, I know I shall, but not just yet.

13

DON'T GO

There would perhaps come a day when the information on a sheet of paper on one desk would automatically be drawn like a lonesome thumb to information on a sheet of paper on a desk not two metres away. It would set off an alarm to say, 'Has anybody seen this?' But at Vientiane police headquarters, three days had passed and nobody had noticed a very significant connection. Sergeant Sihot had been focusing on K6 and the Vietnamese security people and the odd coincidence of victim three's parents having worked at the murder scene of victim one. He'd been attempting to trace the couple through the lists of refugees their spies had sent from the Thai camps. He'd re-interviewed Miht, the groundsman, who admitted he vaguely recalled the couple but that he couldn't be expected to remember everyone as the staff changed so often. Like Civilai, Sihot had a feeling the man was holding something back.

After a long search, Sihot finally found someone with fencing experience. A young attaché at the East German embassy called Hans had learned to fence in Gymnasium. He'd just arrived from Berlin. Through a translator, Sihot learned that the épées used in the three murders were far from normal and were totally unsuitable for competition. Fencing, the young man said, was a test of footwork and accuracy. Scoring was done electronically so there was no need for sharp edges or pointed tips on the weapons. The swords Sihot showed him had certainly been doctored to inflict the most damage.

Finally, Sihot had talked once more to Comrade Chanti at Electricité du Lao and asked why he'd failed to mention the fact he was working on a rewiring project at K6. The engineer had simply put Sihot in his place by saying, 'You didn't ask.' He had been very cool about the whole affair and told Sihot he was busy and, 'would that be all?'

The list of Electricité du Lao employees involved in the project sat on the front right-hand corner of Sihot's desk held down by half a cluster-bomb casing. The third name on that list was Somdy Borachit.

Inspector Phosy had been focusing on the returnees who'd subscribed to magazines at the government bookshop. He was attempting to trace the names on the list. As they hadn't been obliged to provide their addresses, it was a laborious process. He had been sidetracked at one stage after interviewing one bookshop customer: a member of the Women's Association recently returned from Moscow. She had, she said, filed an official complaint against the bookshop clerk for making 'improper advances' towards her. Phosy's enquiries led to the discovery that the poor man had merely asked her if she'd be interested to attend a cultural event with him. That was as far as the advance went and Phosy hadn't seen anything improper about it. Unattached single man approaches unattractive single woman with hopes of romance. A flirtation. He wondered whether the complaint would have been made at all if the clerk had been better looking. He let it pass.

Phosy had been receiving responses too from his Eastern European contacts. The Czech embassy had discovered that Dung, the Vietnamese major, had taken a course in fencing in Prague as part of the physical education component of his course. In fact, his Czech instructor had given him an A and commented that the Vietnamese was a natural swordsman. The major had lied at the interview. As a result, his name was moved to the top of the list of suspects. Over the years, Phosy had come to believe that when all the arrows pointed to one person, that was invariably your man.

To Phosy's surprise, word came back from East Germany via the embassy's diplomatic pouch with regard to the third victim, Jim. Early reports were that she had been a friendly but studious woman who had impressed all her lecturers. She was the perfect student, doing extra research outside the curriculum, not wasting her time with nightlife or parties. Some of her classmates recalled that there had been a man interested in her but nobody remembers seeing him. They only knew from Jim that he was a student on a government scholarship. Jim had once commented with a smile how flattering it had been to have such an attractive man throwing pebbles at a girl's window.

As they'd approached the first round of pre-medical examinations, Jim's comments had begun to sound more desperate. On one occasion, she'd told a classmate, 'I'm starting to get a little impatient. He doesn't take no for an answer.' Some of the Lao had jokingly suggested she invite her 'boyfriend' to one of the weekend balls and she'd become very agitated. 'Really, there's no relationship here. Just an annoyance.' Then, even nearer to the exams a classmate had found Jim walking around outside at midnight in the snow. She'd been crying. She'd said, 'He really won't leave me alone. He won't let me study.'

The classmate had suggested she tell the student representative but Jim had refused. The Lao student said she became concerned for Jim's well-being after that night but Jim wouldn't let her get close. And it was around then that Jim's future came tumbling down. She failed her exams, but more than that it was as if she'd become an entirely different person. One girl commented, 'She'd lost all her warmth. She didn't speak. Didn't answer any questions. Something terrible had happened to her. We thought it must have been him, whoever he was. We didn't know what he'd done to her but she was clearly terrified of him.'

Phosy had gone through the translation two or three times, astonished at what a transformation had come over the woman. Something had happened in Berlin to change a bright, straight-A student with a brilliant future into a frightened failure. In Phosy's mind the killer had taken on a new, more sinister guise. What happened in Berlin might have been unrelated to the K6 murders but he didn't believe so. He immediately demanded a list of all foreign students studying in East Germany in 1977.

Apart from confirmation that victim two, Kiang, had taken no physical education classes and that victim one, Dew, had at one stage been selected to compete in a regional fencing tournament in a very small town in Bulgaria, no other information had arrived to bring him closer to his killer. His desk was a monument of paperwork; his own notes, interview transcripts, and telexes. But, on the front left-hand corner was the list of subscribers at the government bookshop. It was on the top of a pile, weighted down with a tiny plaster cast of Malee's left foot age one month. Eleventh down that list was the name Somdy Borachit.

'Sh . . . sh . . . she didn't come back today.'

'Who's that, Geung?'

Dtui was sitting on a stool facing the freezer controls with the Russian–Lao dictionary open on her lap. Mr Geung was using a long-handled broom to sweep cobwebs from the ceiling.

'The Down's Syndrome. She didn't come b . . . back.'

'Must have been a mirage, hon.'

'No . . . no . . . no. What's a marge?'

'A mirage is something you think you see but it isn't really there.'

'I saw her.'

'Ah, but did you? What if you wanted to see her so much that you made her up?'

'Eh?'

'You made magic and she came.'

'I . . . I . . . I can't make magic.'

'If you want something badly enough, you can.'

'Really?'

'Yeah. Look at Malee. I really wanted Malee in my life and there she was.'

'No. You had s . . . sex and you made a baby.'

'OK, right. That helped too. But it all started with a dream. And then I wished.'

'I wouldn't w . . . w . . . wish for a Down's Syndrome to come.'

'Why not?'

He put on a deep voice.

'That lot are f . . . feeble minded.'

'Yeah? Who said that?'

'Judge Haeng.'

'Oh, yeah? Is that the same Judge Haeng who had you sent way up north?'

'Yes.'

'And you found your way back to the morgue all by yourself?'

'Yes.'

'Then, you tell me which one of you is feeble minded. Look, Geung, you've been giving this woman a hard time since she started here. And, as far as I can see, she hasn't done anything wrong. I'll tell you how to look at this. There are times when you feel . . . out of it, right? When people make you feel like an outsider.'

'Yes. Lots.'

'But you have me and Dr Siri, and Civilai and now you have Malee. And we all make you feel better at those times. Right?'

'Yes.'

'Well, maybe, this woman, if she exists, maybe she feels like you do sometimes. But she hasn't got a morgue full of family to make her feel better. People who love her. Maybe she'd appreciate just a friendly "hello" sometimes and she wouldn't feel like an outsider.'

'Just a hello.'

'That's all. Then she'll start to feel like you do.'

'That's all?'

'Right. But I still don't believe there is a Down's Syndrome girl. Nobody else has seen her. I think she's a joke you're playing on us.'

'No. Sh . . . sh . . . she's real. Her name's Tukta.'

On the eve of Siri's departure for Phnom Penh via Peking, he had a bit of trouble getting home from the morgue. As was often the way, he'd sat around for most of the day fine-tuning his report on the épée murders, scratching about for something to keep himself busy, a case, a phone call, a body, a visit, some splattering of bureaucratic foolishness for him to complain about. But there had been nothing until four in the afternoon. Then everything happened. At one stage, Mr Geung came running into the office and spent several minutes catching his breath, attempting to filter out a word or two. Siri had rubbed his friend's shoulders and calmed him down, and finally he was able to say . . .

'She . . . she's back.'

'Who's that, Geung?'

'The Down's Syndrome. Sh . . . she . . . she's a part-time staff in the can . . . the can . . . in the canteen.'

He'd left again, this time realising by himself that he hadn't brought back the coffee he'd been sent for. Siri wondered whether the excitement was hostile territorialism or passion. He suspected the former. In fact, it occurred to him that even though he'd been acquainted with Geung for two years, he knew very little of the psychology that made him who he was. Did he have the same emotions as others? How many of his feelings were instincts? Where did his heart settle along the parameters between human and beast? Siri was disappointed that he could work alongside a man and not understand him. Perhaps his library could shed some light on what went on in Mr Geung's mind.

It occurred to Siri that he himself had recently emerged from a long hibernation of ignorance. Suddenly he'd become aware of the deep feelings of those around him. He'd always focused on physical well-being and danced lightly around emotions. He wondered whether this awakening might be just one more stop on his journey through the senses. Was the spirit world leading him on a guided tour through the various rooms of the other world, or had he arrived at the garden of love all by himself like some long-haired hippy ganja smoker? Was he closer to heaven? After all the years of war and killing he'd suffered, with his heart as heavy as mud, was this the natural conclusion? After so many years of hate, there could only be—

Hospital director Suk had interrupted his transcendental

train of thought. Siri caught him out of the corner of his eye striding past the office door towards the cutting room. He had a tall foreigner beside him. Siri counted on his fingers, one . . . two . . . three . . .

'Siri, come here!' the director yelled.

Siri smiled, and put on his white coat. It always seemed easier to lie in a white coat for some reason. He strolled casually into the cutting room with his hands in his pockets.

'Siri, can you explain this?' said Suk, pointing at the single strip light overhead and the two vacant fittings. Dtui came out of the storeroom and looked at the doctor, hoping he had an excuse at hand.

'Can *you*, Comrade?' Siri asked.

'Can I what?' Suk replied.

'Can you explain why those Chinese engineers came to take away our perfectly good lights?'

Dtui smiled and returned to the stores. All was in order.

'Chinese? What Chinese?' Suk asked.

'How should I know?' Siri replied. 'They had a work order written in Chinese and the interpreter said something about the wattage of the lamps being inappropriate for the size of the room. She said you'd sent them.'

Director Suk spent several minutes in stunted dialogue with the Russian engineer who was clearly upset. Siri stood there, indignant, with his arms folded. He knew the hospital administration had no idea who was donating what and which experts were due when. He was sure this small matter would be lost in the war of dominance between the superpowers. Suk and the Russian walked out of the morgue without another word to Siri.

The doctor thought that incident would be the grand total of excitement for the day. Geung returned again without the coffee and too grumpy to talk to anyone. Dtui left at five to pick up Malee from the crèche. Siri did his rounds, closing the louvres in the cutting room and checking the water level in the ornamental flood overflow pond which now sported two attractive lotus flowers. He stacked the papers on his desk and began to write a list of duties to keep his morgue team occupied for the next four days. Halfway through the list he looked up and saw his angel mother in the doorway. He smiled, as was his habit. She chewed betel and frowned, as was hers.

'Hello, darling,' he said. 'Enough rain for you these days?' He wondered whether spirits felt rain. Did it just pass through them? He'd never seen one with an umbrella. He knew that, apart from mermaids, folk from the beyond couldn't travel on water. That probably explained why so many royalists had crossed the Mekhong, leaving their evil spirits behind on the Lao bank. Beginning a new life on the Thai side. Not realising there was an entire army of equally evil spirits waiting for them over there. Siri's mother didn't reply. She had never spoken. She was a vision without a soundtrack. Siri had become used to his one-sided conversations. He was concentrating on his list.

6. *Make inventory of all the body parts we have in formaldehyde in the storeroom.*
7. *Write justification as to why they're there.*
8. *If you can't think of any, dig a hole behind the morgue and bury them deep away from dogs (with a few kind words of spiritual praise to the body parts).*
9. *...*

'Don't go, Siri.'

'What?' Siri looked up, expecting to find a visitor in the doorway but there was nobody there but his mother. The voice had been clear. A woman's voice. An old woman, crackly but clear and loud. He stared at the old lady who sat cross-legged staring back at him, chewing her betel.

'Did you speak?' he asked.

If only she could. It was his dream to talk with them. Enough of these guessing games. Had she spoken? Had the words, 'Don't go, Siri' come from her?

'Don't go where, mother?' he asked.

But she sat and chewed and into her body stepped a large chocolate-skinned man in a nightshirt. He didn't seem aware of the mess he'd made of Siri's mother.

'Good evening, Dr Siri,' said Bhiku. 'I hope you are talking to yourself because, as you clearly see, I am not your mother.'

Mr David Bhiku, the father of crazy Rajid, weighed some 100 kilograms. With his chocolaty gleam and gum-bubble of a nose it was evident he could never be a relative of the doctor, mother or otherwise. Siri rose from his seat to greet his friend but old habits died hard and the Indian buried his head deep into Siri's gut and pressed his palms together in greeting.

'Krishna save us, Bhiku,' smiled Siri. 'I look forward to the day when we can just shake hands and dispense with all this bowing and scraping. You outweigh me by several sacks of rice. It looks silly.'

'Yes, sir. Worth is not decided by weight, Doctor. If that were so I should be kowtowing to every buffalo I meet.'

'Come and sit . . . and *not* on the floor.'

'I am an honoree.'

Siri forced him onto the chair and glanced at the doorway to satisfy himself that his mother hadn't been crushed back to life by the big Indian. There was no trace of her.

'I have some tepid tea,' said Siri, reaching for the thermos.

'I have already indulged, thank you.'

'I haven't seen your son, Jogendranath, for several days. My wife and I are worried. With all this rain and nowhere to sleep . . .'

'Ah, yes. My son has found a dry place to sleep. Thank you. That's what I have come to tell you.'

'You've seen him?'

'I see him every night,' Bhiku smiled. 'He curls up like a civet cat beneath the canvas which covers my cooking area at the rear of the restaurant.'

Siri raised his eyebrows.

'He sleeps at your restaurant? That's marvellous.'

'Most nights, now. Yes. He is reminiscent of a small animal sheltering from the rain. Life to a street son like mine must be very unpleasant if there is no star-filled sky to pull over you when you go to bed. He has not yet built up the confidence to eat the food I leave out for him or to come inside out of the wind, but he's there often. I like to sit on the back step watching him sleep.'

'Has he spoken?'

'Sadly, Doctor, my poor son is still mute. But in his dreams the spirits speak through him. I hear them sometimes. In his dreams there are words.'

Siri smiled, delighted.

'With just a little more faith, friend, I wouldn't be surprised if you could reach in and pull out those words, bring him back his voice,' he said.

'Would that it were so.'

'One rung at a time, Bhiku. One rung at a time.'

The Indian hadn't been gone more than five minutes. Siri had begun to pack his cloth shoulder bag. The words from his mother still hung at his neck. 'Don't go, Siri.' He was walking absently towards the door when a third unexpected visitor appeared there. Colonel Phat was tall and gaunt. He smiled warmly with the few teeth he had. He was the Vietnamese advisor at the Ministry of Justice. He and Siri had become close since his arrival in Vientiane. Their opinions of Judge Haeng's suitability for his position had dragged them together.

'Brother Siri,' Phat said as he walked into the office.

'Phat, did you lose your way? I've never seen you near the morgue before.'

'Just pacing out those final steps.'

'And they lead you here? Are you expecting a violent death, brother?'

'A knife in the back. It's a feeling I've held since I first arrived at Justice.'

Phat walked past Siri and sat on a chair, ignoring the fact that the doctor was clearly on his way home.

'I only have cold tea to offer,' Siri said, returning to his desk.

'I come as a harbinger of doom,' said Phat.

'That's a pity. I was planning on having a good-news-only day. Are you sure it can't wait till I come back from Cambodia?'

'That's the point, brother Siri. I am here to strongly recommend that you don't go there.'

'I think the trip's all booked and paid for.'

'Then, come down with something that makes it impossible for you to travel. And tell your friend Civilai to do the same.'

'What on earth for?'

'Dr Siri, what exactly do you know about what's happening in the swamp they call Kampuchea?'

'Not much. The orientation only took half an hour. Most of it was read from some sort of travel brochure. Then they gave us an itinerary and a summary of the Red Khmer manifesto. It looked a lot like ours.'

He didn't bother to mention the warning he and Civilai had been given that they might get some subtle pressure from the Vietnamese not to go. Hanoi had mentored the fledgling Khmer Rouge and encouraged its overthrow of the corrupt Khmer royalists. But its plan to have Laos and Cambodia sit at its feet like tame naga dragons had been thwarted by the new revolutionary leaders in Phnom Penh. It was no secret that the Khmer and the Vietnamese had long since separated on ideological grounds, but, since the beginning of the year, the war drums had been beating on both sides of the border. Once an ally, Cambodia, now Kampuchea, had become a threat. Phnom Penh was drifting closer to China, just as Vietnam drifted further away from the big Red mother ship.

'We are hearing terrible things from Khmer refugees at our borders,' Phat said. 'I am seriously concerned for your safety, Comrade.'

'Refugees have a habit of saying what they think their saviours want to hear. I wouldn't worry about it.'

Phat rose. He seemed to be offended by Siri's attitude.

'I came here on my own time and against the wishes of my embassy. I came out of friendship with a sincere warning.'

Siri wondered whether Civilai was encountering his own delegation of Vietnamese friendship ambassadors.

'I appreciate it,' Siri said. 'But, I think it's too late to get out of it, Comrade.' He stood and held out his hand to Phat. 'But thank you for the warning. It was good to see you again.'

Phat didn't return the handshake.

'It's far more than a warning, Siri. Putting a man with

your character in Phnom Penh at this time is like dropping petroleum on a bush fire. If you go to Kampuchea you will burn, Siri Paiboun. Trust me.'

He turned and walked out.

Siri had never seen him like this. It had been an impressive and – he had to admit – an unnerving visit. The Vietnamese certainly knew how to squeeze. The colonel's words were still on his mind as he put the welcome mat inside and locked the front door. And the old woman's voice telling him not to go. He liked his omens in threes. One more and he'd call in sick and let Civilai go by himself. All by himself to sample the fine wines and tasty Khmer food. The beautiful Khmer women. The charm of Phnom Penh. The memory of walking along Boulevard Noradom with Boua. The smiles of the locals. The music. What was a little prophecy of doom against all that?

A voice from across the flooded hospital grounds reached him through the drizzle.

'Feel like a drink?'

Cast in silhouette against the gaudy strip lights of oncology, Phosy stood astride his Vespa in a foot of water. Siri took off his sandals, rolled up his trouser legs, and waded to the inspector.

'I thought you'd given it up,' Siri told him.

'Just saving myself for Lao new year and very special occasions,' Phosy smiled. Siri hadn't seen him in such a good mood for a very long time.

'Well, new year came and went without anyone noticing,' Siri said. 'So what's the occasion?'

'Another solved case.'

'You haven't . . . ?'

'We have. Not only do we have our fencer, we have irrefutable connections to each of the victims and to the three crime scenes. It's all over.' He shook the doctor's hand. 'Congratulations.'

There were fewer and fewer places to drink of a night in a city whose sense of *muan* – of innocent pleasure – had been slowly wrung from it by two and a half years of socialism. The logical hot spots were roofless snack and drink stalls along the riverbank and, as long as that one unstoppable April shower persisted, they would remain closed. There was the Russian club, a bustling, beery night-eatery populated by Eastern European experts. But that was beyond the budget of a Lao policeman and a Lao doctor. So Siri and Phosy took their drinks under an umbrella at Two Thumb's humble establishment behind the evening market. They drank rice whisky and worked through a plate of steamed peanuts in soft shells. Siri knew he should have been packing, spending the night with Madame Daeng, but she'd always understood the power of celebration, particularly when victory was the prize.

'If we'd only checked sooner,' Phosy said. 'Or if one of us had remembered the names on the lists. But, why would we? We were only interested in the team leader on the rewiring project. I doubt we gave the other names on the Electricité du Laos work roster more than a cursory glance. But I'd arrived at the name Somdy Borachit on the subscriptions list and I read it out loud. And Sihot had just worked out his schedule to interview all the electricians on his list and he asked me how it was spelt. And, sure enough, it was the same name. We had him: Somdy Borachit, who everyone knew by the nickname of Neung. We drove over to Electricité du Laos and he was there, calm as you like. Confident. And I asked him if he had an acquaintanceship with the three victims and he admitted he did. No pretence at all. He came straight out with it.'

'That he'd killed them?'

'That he knew them all. I asked why he hadn't come forward when he heard about the killings and he said, "It's complicated." Complicated? You bet it's complicated. We took him to HQ and questioned him. And it was as if every answer he gave tied him tighter and tighter to the murders. It was as if he didn't understand the implication of what he was saying. Everything in this case points directly to him. Every damn thing.'

'He didn't have an alibi?'

'Claims he was babysitting his son all weekend. His wife was off at a seminar. It's just one more story that doesn't work.'

'Start at the beginning, Phosy.'

'All right. You'll never guess who Neung's father is.'

'Then, tell me.'

'Miht, the groundsman at K6. And when the Americans were still there he used to go to help his father with the gardening work.'

'So, he would have met young Jim there. Attractive girl. Got chatting . . .'

'He admits it. Said he knew her before he went off to study. And where do you suppose he takes his scholarship course in electrical engineering?'

'East Germany.'

'Precisely where Jim was headed. And he studied not two blocks from her school. Amazing coincidence? I don't think so.'

'So, he could have been the mystery man who hounded her there. Followed her to Berlin then stalked her.'

'Forcing her to come home early,' Phosy went on. 'He returned at about the same time. Which brings us to victim number two, Kiang. It's easier to do this in reverse order. In the beginning he told us he'd met Kiang at the government bookshop and they'd chatted about being overseas and he said he'd never seen her outside the reading room. Never socialised with her. And it was so obvious he was lying even Sihot could read it. I was so certain we had our killer I decided I could push as hard as I liked at that stage. But Neung didn't take much pushing. As soon as the word "murder" came up in the interview, he admitted that he and Kiang were . . . "dating", I think is what he called it. I asked him why he'd lied and he said he hadn't wanted word to get back to his wife. His wife? Can you believe it? He's got a wife and a child and he's dating. And it doesn't seem like killing the girl was nearly as important as his wife not finding out.'

Phosy's reaction surprised Siri but he decided that matter could wait.

'And is the school connected? The scene of the murder?' Siri asked.

'Is it ever! It's where he went to school, Siri. It was his own classroom. He pinned his dead girlfriend to the blackboard he'd copied notes from for seven years. This is a very sick character, Siri.'

'How's he taking it?'

'You know how they are. Denying this. Denying that. He had himself in tears at one point.'

'So he hasn't actually confessed to anything?'

'He's denied killing them but there's no getting away from the fact he knew them all. He met the wife of his boss through work. I wouldn't be surprised if he was "dating" her as well. And get this. The syrup on the shaved ice is that our comrade Neung was a fencing star. He was the champion on the university team while he was in Munich.'

'No, wait. How long was he there? Two . . . three years? How do you get to be a champion in so short a time?'

'You don't. He was already an expert before he left Laos. He learned from childhood from his own father.'

'Miht, the groundsman?'

'His father had grown up in a boys' orphanage in Vietnam run by French priests. They had an extensive programme of sports organised for the boys to keep them on the straight and narrow. One of the priests had been a fencing champion and he trained the most promising of his students in sword-play. It appears Miht was the star pupil. If the opportunity had come up he might have even been good enough to compete in Europe, but the war put paid to those plans. Miht came to Laos and put all of his efforts into teaching the skill to his son. Neung had the same natural flair as his father. The old man has a collection of swords at his home.'

Siri thought back to his relaxed conversation with the groundsman. His confident air. He recalled how the fellow had observed the crime scenes so intently. Siri wondered whether he'd known something. Whether he suspected his son might have been involved. Surely, when he discovered that the weapon was an épée . . .

'It does all seem to fit together,' Siri agreed, pouring the last of their half-bottle into the glasses.

'Seem? It's a perfect fit, Siri. Your Judge Haeng is so pleased about it he's decided to make this his first open court murder trial.'

'Wait! He's what? We don't even have a constitution. How the hell can he run a murder trial without laws?'

'Not sure, but he's got the go-ahead from the minister and a couple of the politburo. A lot of people have been upset about all the killing that's been going on lately. I get the feeling they want the country to know that justice is being done and criminals aren't going to get away with it.'

'When's the trial?'

'Next Tuesday.'

'That soon?'

'It is pretty open and shut, you have to agree.'

'There's no physical evidence, Phosy.'

'You mean, no fingerprints?' Phosy laughed.

'I mean no nothing. No eye witnesses, no blood matches, no connected murder weapon, no confessions – no nothing. But I suppose none of that matters if there's no law. That doesn't concern you?'

'Come on, Siri. There's so much circumstantial evidence you'd have to be a halfwit to think he was innocent.'

'It's called circumstantial because circumstances happen to coincide. And it's almost as if he's gone to a lot of trouble to point every finger at himself, circumstantially. But it isn't proof. What was your impression of him, Phosy?'

'My what?' Phosy was getting frustrated.

'As a person. What did you feel? How did he affect you?'

'Siri, you're taking all this philosophical psychological bunkum a bit too far. This is a murderer.'

'All right, forget psychology. What does your gut tell you? Your policeman's instincts. You've met enough killers in your life. What did your gut tell you after a day with Neung?'

'You really want to play this game?'

'Humour me.'

'All right, I felt he's very cool. That he knew we had all this evidence against him and he was smart enough not to lie about any of it. He was convincing as an actor. But men with the ability to plan and execute cold-blooded murder would have the ability to convince others . . .'

'Did you like him?'

'Some of the worst villains are likeable, Siri.'

'Did you?'

'Yes.'

'Right. Is anyone representing him in this play trial?'

'I assume there's somebody.'

'In a land without lawyers?'

'The military, probably.'

'The military conduct court martials and executions. This is a completely different thing. This is no war trial. This is an affront to democratic principles. This is a chance for the public to see Marie Antoinette's head roll.'

'Who?'

'Doesn't matter.'

'Siri, slow down. You sound as if you're on his side. What are you playing at?'

'Not playing at all, Phosy. Looking at all the facts, I'd probably agree that he's as guilty as the devil himself. Anybody would. Which is no doubt why Judge Haeng selected this as his opening number. Easy. No complaints. An evil killer gets what's coming to him. Accolades all round. The only loser here is justice. The rightful course of law. Without that we have nothing to believe in.'

'What would you do, Siri? Lock him up till the constitution's finished? He could be an old man by then.'

'Good point. Can I see him?'

'Who?'

'The accused.'

'What for? Why? When? You have to be at the airport by six.'

'How about now?'

Phosy laughed. Siri was staring at him with those emerald-green eyes. No smile. No bluff.

At the doctor's insistence, Phosy let him walk back to the cells by himself. Neung sat on the wooden bench, his slumped frame diced by the shadows of the metal mesh of the prison bars. He was long-limbed, a strongly built young man, but his face was soft, the type a woman would find more attractive than a man. It was the face of a child that some would feel an urge to mother.

'Are you Somdy Borachit? Also known as Neung?' Siri asked.

The prisoner seemed stunned, even shell-shocked. It took him a while to acknowledge Siri was there outside the bars.

'Yes.'

'Did you kill Hatavan Rattanasamay, Khantaly Sisamouth and Sunisa Simmarit?' Siri asked. No point in preliminaries.

Neung looked at Siri coldly.

'Who are you?'

'You answer my question and I'll think about answering yours.'

Neung stood, walked to the bars and glared. Siri resisted the temptation to take a step back.

'Why would I want to kill three people I hardly knew?'

Siri nodded.

It was a bad response. A murderer's answer.

'But, it isn't true, is it?' Siri said. 'That you didn't know them, I mean. One you were having an affair with. Another you'd known since she was a child. You travelled to Germany with her.'

'What's the matter with you people? Don't you listen? We didn't travel anywhere together.' Neung had raised his voice. 'And I'm not answering any more of your questions until you tell me who you are and what you're doing here.'

'You aren't exactly in a position to call the shots. But I have no objection. I'm Dr Siri Paiboun. I'm the man who conducted autopsies on the three women you killed.'

With a speed and ferocity Siri couldn't have expected,

Neung smashed the heel of his right hand into the concrete wall of the cell. Siri took that step back after all. He was certain the prisoner had broken several small bones in his hand. But there was no pain on the man's face, only anger.

'That's quite a temper. Are you prone to violent outbursts like this?' Siri asked.

'Of course, I'm a violent maniac. Even more evidence for you. Shoot me before I lose control, why don't you?'

He slid down the wall to a sitting position on the floor. He massaged his wrist and looked up at the ceiling.

'Anger and sarcasm aren't going to help you in here,' Siri reminded him.

'And what is going to help me, Comrade?'

'The truth might be a good place to start.'

'I've tried. Believe me, I have. But your police friends have their own truth and they've been backing me into it all day.'

Siri sat cross-legged on the floor and looked at him. He took a few seconds to consider the consequences of what he was about to do.

'Has anyone told you what the evidence is against you?' he asked.

The prisoner looked up.

'I've picked up bits and pieces from their questioning. But not everything. No.'

So, for the next ten minutes, Siri laid it all out for him. He told him about all the circumstantial evidence that was ganged up against him. And, as he spoke, Siri watched the man's reactions. He watched for nonchalance and feigned surprise but Neung listened intently and asked questions at the right times. He was like an acolyte listening to the teachings of a monk. Siri tried to see inside him. The doctor had made mistakes before. He'd seen guilt when it didn't exist. He'd failed to notice evil when it was right in front of him.

The danger was that a man with the temperament to put detailed planning into three murders had to have a special type of mind. And Siri wondered whether he had the ability to see beyond that deceit.

Once all the evidence was mapped out, Neung fell back against the wall and bumped his head several times on the concrete. It was as if he suddenly understood how bad the situation was.

'Everybody thinks you're guilty,' Siri said.

'You too?'

'Yes.'

'I see,' Neung sighed. 'Then I'm on my way to hell on an ox cart.' He stared deep into Siri's golf-green eyes. 'Are the police aware you're here telling me all the details of their case against me?'

'I didn't even know myself when I came back here.'

'So, why?'

'You're just about to go up against the whole injustice system. They'll give you some token representation but ultimately, it's you against them. And I don't think those odds are fair.'

'Even though you believe I'm guilty?'

'Irrespective of my thoughts as to your guilt, you still have the right to defend yourself.'

'Thank you.'

'It isn't much.'

'Will you be attending their kangaroo court?'

'I'm off on a junket in Cambodia, me and the only qualified lawyer in the country. That's why I'm here at midnight. We leave tomorrow morning.'

Neung sighed and thought for a moment. A toad was practising its baritone beyond the window.

'OK. Can I tell you my story?'

Siri was surprised. He was afraid he was about to hear a confession and he didn't know how to handle things. He wondered if he should call Phosy.

'I don't—' he began.

'I want to tell you everything I know,' Neung said. 'I want at least one person to have my side of it.'

'If you're going to give me that "I hardly knew them" routine, I don't think I want to hear it.'

'I'm sorry about that. I did. I knew all three of them. And somebody's obviously aware of that.'

'Yes? What *somebody* might that be?'

'If we knew that, we'd know why I'm here.'

'So, you'll be going with the "I was framed" defence? Good choice.'

'Do I have any other hope?'

'No.'

'So . . . ?'

'So, I'm listening.'

'All right.' Neung shimmied across the concrete floor till his nose was no more than a few centimetres from the bars, his hands within grasping distance of Siri's neck.

'Dew,' he began. 'She was the wife of my section head, Comrade Chanti. I met her once at the company's New Year children's party before I went off to Germany. It was about five years ago. Chanti and his family had just arrived from the north-east after the ceasefire in seventy-three. My boss introduced his wife to everyone. She wasn't particularly friendly. She seemed reluctant to be there. She had one baby in arms and one toddler. I don't recall seeing her talk to her husband at all that afternoon. Then I met her once more at the government bookshop in the reading room when I got back from overseas. She was more friendly then. I had to remind her who I was, told her our kids had played together at the party. She said she'd just come back from Moscow. Then she was off somewhere in a hurry.'

'That's it?'

'The sum total. Two meetings, a dozen or so words. She was more polite the second time but we didn't actually hit it off.'

'But there was somebody from the reading room you did hit it off with.'

Neung blushed.

'That was my one guilty secret in all this,' the man confessed, 'and it doesn't surprise me I've been found out. I deserve it. I don't know how my wife will ever find it in her heart to forgive me.'

'I get the impression your wife's a very understanding woman. I passed her in the entry. She's been sitting out front of the prison since she found out you'd been arrested. She and your father. They've both refused to leave.'

'Do you think . . . do you suppose the police have told her about Kiang?'

'Of course. They have to mention details like that to the family to see whether they register any surprise. To see whether the suspect is a serial philanderer.'

'It'll break her heart.'

'You should have thought of that before you started fooling around.'

'I had no intention of being unfaithful.'

Siri's eyebrows reached for the ceiling.

'Really. Before Kiang came into my life I was perfectly content. And it was she who approached me. I was in the reading room at the bookshop and she got my attention by telling me I reminded her of somebody. She didn't ever give me any details but I got the impression it was someone she'd known when she was younger. Someone who'd left or died.'

Siri considered that point. It fitted into the mother's account of Kiang's soldier-lover killed in the north.

'Of course I'd noticed her before at the shop,' Neung continued. 'She was a striking-looking young lady. And it was as if she was attracted to me. I could sense it. But I kept things polite and I didn't encourage her.'

'Why not?'

'I'm a married man. And, I don't know, I suppose I thought she wasn't interested in me exactly. Just my similarity to that other man.'

'But the flesh was weak.'

'Doctor! A beautiful woman begging to make love to you? What would you have done?'

'Strange as it may seem, the opportunity doesn't arise that often. But I get your point.'

'And it was all so wonderful. Kiang was sweet and loving. She had a passion. It was as if she were saving it up for someone. It got to the point that I didn't care who she thought I was. Of course I fell in love with her. In fact, it was more like an addiction. I couldn't get enough of her. We got together when we could, made love, talked about our times in Europe. But she didn't ever introduce me to anyone. I never met her family or friends.'

'When was the last time you saw her?'

'Midday Saturday. We met for lunch. We had this place by the river where we'd meet up. An old guesthouse. We'd found the key under a pot of dead plants once when we were sheltering from the rain. It became our rendezvous spot.'

'Saturday was when she died.'

Neung nodded and his eyes glazed over.

'She didn't show up for our lunch date on Monday.'

'You weren't curious why not?'

'Of course.'

'Did you make any effort to find out why she didn't turn up?'

'We had an agreement. I wasn't to contact her. I couldn't go to her house or the library. I didn't even have her phone number. All the contact came from her. It's the way she wanted it.'

'And that arrangement was all right with you?'

'I had a wife. I wasn't really in a position to insist on visitation rights. And I was crazy about her. She could have done and said anything and it would have been fine with me. I was just glad to be around her. I loved her.'

'And your wife?'

Neung nodded.

'You're a generous man,' Siri told him. 'So much love to share with so many women. Which brings us to victim number three, Jim.'

Neung sighed with frustration.

'There isn't much to tell,' he said. 'I vaguely remember her pottering around K6 when she was a kid. She was podgy then. One of those keen young things who follow you around asking questions. I heard they'd taken her on as a trainee at a clinic up north. I didn't see her at all after that until Germany. I was on the fencing team at my college. There were local and regional competitions every weekend. And who should show up at one of them but Jim. I was totally surprised. I didn't recognise her at first. She'd lost a lot of weight. In fact she was looking very fit. She told me she'd come to Berlin to study medicine. That didn't surprise me. I knew she was smart. But what did surprise me was that she could fence. And she was good. Really good, and strong as an ox. She'd obviously put a lot of time into it.'

'Where did she learn?'

'I asked her, of course. But her answers were always

vague. Things like, "I can't tell you all my secrets so soon". I assumed the Americans . . . but I never really found out for certain. She asked if I had time to tutor her, work on her techniques. I told her I'd be happy to.'

'I bet you were. One on one, was it?'

Neung glared. 'No. She attended a class I helped out at. It was a fencing school for local teenagers. I was a volunteer. The instructor and I agreed that Jim had potential. In fact, the instructor had a friend from one of the big clubs come to look at her. It was one of those serious places, the type that gear you up for the Olympics. They agreed that with the right coaching she could have a future in fencing. They made her an offer. They said they could arrange for a permanent visa, perhaps even citizenship if she made the grade.'

'But she didn't go for it.'

'She was good but I could tell her mind wasn't in the sport. The difference between competence and greatness is in the heart. She didn't have a heart for fencing.'

'Odd, considering she'd obviously put a lot of effort into it.'

'That's what I thought.'

'Do you recall her talking about another man? A boyfriend. Someone who might have been showing an unhealthy interest in her?'

Neung put his fingers against his face as if he were raking for a memory or two.

'I don't remember anything specific,' he said. 'But I did get the feeling there was something troubling her. She'd lose concentration now and then as if she were on another planet. It was a little bit worrying when you're playing around with swords. It might have been because of a boyfriend but I don't know. It wasn't the type of thing I talked about with my students. We really weren't that close.'

'Did you see her again after Berlin?'

'Once. Recently, in fact. I was surprised to see her back in Laos so soon. I thought she'd be in Germany for another four years. She was outside the bookshop when I came out one Saturday. I asked her what was wrong and she told me she'd failed her exams and they'd sent her home. She didn't seem that upset about it. In fact, I got the impression she was happier than I remembered seeing her in Berlin. Being back in Laos seemed to have freed her soul somehow. She said there was some matter she needed to discuss with me, urgently. She was always asking this or that question, usually about things that weren't really important, so I didn't take it too seriously. She gave me her number at Settha Hospital. I meant to call, but with all the work out at K6 and family life . . .'

'And Kiang.'

'And Kiang, yes. I forgot all about calling Jim.'

Neung's brow arched as a realisation seemed to drop over him. 'I wonder, if I'd phoned . . .' he said. 'If she'd wanted to talk about her problem. I wonder if I could have prevented her death.'

'I wonder.'

Siri sat silent. It was a great line. Convincing. The doctor wasn't about to be sucked wholly into Neung's version of events, but he'd earned himself a second hearing.

On his way out of the station, Siri woke up Phosy at his desk and told him,

'Tomorrow, when you're feeling fresh, I'd like you to go and listen to that boy's story one more time. Just listen.'

14

A HINT OF ROUGE

The Shaanxi Y-8 lifted off from Vientiane's Wattay airport three hours after the scheduled departure time. No plane, no bus, no donkey cart ever left on time in the People's Democratic Republic of Laos. Timetables were in the same section of the government bookshop as legends and folklore. They were fictional beasts that lied without trepidation. Yet, despite this knowledge, no passengers ever came prepared for a wait. Nobody ever brought books or puzzles or letters to write or darning or weaving or embroidery to fill in the hours. It was as if, deep down, the Lao believed that today would be different. A miracle would happen. Today, a flight would leave on schedule. So they sat staring hopefully at the runway, at the rain on the window, at the other passengers, and then they dozed. And they awoke with a refreshed belief. Always disappointed.

Siri had arrived with stories to fill the hours. He'd informed Comrade Civilai in great detail of the neat slotting of engineer Neung into the evidence of the épée case. He'd left nothing out, neither fact nor feeling. Civilai, in clean but not necessarily ironed clothes, had sat nodding as he watched an incoming aeroplane break through the pudding clouds and splash along the runway like a stork in pursuit of a giant snakehead. Unlike his usual self he had nothing to ask, no clarifications to seek. Siri had done a very thorough job. The doctor was just about to tell his friend about the meeting with Neung at police HQ when a Lao Aviation official stood in front of the eleven passengers with a megaphone and yelled an announcement that flight CAAC23 would be leaving in twenty minutes. Passengers were invited to bring their luggage out to the runway and to help the pilot load it into the hold.

Siri and Civilai travelled light. What you wore today you washed tomorrow. All being well, it would be dry by the following day. The only thing of any substance in Siri's shoulder bag was his Camus compendium, a sort of greatest hits volume. He'd debated not bringing it but he was certain there'd be long periods of waiting or listening to speeches when Monsieur Camus could entertain him.

Madame Daeng had enjoyed no more than four hours with her husband between jail and the airport. But she'd found the time to ask whether somebody along the trail might take objection to the writings of a man who had converted from communism and proceeded to argue heatedly about its futility. Before attempting to steal an hour or two of sleep, Siri had assured her that nobody would dream of looking in his bag. He was a representative of Laos: a makeshift ambassador, and, as such, he would have makeshift diplomatic immunity.

Their parting words, which both of them would later come to rue, had been,

Siri: 'See you in a few days.'

Daeng: 'Don't forget your noodles for the flight.'

No pledges nor confessions of emotion. No hopes. No fears. Just noodles and an imprecise calculation of time.

The only thing of substance in Civilai's shoulder bag was a wad of five hundred dollars rolled into a secret compartment in the thick handle strap. He always travelled with it 'for emergencies' and it was no secret to Siri. To date they hadn't had cause to use it.

They were scheduled to spend the night in Peking before their onward journey. The hosts really outdid themselves. A permanently smiling Lao-speaking cadre, who appeared to have no idea who Civilai and Siri were, had been assigned to look after them for the evening. They were stuffed with food and drink and given little time to burn it all off between courses. In the car back to their ostentatious hotel – the Sublime – the cadre had asked whether they might enjoy fourteen-year-old girls before they slept. Neither Siri nor Civilai could envisage what they might do with a fourteen-year-old girl other than a quick game of badminton. It was late and they were tired so they had returned to their adjoining suites alone.

Civilai knocked on the common door at exactly the same time as Siri.

'I feel like a hastily put together tractor on an assembly line,' Civilai said. He went to sit on Siri's trampoline-sized bed. 'Is it my imagination or has the world speeded up considerably?'

'I'm still dizzy,' Siri confessed. 'It's as if we've just been given the next month's intake of food and drink and we'll have to live off it till June.'

'I certainly could,' Civilai agreed. 'We were five plates in before I realized we hadn't yet seen the main course.'

'Do you think there's a point to it?'

'Absolutely. Stick with the Chinese and you can have all the food, drink and virginity you can handle. They think we'll go back and push for a bilateral trade agreement. Maybe hand them a province or two in thanks.'

'But we aren't anybody. We couldn't push for a hand cart.'

'They don't know that. They assume that if our country

has selected us they'll listen to us when we go home. They're canny, the Chinese. They know when it comes down to it, it really has little to do with policy or diplomacy. When a politburo member makes a casting vote, at the back of his mind is the night he spent with identical triplets in a tub of honey. We're men and it's a proven scientific fact that eighty per cent of the decisions in our lives are made with our stomachs and our sexual organs.'

Siri thought back.

'I don't—'

'Of course, I'm not including you and me, Siri. We're men of integrity. Our lives have been complicated by the burden of conscience. But we are freaks. Ninety-six-point-three per cent of males are born without.'

'That's what I admire about you politicians. Figures at your fingertips. Debates won at the drop of a made-up number.'

He found his hand caressing the silk coverlet.

'I really had been expecting something more austere,' he confessed. 'You know? A wooden cot in a concrete room. That strikes me as more fitting for Chinese revolutionaries.'

'That really wouldn't have achieved anything, would it?'

'Do you suppose we're being . . . ?' Siri mimed headphones and a microphone.

'Probably. And . . . (Civilai mimed the use of a hand-cranked movie camera) no doubt.'

'So, then romance is out of the question?'

'Wait, I'll turn out the lights. Our love cannot be denied.'

Both men laughed at the thought of the poor translator reaching this point in the tape and rewinding, and rewinding. Were the two old men speaking in code or were they actually . . .?

Sobering up, Siri finally managed to describe his meeting with mass-murderer Neung.

'Very impressive. He's either a very very good liar – and don't forget, psychopaths can convince themselves to believe what they're telling you, even fool lie detectors – or . . .'

'Or somebody really did set him up.'

'And you believe the latter.'

'I didn't say that. But I convinced him . . . at least I think I did, to tell his story to Phosy exactly as he'd told it to me. He was reluctant. I think Phosy had given Neung short shrift during the interrogation. But I told him Phosy was a friend and a good policeman. Then I woke Phosy and told him to shut up for half an hour and just listen to Neung's version of events.'

'Too bad we won't be back in time for the trial.'

'No, but we'll only be away for four nights. We should be back in time for the execution.'

'Mm. Something to look forward to.'

'No, I mean it gives us time before the execution to follow up on some of Neung's claims. I'm hoping Phosy's sense of fair play might push him to reconsider whether this is a closed case and take another look at the facts.'

'Good. That's settled then. And, in the meantime we enjoy a little holiday, drink a bit too much, embarrass ourselves and our country, and take lots of nice tourist shots as evidence that we actually went.'

'Hear, hear to that.'

The enthusiastic Lao-speaking guide who'd offered Siri and Civilai fourteen-year-old badminton partners the previous night knocked on their doors at six a.m. He forced them into partaking of a full morning of breakfast, sightseeing, meeting people who didn't want to be met, and early lunch. The meal was another eight courses with fruit wine which left the Lao delegation so bloated they were certain they'd exceed the baggage allowance on the afternoon flight. Scheduled to leave at three forty-five, the airplane left at three forty-four and, as far as they knew, nobody was left behind at the airport.

Their fears that Civilai might embarrass the Chinese delegation, and himself, were put to rest when it became apparent the Chinese diplomats were all in the front section of the plane, separated from Siri and Civilai and a number of state media representatives who had the rear all to themselves. A red curtain – polyester rather than bamboo – had been drawn between them even before take-off. The members of the media spoke amongst themselves. They'd brought their own dinners on plates clamped together and tied in cloth. They seemed to know there would be no service, no meal, and certainly no in-flight film. All three lady air cadres were busy in first class.

When they landed on the bumpy tarmac at Phnom Penh airport, the Chinese left the plane first. Civilai watched through the window. Five jet-black limousines had driven out to meet the plane with their headlights blazing. Three heavy-set Chinese-looking men and two dowdy Chinese-looking women were at the bottom of the portable steps to shake hands and hug the delegation. They hung limp mimosa lei around the visitors' necks and smiled a good deal. On the short walk to the cars, the Chinese either handed the smelly necklaces to their aides or surreptitiously dropped them on the runway. The cars consumed the guests, turned in formation, and headed in a direction that appeared to contain nothing but the beams of the limousines.

'Is this our stop, do you think?' Siri asked.

'I didn't see a sign,' Civilai replied. 'In fact there's nothing outside the window but blackness.'

The press corps had fled at some stage and none of the

Mao-jacketed stewardesses had brought them barley sugar to suck or little metal aeroplane badges to pin on their lapels. In fact, but for the propellers whirring slowly, there was no sound. The two old comrades laughed.

'Do you think we should get off?' Civilai asked.

'I'm not going out there to stand on a dark wet runway,' Siri said. 'If they want us, let them come and get us.'

After five more minutes the pair was starting to believe they weren't wanted. But then a short man appeared from behind the red curtain. He was dressed in black pyjamas and had sandals made of thick chunks of old car tyres on his sunburned feet. Around his neck was a faded black and white checked scarf. His hair was slick and angled across his forehead in the style of Adolf Hitler. But his face was boyish, not yet ready for a moustache. In his hand was a large grey card with the names Dr Siri Paiboun and Comrade Civilai Songsawat written in pencil, camouflaged, grey on grey. In the wrong light it might have been illegible but the cabin lights reflected silver off the carbon letters.

Siri and Civilai raised their hands and the young man nodded. They collected their baggage from the overhead container and followed him down the steps and across the runway. The old fellows attempted one or two questions along the way, in Lao, then French, then Vietnamese. Then the odd phrase in Burmese, English, Chinese, and Mauritian Creole (Civilai had learned to say 'I would like to meet your sister' from a very personable Mauritian he'd met at a conference in Havana.) Their guide responded to none of these.

Their own limousine was parked beside a wire fence. They sat, the three of them, in the rear seat, the scent of the leather hinting that the cow had not long been slaughtered. Siri and Civilai exchanged a glance and chuckled. The limousine, lit only by the distant lights of the aeroplane, was missing a driver.

'I've read about this,' Civilai whispered. 'They're remote controlled. This fellow pushes a button and it heads off all by itself.'

But then a skinny man with a cigarette hanging from his bottom lip, wearing his black pyjamas and scarf with less panache than their guide, walked out of the darkness adjusting his crotch. He stopped, looked at the shadows in the back seat, and took one last puff of his cigarette before flicking it over his shoulder. He climbed in the driver's seat, slammed his door and started up the car. He glared into the rear-view mirror with eyebrows hacked from old door mats.

'If they ever come to visit us I'm not sure we'll be able to match a reception like this,' Siri whispered.

'I can't begin to imagine all the planning and expense that went into it,' Civilai agreed.

The new limousine started silently and the gear lever danced from first to second without effort. When they reached and passed the fortified guard post, the guide also slipped into gear. His Lao was fluent but accented. Somewhere from the border up towards the Kong Falls. The product of a mixed marriage, they guessed, although something about him suggested one of his parents was a machine.

'Welcome to Democratic Kampuchea,' he began. There had been no eye contact and even now he stared straight ahead at the driver's bald patch.

'And we're very happy to—' Civilai began.

'Our two countries have a great and mutually respectful history,' the guide continued. 'As the two honoured guests know, we are the first two Marxist states to have shaken off the shackles of Therevada Buddhism, leaving our peoples free to think without superstition and religious propaganda.'

'What's your name, son?' Siri asked.

There was a confused moment like a tape sticking in an old recorder, but it was fleeting. The boy continued.

'We are happy to receive such honoured representatives from the People's Democratic Republic of Laos. I am your guide, Chan Chenda and I will be accompanying you during your visit here. While you are—'

'I think I detect an accent in there,' Civilai said. 'Don't you, Siri?'

'I picked it straight off,' Siri agreed. 'I'd wager one of your parents is Lao. Am I right?'

'My family . . . I am proud to serve Angkar,' the guide said, flustered. He glanced briefly at the two guests then looked away, embarrassed.

'I bet you are,' Siri said, not really knowing what Angkar was. 'Such a lovely place. Travelled around much, have you?'

'Thank you,' said the guide. It was the type of "thank you" heard at the cinema when somebody's trying to hush up a chattering couple. Siri and Civilai recognised it at once and they shut up.

'Here in Democratic Kampuchea,' the guide continued, 'we have drawn upon human resources to develop the ambitious aims of our great country. Through direct consultation with our Khmer brothers and sisters, we have reached an exciting period in the development of cooperatives. As laid out in our four-year . . .'

The boy droned on like an automaton, leaving the guests with no entertainment but the occasional brown light of a wax lamp glowing from a passing hut. It was too dark to read so Siri left Camus in his bag. The old friends had endured enough government propaganda sessions to know a prepared script when they heard one. The guide was on "play" and they wouldn't get in a word until he reached the end of the reel.

'. . . laid out in our four-year agricultural template for the future, drafted in 1976, collectives will be the key to unlocking the door to independence and prosperity. We have almost tripled our rice yield and in five to ten years we anticipate that eighty per cent of farms will be mechanised. In fifteen years we should have established a base for industry. We currently have . . .'

'Any idea how far the airport is from the city?' Civilai asked Siri.

If the guide was upset by the interruption he didn't show it.

'. . . of our new National Technical college which already has three-hundred students and will . . .'

'No more than twenty minutes, according to the map,' Siri replied.

'Could be one of those Einstein twenty minutes,' Civilai sighed.

It was only the sight of one or two large buildings showing off with actual electricity that signalled their arrival in Phnom Penh. Most of the city was black blocks and empty unlit streets. There were no other car headlights to guide them. At last, the large wooden sign, HÔTEL LE PHNOM was exposed in the full beam. Half hidden beneath untrimmed trees, it seemed to issue a plaintive plea for help rather than a welcome. Siri recalled the hotel from his previous visit. It had been a gay, noisy place then, with elegant French high-socialites taking cocktails around the pool. Fawning French-speaking servants in starched white uniforms running back and forth with trays. Floodlights flaunting the new white paint of the façade and highlighting the greens of the tropical garden. Two uniformed guards in

white caps had stood guard at the front barrier to keep out
riff-raff. Siri and Boua hadn't been allowed inside. After
speaking to them rudely in Khmer, the prim bouncers had
asked in French,

'Are you guests?'

'Mais, oui,' Siri had lied.

'Show me your receipt.'

'It's in our suite. My personal French secretary has it in
her purse.'

The guards had eyed their peasant clothes, their sandals
and their cloth shoulder bags and laughed at them. They'd
laughed right in their faces and pointed to the street. Phnom
Penh had been a city back then in which natives were not
welcome. The Khmer made up ninety-three per cent of the
population but the Chinese had all the money and the
Europeans handled the culture. The Khmers cooked and
cleaned and begged and threw scum out of luxury hotels.
Such was their lot.

The floodlights were gone now, the grounds overgrown.
Only one or two lights glowing from rooms here and there
gave any suggestion of the size of what the guide told them
was no longer Hôtel Le Phnom, but House Number Two.
They pulled up in front of the large entrance but nobody
came running down the steps to open the door for them. The
driver switched off the engine but the guide was still
running.

'. . . that worklessness no longer exists in Democratic
Kampuchea. All our citizens work with vigour to the hours
of the sun. There is no longer salaried employment and our
Khmer brothers and sisters voted unanimously that we
should do away with money. We use a system of . . .'

'You don't have money?' Civilai asked.

'We are a . . .'

'So we can't give him a tip,' Siri lamented, climbing out of the car. 'Too bad because he's been so helpful and informative.'

The guide continued to drone on in the background.

'Then we'll show our gratitude in some other way,' Civilai decided. 'We'll tell his president what a good guide he is.'

The guide stopped.

'We don't have a president,' he said.

'No? What do you have?'

'We have Brother Number One.'

'Is that so?' Siri asked. 'And does Brother Number One live in House Number Two?'

'No. He lives in House Number Three.'

'I might have known. Then it is Brother Number One whom we shall inform of your diligence.'

'It is my pleasure to serve Angkar,' the boy said.

'I bet it is.'

The car pulled away and there was faint but undeniable pride on the face of the guide as he peered from the rear window. But it quickly became clear they shouldn't have dispatched their interpreter so soon. From that moment on they could communicate with nobody. The hotel staff, or at least the figures standing in strategic positions around the reception area, were dressed exactly as their guide. The women had short hair and stern faces. The men glared accusingly. There was not a pretty or handsome one amongst them. Nobody smiled. Nobody was animated. It was like a visit to a slowly melting waxworks.

Siri and Civilai pointed to their names on the hotel guest ledger and a serious man with a limp led them up to the second floor. He unlocked two doors and left the keys in the locks and the guests in the hallway.

'Is this weird enough for you yet?' Siri asked.

'I suppose room service is out of the question,' said Civilai, looking up and down the deserted corridor.

'There's still half a ton of Chinese inside you. You can't be hungry?'

'I was thinking of a nightcap.'

'Perhaps they've left us a little something in the rooms. Sandwiches and a bottle of Beaujolais perhaps?'

'Now, why do I doubt that?'

In their rooms they found beds, chairs, cupboards, unlabelled bottles of water and slightly grimy glasses.

'What time is it?' Civilai asked.

'The only working clock in reception said it was eight o'clock in Mexico City.'

'Well, assuming that's eight a.m. then it's only about nine p.m. here. Fancy a stroll around town before bed?'

'I can't imagine what else to do.'

They emptied their bladders in their respective bathrooms and regrouped in the hallway. As they walked along the light green carpet they heard a loud squeaking, grating sound coming from the floor below. It was unmistakably the sound of Godzilla chewing on a Volkswagen Camper. They walked down a dimly lit stairwell to a reception area whose lights, all but one above the desk, had been extinguished. The staff had fled but for one of the male cadres. He was now shirtless and tending to some business behind the counter. The entrance to the hotel had been blocked by a huge metal roller-grill. Phnom Penh beyond was apparently out of bounds. They were trapped.

They walked to reception and discovered that the clerk was connecting a mosquito net. One end was tied to the switchboard, the other wound around the neck of a stone statue, a poor copy of one of the *apsaras* from Angkor Wat. He seemed annoyed to have been disturbed. After ten minutes of mimes and gestures; bottles, drinking, staggering drunkenness, then down the scale to eating, rice, peanuts, bananas, the cadre was positively livid.

'My brother, Civilai,' Siri said at last, 'if our friend has a weapon of any sort down there behind the counter, I feel he's reached the point at which he'll use it.'

'Then, I'll say goodnight.'

'Goodnight and sweet dreams,' they wished the scowling receptionist.

There was no sweetness in Siri's dream that night. That same disconcerting nightmare was waiting for him. But everything was so much more vivid. The streets through which he walked had acquired a scent, a rancid smell he knew well from his work. The song came at him from everywhere like a sensur-round soundtrack with strings and a harmonious backing group. But it was certainly the same eerily beautiful song.

The boy-soldier who approached him with his pistol raised had a history now. He had a family, brothers and sisters, all hungry, others dead because there were no medi-cines to cure simple ills. He had been drafted into the military because his mother had no rice to feed him. Siri knew all this, not because he'd been told, but because, in the place where dreams are produced, this was a logical plot development. It made the character more dimensional. We now had reason to feel sorry for the antagonist, to side with him. It created an element of conflict in the conscience of the viewer, in this case, Siri. Something in him wanted the boy to pull the trigger. And, with so much unexpected support, that's exactly what he did. Siri's head was gone. Splattered like a kumquat on a busy highway. And the dream-Siri was filled with dread, not because he was headless – inconven-ient though it was – but because he was afraid he might stumble into the singer and that would be the end of mankind. He knew there was nothing to pull him back. Finding the origin of the song would signal the end of all hope, worse than anything he'd ever experienced.

The explosion of the gun had reduced the soundtrack to a single beautiful voice. Headless Siri was on his hands and knees. He reached a plot of earth where the sounds climbed up through the dirt and lingered there like invisible music plants. He began to dig down. Something beneath the ground was attempting to dig upwards. Siri was over-whelmed by the wonderful song. The refrain squeezed at his heart strings, squeezed blood out of them, squeezed until they snapped, one by one. His heart, stringless, broke away from his chest like an untethered blimp and was carried off by the music plants, rising, lost in the blood-red sky. As his seventies cultural attaché, Dtui – self-confessed addict to Thai pop magazines – would say, it was all very Beatles.

A breath fanned his hand and his fingers felt the outline of a mouth deep in the dirt. These were the lips that sang the love song. He raked away the debris with his fingers so the singer could breathe fresh air. He hurriedly brushed dirt from the nose, from the eyes. The voice was beginning to break. It slipped off key and fell, tumbling through octaves. It came to rest on a deep, bronchial B flat. Siri knew he had to save the tune. With increasing desperation he strove to free the singer from his tomb. He lifted the head and cradled it in his arms, willing the song not to die. And that was when his fingers knew. Beneath their touch the cheekbones rose, the eyebrows bristled. And as he swept back the thick hair, his thumb and forefinger traced the outline of a left ear, missing a lobe.

15

A MOSQUITO INSIDE THE NET

'I really don't know what he's getting at,' Phosy said, not for the first time. Even though his desk was directly behind that of his superior, Sihot shook his head in response. Phosy held a note from Dr Siri. Daeng had dropped it off after Siri's departure, a last-minute memo scribbled in Siri's barely legible hand. Against his better judgement, Phosy had done what the doctor had suggested. He'd listened to Neung's story. It had been very slick. It explained everything apart from why three victims, all known to the suspect, had been killed. Phosy was disappointed that the doctor could have fallen for it. Of course Neung had it all worked out. It was easy enough to do when the evidence has been handed to him on a plate. Even Phosy could have done that. He was furious that Siri could have been so naive, presenting the accused with the police department's entire case.

But Phosy had listened patiently and asked the appropriate questions at the end. 'Who would want to frame you? Do you have any enemies? Has anybody threatened you?'

And all the answers had been negative. If Neung was about to go to all the trouble of inventing innocent relationships with the victims, surely he could have come up with a scapegoat to divert attention from himself. But, no. And, if it were possible, he made it worse for himself. Phosy had thought to ask whether the initial Z meant anything. And rather than deny it, Neung had the impudence to boast that they'd called him Zorro in Berlin. Something about his style, evidently. He'd been christened by his coach and the name had stuck with his students. Neung hadn't even the common sense to withhold that juicy fact. So, Phosy had his water-tight case and had no doubts in his own mind that he had the right man. No serious doubts. Of course, all criminal cases leave some gaps. But Siri's note rankled him. It wasn't a list of chores so much as unanswered questions. And of course he knew the questions. He had them on his own summary paper. He didn't need Siri to remind him.

> *Did Chanti suspect his wife was having an affair with Neung?*
>
> *Did he care?*
>
> *Why were the Vietnamese so reluctant to hand over the case to us?*
>
> *Did Kiang see her affair with Neung the same way he did?*
>
> *Did they fight?*
>
> *What was the timing of Neung and Jim's respective arrival in/departure from Berlin?*
>
> *Who was taking painkillers and why? (Does Neung have an injury?)*
>
> *Does Neung still have the knife used to cut out the signature?*
>
> *Does his father think Neung is guilty?*
>
> *Do you?*

Certainly, a lot of it was merely the tying up of loose ends. As a good policeman he would have done that anyway . . .

if they hadn't been so understaffed. Just him and Sihot and so many reports to write. And what was the point? They had their man, didn't they?

It was the post script to the note that had most riled the inspector. Just who did this little doctor think he was? Not satisfied with playing detective and telling him how to do his job, he had to interfere in Phosy's personal matters, too.

Phosy, I'm sorry. I meant to tell you this earlier this evening but I was distracted by the visit to Neung. It would have been better face to face but I've lost my chance. It's quite simple. If you aren't having an affair, tell your wife, immediately. If you are, stop it.

Phosy scratched out the entire postscript with his black biro, slashed at it till the paper tore. Still not satisfied, he took a pair of scissors from his pencil drawer and snipped off the bottom of the page. He scrunched it up and threw it into the wastepaper bin.

'Interfering little bastard. None of your business,' he thought. 'Who are you to tell me what I should or shouldn't do? You aren't even a relative, certainly not my father. Too late now, Siri. Where were you forty years ago when I needed you?'

There weren't any orphans in Laos, not government-sponsored or otherwise. And that was due to the fact that folks didn't give children enough time to think they were unloved. If you lost your parents, a relative would step in and fill their sandals as quickly as blood clotting on a wound, barely a scab. If you had the misfortune of losing your whole family, a neighbour would take you in, or someone in the next village. A local headman, perhaps. But, either way, you'd wake up next day with a new family and nobody would harp on your loss. They'd tell you what happened without drama and, no matter how poor, they wouldn't complain about what a burden you were. At least, that's the way it had been in Laos. That's the way it had been for Phosy.

He'd been studying at his primary school one day in the little northern village of Ban Maknow, Lemon Town. His mother and father just happened to be working in the wrong field at the wrong time and were mowed down in crossfire between this or that faction. Someone had come by the school and whispered in the teacher's ear. As Phosy had no uncles or aunts, he went home that evening with his friend, Pow. Pow's mother and father already had three other children living with them who had lost their parents in a civil war nobody really understood. It was such a clinical transition that it was several days before Phosy fully realised that he'd never see his parents again. He'd cried, of course. He missed them. But he was already safe and happy before loneliness had a chance to take hold.

His new father was a carpenter. He carved temple doors and fine furniture and all seven of the children, five boys and two girls, learned to use woodworking tools at an early age. There was no secondary schooling in those parts so Phosy had hoped his new father would take him on as an apprentice as he had done with his eldest son. But when Phosy was ten, a young man had come to the village. He was educated and well-spoken. In the open-sided village meeting hut, he explained to all the parents how he had been plucked from a place very much like this when he was a boy. How he'd been given the opportunity to study in the liberated zones in the north-east. He'd graduated from high school there and gone on to further education in Vietnam. He told them that they'd recently opened a new school and that they could take eight hundred new students. All food and board would be taken care of.

A week later, Phosy, Pow, and their sister, Beybey, were in a covered truck heading across the country. Phosy felt something in his stomach that he would later come to recognise as betrayal. They'd given him away. The family he'd loved had handed him over to a stranger. He couldn't understand it but life was travelling too quickly to analyse. They taught him things in the liberated zones. He learned how the French colonists had stolen their land. He learned how the rich landowners had taken advantage of the common people. He learned how to be angry and to punch his fist into the air and shout, 'Liberation!' He learned how to shoot guns and kill. And, by the time he reached seventeen, he and his false siblings were junior officers in the new Lao People's Liberation Army. All three of them were so entangled in the revolution they hadn't found time to go back to visit the family that had raised and cared for them . . . and given them away.

Phosy rose fastest through the ranks. He had an inquisitive mind and, once he reached the position of colonel, he was transferred to military intelligence and trained in the art of espionage just outside Hanoi. With a new identity, he arrived in Vientiane in 1965 and began work as a carpenter. Other LPLA men and women had been trickled into the mainstream of royalist society, spreading their beliefs subtly from the inside, passing on intelligence, preparing for the day revolution would come. They became known as the mosquitoes inside the net, these sleeper agents, ready to sting when the time was right.

But, while he was waiting, something occurred that Phosy hadn't prepared for. He fell in love. There was probably a whole chapter in the Indochinese Communist Party spy handbook detailing the dangers of falling in love whilst engaged in subversive activities. But Phosy was emotionally lost and in need of confirmation that someone might want him. He married and they produced first a boy, then a girl, and that old feeling of family returned to him. That warm comforting glow of belonging took over Phosy's life. At times it seemed more important than nationhood. The revolution took a back seat to Phosy's family.

But the revolution came anyway. It came swiftly on the heels of the Vietminh victory in Saigon and without the wholesale bloodshed that had been envisaged. And the Pathet Lao moles in their burrows in Vientiane celebrated quietly. The status quo had changed but there were still enemies. The new socialist government couldn't decide what to do with its spies. Under the guise of re-education, Phosy and his colleagues were recalled to the north-east and new roles were allocated. He was away for three months and when he returned to the capital, his wife and children were gone. Gone, the neighbours said, to a refugee camp on the Thai side. They'd paid a fisherman for a night passage to Nong Kai. Gone because his wife was afraid of the communists. Afraid of what they might do to her. Gone because Phosy hadn't been able to tell her he was the enemy.

Phosy left Vientiane and rejoined his unit in the northeast. Three families had deserted him. Phosy was a serial orphan. Love crumbled in his hands like hearts moulded from fine sand. Why invest? Why waste all that emotion? He'd met nurse Dtui. He'd liked her. He'd made her pregnant. He'd offered to marry her. She'd asked him if he could love her and he'd told her no, but he was prepared to marry her anyway. That had been good enough for Dtui and for him, companionship without fear of heartbreak. Then Malee had come along, the sweetest button of a babe. She had smiled and he'd remembered all the other smiles that had trapped him. He watched them together, Dtui and her baby, and he'd seen treachery in their eyes. He watched how she controlled the mind of the little girl. How would they break him, these two? Every day he was afraid he'd come home and find them gone. And the conflict was killing him, splitting him apart. On one side was the feeling that there was nothing on the earth so full of wonder as the love of a family. And on the other was the certainty that they would desert him. Either in death or in deceit they would go away and leave him without hope. How dare he tell them he loved them?

Siri tapped on Civilai's door at eighteen thirty Mexico City time. Civilai's voice carried dully from the bathroom.

'Come in if you're carrying food.'

Siri walked into the room. From the crumpled sheet and deformedly dented pillow, it appeared his friend hadn't slept any better than he had. He walked to the window. The view was similar to that from his own. Grounds that had once been landscaped were now jungle. A giant lucky hair tree craved attention not two metres from the glass. The city wasn't visible. Civilai walked from the bathroom wearing only shorts. He looked like a medical school skeleton with a paunch.

'I bet with a couple of chopsticks we could get a decent tune out of those ribs, brother,' Siri laughed.

Civilai ignored the taunt.

'Did you get your early-morning call?' he asked.

'I thought it was my imagination. It was a gunshot, wasn't it?'

'Pretty close too, by the sounds of it. Perhaps they were killing something for breakfast.'

'Good. I prefer my breakfast dead. I'm starving. Do you suppose the restaurant's open?'

'It's on the itinerary.' Civilai picked up the single sheet of paper they'd given him in Vientiane. '"Seven a.m. morning meal at House Number Two."'

'Good, hurry up and put on a shirt so we don't frighten anyone.'

Breakfast in the spacious dining room was uncomplicated but tasty. Other delegates sat at other tables minding their own business with great deliberation. The only noise was coming from the three Chinese tables whose breakfast banter bounced around the dusty restaurant like early morning ping-pong balls. Mr Chenda, their guide, joined the Lao at their table but refused food. He had a copy of their itinerary and he proceeded to read through it, expanding politically in one or another direction from notes he'd made on the sheet.

'Before lunch,' he said, staring towards the door, 'you will have the opportunity to visit your embassy. There, your ambassador will brief you on your country's relationship with Democratic Kampuchea and the ongoing role we expect the People's Democratic Republic of Laos to play in our development. You will sample a lunchtime meal of fresh food supplied directly from one of our cooperatives and then you will join representatives from other legations to visit our model collective in District Seventeen. You will return in time to change, whence you are invited to attend our grand May Day reception where you will have the great honour of meeting our respected and glorious leaders.'

'Including number one brother?' Civilai dared ask, not really expecting a response. But the guide became enlivened at the mention of the great leader.

'Brother Number One will most certainly be in attendance,' he beamed. 'Our leader is excited at the prospect of exchanging views with our respected allies.'

'Does Big Brother have a name?' Siri asked. He noticed indications of a short circuit deep in the guide's brain. His face shut down for a few seconds then rebooted.

'Tomorrow you will have the opportunity to visit a truly spectacular irrigation project where you will see what our peasants have been able to achieve, working hand in hand, shoulder to shoulder . . .'

'. . . heel to toe, thumb to nose,' Siri mumbled. He was becoming frustrated by the boy's inability to answer questions.

'What?' The guide seemed angry.

'Nothing. Go on.'

'As I was saying. The irrigation project is an example of what it's possible to achieve with nothing more than a love of Angkar, determination and hard work.'

'And Chinese funding,' Civilai added.

'They don't believe in money,' Siri reminded him. 'Isn't that right, little comrade? You see? I was paying attention. But I didn't catch Big Brother's name. What was it again?'

The guide put both his palms on the table and pushed himself stiffly to a standing position. He still hadn't looked either of the old Lao directly in the eye, but he glared menacingly at the condiment tray.

'You must be ready to leave from reception in ten minutes,' he told the fish sauce.

Considering the fact that Siri's old map showed Hôtel le Phnom to be no more than five city blocks from the embassy section of Boulevard Manivon, the limousine drive was curiously circuitous. As they pulled out of the hotel grounds, the first landmark his map said they'd pass was the Catholic cathedral. He'd visited it with his wife. It was gone. All that remained was a pile of rubble. They proceeded past the railway station which stood like a deserted castle and cut through a number of streets, none of which had signs. At every corner stood a sentry in black pyjamas with an AK47. They were men and women, old and very young, but all of them slouched and glared at the passing car. The limousine swung around the gangly Olympic stadium, one more example of the royal family's nouveaux Khmer architecture of the sixties, and headed along an empty Sivutha Boulevard. Its old sandalwood trees pointed their dead or dying fingers as they passed. The streets and buildings they saw were all immaculately clean, windows smiled reflections of the early sun. The journey might have given a guest the feeling the roads had been closed off for their safety, the people told to remain in their homes, but Siri had goose pimples as he looked out of the window. Something was wrong here.

They eventually entered the diplomatic section of Boulevard Manivon from the south. The entire road had been partitioned off with a heavily guarded barrier blocking the entrance.

'We provide maximum security for our foreign representatives,' the guide told them.

'Who from?' Siri asked.

'I'm sorry?' Every time the doctor interrupted, the guide became more impatient.

'Who are you protecting them from? Didn't you say you were at peace?'

'We are, indeed, a peace-loving nation, and the population has joined hands with us to form a unified democratic state. But there will always be insurgents out to embarrass us. We have enemies jealous of our successes. We need to remain vigilant.'

The limousine drove into the newly created compound and pulled up in front of an old sand-coloured colonial house. It was surrounded by a white wall like a temple. For the first time that day they saw people walking along footpaths, sitting on benches, locked in conversation. All of them foreigners. But Siri noticed the others; the silent, unmoving ones. They stood in strategic positions in their black pyjamas watching, minding. They reminded him of the ghosts who hung around temple fairs. They never joined in, were never seen, were not really there.

Both Siri and Civilai knew the Lao ambassador, Kavinh. They had fought campaigns together. He was only slightly taller than Siri and he too had been a fearless warrior. Yet they noticed immediately, as he walked along the path to greet them, that time had sandpapered the ambassador down to a spindle of the man they remembered. He had no spring in his step, no truth in his smile. Beside him was his own black-suited minder, a short-haired peasant with a sun-blistered face.

'Comrades,' said Ambassador Kavinh. 'It's been a long time.' They shook his unsteady hand and reminded each other of when and where they'd last met. But he was less than enthusiastic, not at all warm. He didn't introduce the man at his side. He turned and led them back inside. Siri caught Civilai's eye. Nothing was relaxed here. Nothing natural.

There followed a two-hour briefing, not from the ambassador or his diplomatic aides, but from the Khmer minder. He read from a prepared sheet. His Lao was heavily accented, comical at some points. But the old men found it prudent not to make comment. They sat on a circle of chairs in the front room of the embassy with their guide, the ambassador, two Lao aides and two more Khmer. Time became a heavy log towed by an ancient elephant. Siri could do no more than merely will it all to end. He took advantage of the opportunity by going over the case of the three épées in his mind. He had time to look at the circumstances through the eyes of each of the victims. And it was from the perspective of one of them that a completely different picture presented itself. He played a new hypothesis through to its gory conclusion and all the parts fitted. Only one question remained to be answered and, by the time they announced lunch, he was just a breath away from solving the mystery.

The fish and vegetables they served were fresh and, they had to admit, delicious. But the lunch table conversation was torturous. Every topic was a slow drip of water onto the forehead. Whenever light and jovial threatened, the Khmer would step in to redirect the mood in the direction of sombre and dull. There were no servants. The Lao diplomatic staff delivered the meals and collected the dishes without speaking.

It was during the distribution of the pumpkin custard slices that one young diplomat dropped a spoon on Siri's lap. It was a minor inconvenience as there had been nothing on the spoon at the time. Siri reminded him that, as far as he knew, they didn't teach the dishing up of pudding at the foreign diplomats' school, but the young man made a terrible fuss. He bowed and threw his hands together in apology and berated himself. And, as he leaned over to right whatever wrong he thought he'd done, he dropped a folded napkin into the doctor's lap and engaged his eyes briefly.

Siri finished his dessert, asked where the bathroom was, and excused himself. There was no lock on the bathroom door so Siri leaned against it and unfolded the white cloth serviette. In laundry pen were written the words:

Siri. Find an excuse not to go on the p.m. trip. Stay here. Urgent. Kavinh.

Siri pulled the chain, climbed onto the porcelain toilet and dropped the napkin into the overhead cistern. He waited a few minutes before returning to the table. His rendition of a man suffering from diarrhoea and stomach cramps was spectacular. He'd obviously seen his fair share of victims. The noises he somehow produced from his bowel region were frightening enough to make everyone in the room fear they might forfeit their own lunches. Siri was led to a camp bed in a back room, covered in a blanket, and left to groan. Knowing his friend's solid constitution, only Civilai saw anything suspicious about the attack and he kept his doubts to himself.

'I'm not really feeling too well, myself,' Civilai announced. 'I'm wondering whether something in the lunch was off.'

'I assure you—' the short-haired minder began.

'But, at least one of us should make the effort,' Civilai decided. 'I'll carry our flag to your collective, comrades. Let's hope my colleague is well enough to attend the reception this evening. I'd hate for this to turn into a diplomatic matter.'

He told them he wouldn't push the issue with the Chinese as long as the doctor was given care and rest for the afternoon. The guide seemed almost relieved to leave Siri there. And so it was that Civilai and Comrade Chenda boarded the bus to District Seventeen and Siri did not.

Phnom Penh, under whatever tyrant or warlord, had always observed the colonial French custom of sleeping after a good meal. Those two hours during the hottest part of the day belied the claim that Kampuchea did not know worklessness. Comrade Ta Khev, the sun-blistered cadre

attached to the Lao embassy, was no exception. As soon as
the man began his customary afternoon nap, and the bestial
sounds of his snoring could be heard behind the door of his
room, the embassy came alive. One diplomat was posted in
front of the cadre's room. Ambassador Kavinh was kneeling
on the floor at Siri's cot, hugging him like a newly deceased
relative. It was a desperate and unexpected gesture.

'Siri, Siri, my old friend,' he whispered.

'Kavinh? I thought you'd forgotten me.'

'My past is the only thing I can think fondly of,' he
replied. It was a curious comment but Siri instinctively
understood it.

'Come, we don't have much time,' Kavinh said, climbing
slowly to his feet. 'And there's a lot to do.'

Siri was led through the house to the larder. In the corner
stood a stack of wooden crates. Those on the top contained
cans of meat and fish. The lower boxes were apparently
empty. Two of the junior diplomats quickly slid the stack to
one side and revealed a large metal ring on a hinge
embedded in the wooden floorboards. They prised the ring
upwards and pulled. A heavy trapdoor lifted slowly and
without sound and Siri found himself staring down into a
black pit. The embassy staff looked at him and gestured that
he should go down. Siri, it had to be said, had a problem
with black pits. Some of his worst living nightmares had
taken place in such places. He baulked.

'Really, Siri,' said Kavinh. 'We don't have much time
before the bastard wakes up.'

'Oh well.'

A metal ladder led down into the darkness. Siri took a
deep breath and began to descend. The ambassador
followed close behind. Siri arrived at a concrete floor. He
stood aside and Kavinh stepped down. The trapdoor closed

and Siri could hear the rearrangement of the crates over-head. The darkness was total and overwhelming.

'Bien,' said the ambassador.

There came a tinkle of glass, the strike of a match, and Siri saw a disembodied hand suspended in mid-air. It carried the flame to a wick and a dirty yellow light from an oil lamp bathed the cellar. Twenty eyes looked out of the ochre shadow.

'Good afternoon,' said Siri.

There was a long moment of hesitation before four men and six women stepped up to him, smiling, taking his hand, squeezing his fingers. None of them spoke.

'This is the real briefing,' Kavinh whispered. 'It will have to be quick. But this is the information you need to take back to Vientiane when you leave.'

'Who are these people?' Siri asked.

'They're Khmer. All of them. Some we found. Others found us. This room is ventilated and sound doesn't carry. But we have to be careful. If they're found we'll all be killed.'

'But, why are they here?'

'Siri, you're going to learn a lot today that will stretch your belief. Things so horrific you won't sleep well for a year. We haven't had direct contact with Vientiane for eight months. We have no phone here. We can't travel without our minders. Every document passes through censors at the foreign ministry. So I haven't been able to alert our govern-ment as to what's happening. When I learned there would be a May Day reception and that a Lao delegation was invited, I knew it would be our best chance. Perhaps our last. I was so happy when I saw your name on the list, Siri. You're exactly the type of man I need to fight for us, for the Khmer.'

The situation seemed somewhat ridiculous to Siri, far too melodramatic. A lot of film extras overacting. Anne Frank-

like whispers in the attic. So the Khmer Rouge were para-
noid. Weren't their own Pathet Lao? Didn't they also
over-regulate Laos into a societal straitjacket? But, "we'll all
be killed"? Come on. Siri was tempted to smile and would
have done so but for the serious expressions all around him.
A girl, probably no older than twenty, brought over two
stools. She gave one to Siri and sat on the other. Ambassador
Kavinh and all the pale dwellers of the cellar sat on the
ground with their legs crossed and their backs straight.

The girl was paler than the others. Siri wondered how
long she'd been here in this sunless place. She was pretty but
her young face was drawn now and her eye sockets were
hollow and grey. She began to speak in French.

'My name is Bopha,' she said. 'My father was the curator
of the Khmer national museum.' Her voice was like thin ice
disturbed by the rippling of a pond. Her grammar was
perfect. Her accent suggested she'd lived in France for some
time. She spoke carefully, searching for exactly the right
words.

'I was his assistant,' she continued. 'I studied museum
sciences at the Sorbonne. On April the seventeenth, 1975,
my father and I were given an hour's notice to pack our
belongings and join the exodus from Phnom Penh along
with two and a half million other people. The Khmer Rouge
told us we were all to go to the countryside to work. My
father had been entrusted with the safety of our heritage, our
national identity, our treasures. He refused to leave and
asked to speak to a commanding officer. A young soldier
spat at my father and cut off his head with a machete. I was
standing beside him.'

She spoke for exactly thirty minutes, this brilliant, fluent,
destroyed young person. She told tales and recounted scenes
so awful that if a listener considered for one moment they

might be true, he would never be able to trust another human being. He would be left with the impression that there was nothing in the world save hate and evil. Hundreds of thousands executed, abused, left to die by the roadside. The genocide of intellectuals. A one-sided war against pale skin, Chinese faces, soft hands and spectacles. Two thousand years of Khmer history erased like a pencil sketch from the compendium of time. She spoke so bluntly of atrocities that she might have been a newsreader. At the end of her account she apologised for her poor French. As a sort of ironic after-thought, she mentioned that she'd been there in the cellar for four months. She said they had received no credible news of the world for four years and was wondering who had won the Nobel prize for literature in 1975. She had been following the judging when . . .

Siri couldn't give her an answer to her question. Nor could he speak. His stomach was a sack of lead shot. She had crushed his heart with her story, this innocent girl. When he eventually found words, his voice wasn't one he recognised.

'How did you get back to Phnom Penh?' he asked.

'I'd worked for two years carrying earth at the irrigation site,' she said. 'Digging latrines. Pleasing cadres. But they had my autobiography. They knew who I was. Somebody decided they needed to be seen to preserve our birthright. Incredibly, they had locked our treasures away. They brought me back to supervise the museum. I had no heart for it. It wasn't just the messages the Khmer Rouge had beaten into us, that rich is bad, poor is pure and good. I looked around me at all the opulence in the museum. The statues, the paintings, the gems. They had taken on a new meaning to me. They were the spoils of other warlords, other oppressive regimes who had stolen enough treasures to make their mark on history. They were symbols of tyranny. I hated it all.

'I knew Ambassador Kavinh. He had supported some of my father's projects. I ran away from the dormitory and came here. He has risked his own life to look after us. I am grateful to him and some days I think I am lucky to be alive. But mostly I regret that they didn't bury me out there with my sisters. I know these years will live inside me until I am old. All of us here, by the Lord's good grace, we all survived, but the killing fields will not leave our hearts. We are all charred by the flames of hell.'

Comrade Ta Khev, the Khmer Rouge cadre, awoke from a blissful sleep. As usual, it took him a few seconds to recall where he was. Good bed. Nice room. This was the life. Enough of all that jungle living. He'd endured poverty all his life and it was shit. This was what they'd dreamed of back then. A cushy city job, good food, and power. The high life and whatever it takes to get there. He rose from his bed, put on his black shirt and walked through the house to the little alcove that had once been the servants' sewing room. A room exclusively for sewing. He laughed. Those French. They certainly knew how to spend it. If he had money he'd build himself a counting room. A room where he kept all his money and he'd sit there all day counting it. He'd drink classy French wine and he'd count his money. He rubbed his full belly and opened the door. The cot was there in the middle of the little room but it was empty.

'Arrogant Lao,' he said to himself. 'I knew you were going to be a problem as soon as I—'

He heard a cistern flush across the hall and a tap run. He went out in time to catch the old doctor stagger out of the bathroom. He looked in a bad way. He used the wall to hold

himself up and tottered across to the sewing room. Comrade
Ta Khev stepped out of his way. He asked the old Lao how
he was but Siri ignored him and stumbled to the cot. It
croaked like a toad as he lay on it. The cadre smiled and
muttered in Khmer,

'Good. Serves you right. Arrogant Lao.'

Siri listened to the footsteps walking off along the hallway
and rubbed his face with his palms. The girl's voice still
crackled in his mind. He didn't want to believe her. He didn't
want to think he could be one of a species that had no
respect for its own kind. He'd dedicated fifty-odd years to
preserving life. It was precious. Every one he saved and every
one he lost. They all had value. Yet, if she were to be
believed, lives here were being squashed and trodden underfoot. There was no logic to it. No sense.

Ambassador Kavinh had heard the Khmer Rouge leaders
describe it as an experiment. An experiment in human engineering. But to Siri's ears it was jealousy, pure and simple.
The have-nots wiping out the haves. The country poor had
swept across the land like a black-suited plague and exter-
minated the rich and the educated. Then they'd moved
against the middle classes, the not-so-rich and the semi-
educated. And, when there was nobody left to hate, the
Khmer Rouge had begun to turn on itself. And here, what
was left of the administration, hanging by a threadbare
noose. A still-kicking corpse, living in fear and paranoia.

Siri couldn't allow himself to believe it. If it were true,
what was there to stop the plague from spreading across the
northern border? Why shouldn't it take hold in the souls of
his Lao brothers and sisters? Why shouldn't his country
become a laboratory for its own inhuman experiment? If
collectivism was an ideal state, then why not slavery? Why
not kill those infected with the capitalist disease and be left

with pure socialist man toiling eight hours a day with no ambition and no dreams? If death proved a convenient way of culling the populace here, why should his own leaders not . . . ?

He opened his eyes and spoke aloud.

'What if it's started already?'

With so little news and such a poor communication system, how could he really be sure there was no systematic slaughter in his own country? What became of all those members of the old regime sent for re-education in the north? What became of the missing hill tribe people attempting to escape to Thailand? Surely the Lao couldn't . . . It was all too much to take in. He felt as if his head was a pot and he was attempting to fill it with all the water from a village reservoir in one journey. He began to drown in the small room. He needed air. He needed evidence of normality. Children playing in front of their homes. Old ladies smiling from windows. Pretty girls ignoring the bawdy comments of street-corner youths. He didn't mind if they were the country poor brought to the city and crammed into rich people's houses like fast-breeding rats. It wasn't important. He just needed to feel humanity around him. For his own sanity he had to be sure that at some level, life went on in this country.

The life he was looking for would not be found behind the barricades of the embassy ghetto. It wouldn't be amongst the prisoners of diplomacy with their huge concrete flower pots and their street cleaners and their ghost minders. He would have to break out of this wonderland and see what genesis of a future he could find in the dirt-poor suburbs.

He went through the back kitchen door and into the garden. He knew that the people in the cellar hadn't walked in past the sentries at the main gate. There had to be another way in and out. The original white wall around the garden was two metres high but another metre of breeze blocks had been crudely cemented on top of that. That in turn was garnished with ugly broken glass. The breeze-block barrier crossed the side street beside the embassy and climbed another garden wall on the far side before snaking off into the distance like the great wall of China. Siri had no doubt it blocked in every yard and every building in the quarter. The embassy compound was East Berlin.

Siri was certain that with a pick and ten minutes he could have a hole in that jerry-built wall big enough to climb through. But he'd have every minder in the street on his back before he could remove one brick. No, he had to believe that those who built the wall saw it as a symbolic representation of power. They wouldn't have imagined anyone in the embassy with the gall to challenge them. He strolled around a muddy garden still lovingly cared for by the Lao. He inspected the original white wall. Where it formed the border to the adjoining yard it was overgrown with a hysterical wisteria. An ornamental rockery leaned against the display with ledges of pansies and other effeminate border plants. From top to bottom ran a sculptured waterfall which no longer spouted.

Siri climbed to the top of the pile, crushing plants underfoot, and looked into the neighbour's property. At one time it had been a mechanic's yard or the car park for some rich man's automobile collection. It was one large oil-stained slab of concrete. But it had its own brick wall. It ran parallel to that of the embassy and was only a metre and a half tall. Why the neighbour would need a wall of his own and why it wasn't built flush with the embassy wall he had no idea. But there was a gap, no more than sixty centimetres, between the two. That, Siri was certain, was the way out. He leaned casually onto the top of the wall, glanced back towards the embassy; then, certain there was nobody standing behind him, he slipped over the wall into the gap.

He felt rather foolish pinned between the two walls and had no idea what he'd do if his theory proved to be wrong. But he sidled to his left to where the Khmer Rouge wall towered above him. The intersecting angle was bricked also but it was apparent that the blocks were not cemented, merely piled one atop the other. From a distance nobody would have noticed. Siri began to disassemble the temporary wall. Brick by brick the far side revealed itself to him. The contrast between the view ahead and the oasis behind was as drastic as that between heaven and hell. The entire block immediately at the back of the embassy compound had been levelled, apparently by a bomb. Rubble and shattered glass and broken lives were strewn fifty metres in either direction. Beyond that, the surviving buildings stood bruised with soot and dejected like mourners around a grave.

Siri stepped cautiously into this other world and carefully replaced the blocks behind him. It was a peculiar *Alice Through the Looking Glass* feeling. He had the over-whelming sense of being behind the set at a film lot. Backstage, there was no pretence, no need for flowers and new paint. He picked his way through the debris until he was on a dirt street. There were no body parts amongst the rubble. No flies in search of lunch. The only sounds were far off and there was no movement. No birds, no dogs, no life. The buildings on either side seemed to stoop forward with curiosity to watch him pass. Some doors were open, others were padlocked. Those windows with glass were shattered. Every building had its own unique display of dead plants: dead orchids in half-coconut shells hanging from an awning, dead crown-of-thorns in a row of coloured pots, dead vines climbing a three-storey building, losing their grip, hanging over the street suspended in free fall.

Another street, open doors and front yards with small cemeteries of dead consumer goods. A toaster oven. A television. A rice cooker. Like fish washed up on a river bank, no life source. No point. Embarrassed cars stripped bare, left with only their carcasses. A dove in a rattan cage, unfed, feathers on a white ribcage. Broken bone china cups crunching underfoot. At each intersection a pyre of the questionably valuable. The sooty smile of a piano keyboard. A child's high chair in charcoal. The black shadow of an antique French bureau, once priceless, now worthless.

Siri walked slowly along the unpaved lanes, his hands clenched into fists. He stepped into unlocked apartments and found himself in interrupted lives. The subliminal message, 'Had to pop out for a minute. Be back soon' was pinned somewhere in the air around them. They sat humble and faithful like stupid dogs waiting for their owners to return. A letter, half-written, undisturbed on a desk. A plate of putrid fruit on a kitchen table. Toy cars parked in front of a Kellogg's packet garage on the floor.

He heard a noise.

He was at a row of two-storey Chinese shop-houses and, illogically, he walked from one to the other trying to locate the sound. His instincts and the amulet at his neck told him to walk away. But the ghostly loneliness of his promenade so far had been unnerving. Noise was a welcome ally. Even if it was a stray cat, or an orphan child, or a cheetah escaped from the Phnom Penh zoo, it made no difference. He could use the company. He stood below a balcony and heard the unmistakable sound of drawers being opened. No animal he knew of had perfected the art of opening and closing drawers.

He walked in through the shopfront. They sold baskets there, finely woven bags and purses, stacks of place mats and coasters. All too delicate to be pilfered by an army. Nothing seemed to have been disturbed or destroyed. The till tray remained open, bank notes were pinned inside it under wire clips. Siri walked up the staircase at the back of the shop noisily, he thought, in his leather sandals. He followed the sounds into a kind of study with cabinets and bookshelves against one wall and bank upon bank of chests of drawers. And, on his knees rifling through them was a child of thirteen or fourteen. He had already amassed a small pile of booty on the floor beside him, mostly ballpoint pens and coloured pencils. He was so engrossed in his search that he hadn't heard Siri enter.

The doctor smiled. He was about to turn and leave the child to his treasure hunt when he noticed the muscles on the boy's neck tense. It was as if he sensed a presence. He turned his head and saw the old man standing there. He seemed to tremble. His eyes widened and he fumbled around him for something on the floor. He found what he was looking for on a shelf in front of him. His pistol was fat and clumsy in his hand, but holding it seemed to give him confidence. He was no longer afraid. His face hardened and it was then that Siri recognised him. He'd looked into those eyes every night for more than a week. This was the young assassin from his nightmare. The boy was real. So was the gun. He climbed to his feet with the weapon in front of him and snarled and spat out words Siri didn't understand. The gun was the child's courage, his image, his personality. Siri knew it had killed before. The boy swaggered up to the old man and levelled his personality at Siri's forehead.

It was a performance that had never failed. Siri was certain men, women and other children had quaked with fear at this same show of strength. Siri knew the boy would have no qualms about pulling the trigger. He smelt death on him like the scent of gunpowder on a shooter's hand. Siri knew that if he spoke just one word of Lao it would be his epitaph. So he kept quiet. He smiled and raised his right hand and he slapped the little boy hard across the cheek. The blow snapped the boy's head to one side and the gun suddenly looked more like a plaything in his hand. He stared at Siri in amazement and the doctor glared calmly back into those young eyes. What thoughts, what memories passed through the child's head in those few seconds? Confidence was suddenly replaced with indecision which rapidly became humiliation, and the boy began to cry. Tears rolled down his cheeks and he huffed back the sobs. At that moment, the little soldier was three years old again, and helpless, and just a child.

Siri turned away from the shaking gun barrel, shook his head, and walked back down to the street. He paused by the front shutter to catch his breath. He didn't know why he wasn't dead. Perhaps, being elderly and white-haired, it was conceivable he was one of the mysterious brothers of the Red Khmer. The boy might have seen the old man in a motorcade or heard him talk at a training seminar. Everyone over sixty looked the same. But, more likely, it was because the doctor had shown no fear, and it was fear that satisfied the blood lust of the little killer. Without it, the kill meant nothing. There was no power-fed adrenalin. Nothing to disguise the fact that every day was a trauma for the child.

A block away, Siri's legs began to wobble and he caught hold of a tree trunk, hanging on to it for dear life until the shakes worked their way out of his body.

'Not the way you'd planned to go, Siri,' he said. 'Not in the script. A Douglas Fairbanks ending for you, old boy. A fitting hero's exit. Not popped by a little lad with a grown-up's gun. No, sir.'

He often talked to himself when he was overwhelmed with fear. He saw it as a more dignified reaction than wetting himself. And, invariably, it helped. With his legs back under control he walked one more short block, looking over his shoulder the whole way. He was at the intersection of a wide street. It was one he knew well. One he recalled often when searching for happy thoughts. This was Boulevard Noradon, named after the fickle regent, the mood-swing prince who rented out his soul to any passing devil. Siri was no fan of royalty but if only half the stories he'd heard today were true, he wouldn't be at all surprised to find Sihanouk's head on a pole on his own street. He couldn't imagine Brother Number One chumming up with the little regent.

He stepped onto the deserted tree-lined boulevard. This was where he and his wife had walked hand in hand back in the forties. It was one of his golden scenes. Those moments had become fewer and farther between as Boua became fanatically entwined in the struggle for independence. He needed to hold on to that Phnom Penh for as long as he could. But there were no smiling faces now. No lovers on benches. No impossible beds of tulips and roses. This was a morning-after Boulevard Noradon. Most of the imported trees had withered through lack of care. There was litter everywhere and evidence of vandalism. One street lamp was bent like a boomerang. Across the street stood half the national bank. A large dented strong room, open and empty, peeked from between destroyed brickwork.

Siri began to walk along the central reservation in the direction of Phnom Temple. He passed a porcelain toilet and, twenty metres further on, waded through slippery puddles of French piastre coins. To his left the central market, the old Chinese quarter, was a graveyard of wrecked umbrellas and shredded awnings. It gave off none of the market scents, no rotten vegetables, no stale cereals, no putrid meat. This was a market lifeless for three years. It was about now that Siri began to hum. There was certainly nothing to hum about. The last dregs of joy at being alive in this world had been drained out of him in the cellar of the Lao embassy. But it was the type of annoying ditty you might pick up from the radio or Thai TV commercials. He couldn't shake it off.

He still had that 'last man after the atomic bomb' feeling as he walked past the impressive École Miche where he and Boua had attended night classes beneath ceiling fans vast as helicopter blades. He reached the European quarter. He had no idea how long he'd been walking but recently he'd been stepping to the tune in his head. He tried to find words for it but nothing came. It was lulling him into a bloated sense of security and self-confidence. Making him think that it was perfectly all right to be walking the streets of a hostile city all alone. He reached Le Cercle Sportif. To his right the Phnom Temple stood defiant at the top of its lion-guarded steps. Across the square was the national library. He knew he was only a block away from his hotel. All being well he could stroll past the guards and nobody would say anything.

Such was his aim. He had survived. He headed off across the untended grass and could see the roof of house number two in the distance. But when he reached the lawn of the national library he stopped cold. His sadness for a beautiful defiled city turned to a bitter acid in his gut. Strewn across the grass were the soggy remains of thousands of books. Tens of thousands. Some old tomes had been set alight and had melded together. Illustrated pages flapped in the breeze.

Precious and priceless volumes providing mulch for the next generation of plants. He crouched and paid reverence to the victims of ignorance and wondered whether anyone else in this city had been able to mourn the death of culture. It was then that he believed it all. If Big Brother could destroy literature and history, he could destroy lives.

He walked back through the overgrown grass of the lawn and raked his fingers through his hair. He had to get out of this place, this country. He was in the dead centre of a dead city. He had to convince somebody of what was happening here, but he had no proof. One more block and . . . The song was playing loudly in his brain now, confusing his thoughts. And finally the lyrics came to him. Not to his mind, exactly, but to his ears. He could hear the male tenor voice as clearly as from a radiogram. It was even more hauntingly beautiful than he remembered it from his dreams. It came to him not from the giant speakers in front of the Ministry of Information, nor from the prayer room of the empty temple, but from the ground beneath his feet.

This was the spot. This was, in some inscrutable way, the answer. He dropped to his knees, put his hands together to show respect and, without once considering the ramifications, began to dig into the rain-softened earth.

16

CAN WE HAVE SEX TONIGHT?

Phosy and Dtui had run out of tears. They were as dry and exhausted as old batteries. Phosy had squeezed his wife's hand bloodless. They sat on the flat roof of the police dormitory on two director's chairs their neighbour had once requisitioned for evidence and forgotten to give back. There was still rain in the air but it was an almost imperceptible mist. The low clouds denied them a view of the universe, and the night all around them was so black they might have been in the belly of a giant river dragon. But still they thanked the stars they couldn't see that only Siri and Daeng had been witness to their foolishness.

Phosy had been astounded at Siri's accusations at first. Why in blazes would he have an affair? Who'd want him? Where would he ever find the time? How would he muster the enthusiasm? And, what would the point have been? He already had a wife and he was doing a poor job of keeping *her* happy. At first he'd wondered whether Siri had been encroaching on the subject because the old fellow himself was on the hunt, or already had his snout in the chicken coop. But then, no. Who in their right mind would cheat on Madame Daeng, a woman very handy with a cut-throat razor? And then the note. Siri's hurried note before he left. Tying up loose ends. Expressing doubts, and then the postscript. The last thought of Chairman Siri. 'If you're having an affair, stop it.'

He'd told Dtui about the note. He hadn't been able to show it to her because he'd destroyed the postscript. But he laughed it off as one of Siri's overprotective moments. A ridiculous thing.

'Are you telling me you aren't having an affair?' Dtui had asked.

'Why on earth would I want to?' he'd replied.

'That wasn't the question.'

'No, Dtui. Of course I'm not having an affair. Don't be ridiculous.'

And that introduction had led into a long painful confessional of the doubts of the pair of them. They'd asked policewoman Wan to look after Malee and they'd fled to the roof where nobody could hear. And all the anxiety, the frustration and stupidity were released into the night like steam from an old rice cooker. Phosy, for the first time since they'd been together, perhaps for the first time ever, had shared his feelings. It was a significant step for a man who kept everything bottled up inside. He told her about his family and his first wife and his fears that one day he'd come home to find their room empty. When the words were all out they both sighed. Phosy noticed that he was holding Dtui's hand in his and it felt squashed and numb, but she hadn't attempted to wrestle it free. The fine rain had mixed with their tears and left them fresh-faced. Everything would be all right. Malee wouldn't be growing up in a single-parent household.

'All you need is love,' said Dtui, in English.

'What?' said Phosy, who didn't speak the language.

'Beatles.'

He had no idea what she was talking about.

'As a medical person, I'm predicting we'll catch pneumonia if we sit up here in the rain for much longer,' Dtui told him.

'That's all right. We can share a bed in emergency. Joint drips.'

'That's so sweet. I think I'm going to like this new romantic Phosy.'

'Don't get your hopes up. If this conversation gets out to anyone else, you and the orphan are on the street. Get it?'

Dtui put her arm around his neck.

'I think we owe Siri and Daeng a meal, don't you?'

'We would have sorted this out eventually.'

'Probably. In two or three years?'

'You're right. When the good doctor gets back from his trip we'll take them somewhere nice. I'll start saving.'

'Good. Phosy?'

'What?'

'Can we have sex tonight?'

'Dtui!' The policeman blushed the colour of a rat-excrement chilli.

'What? We're married, you know.'

'A lady doesn't . . .'

'Sorry.'

They looked out into the vast darkness all around them.

'Phosy?'

'What?'

'Can we?'

'Absolutely.'

It was some two, perhaps three hours later that Phosy, wearing only a loincloth and a grin, brought his papers into the police common room. He tugged on the bobble chain that clicked on the light bulb. He had a report to write about the three-épée case. The commissioner of police had been very pleased with the thoroughness of the investigation and was optimistic as to how the police would look in the eyes of the public once the trial was over. He had mentioned over tea that afternoon that, as far as he was concerned, the case was closed. All he needed was the final report. The trial, he conceded, was just a bit of trumpet blowing from Justice. Phosy didn't have to be involved in all that. He didn't even need to put in an appearance.

Phosy had been confused. He'd asked how they could have a trial without the arresting officer present. How would they present the evidence he'd collected? The commissioner had smiled and leaned close to him, even though there were only the two of them in the office.

'They'll read out your report,' he said.

So, pressure was on to have the report finished to read in evidence the next day. He opened the case of the portable typewriter and clicked his fingers. He had to get his spelling right. He'd have Dtui read through it in the morning to be sure the grammar was . . . Or perhaps not. She'd ask questions and the report would never be delivered. She'd ask questions like, 'What kind of trial doesn't allow the defendant's representative to cross-examine the investigating officer?' She was like that. Logical. He looked at the folder with all his hours of interviews and communiqués from Europe. He stared at the pile like a writer with a block. Apart from Dr Siri, everyone had decided Neung was guilty. It didn't matter what the accused said or did during the trial. He was a dead man.

Phosy put a sheet of paper between the rollers and held his fingers over the keys. They hovered there for a minute playing air keyboard, before he brought them down all at once. The keys wedged together and remained stuck, handprints in metal. What had Siri asked? 'What does your instinct tell you?' And Phosy's instinct told him a lot. Nothing about Neung suggested the man was a mass murderer. Everything about this case was weird. There were more questions unanswered than answered. Ignoring them didn't make the inconsistencies go away. The trial would go on for a day or two. There was time for just a little more police work.

Comrade Civilai sat on the end of the bed in House Number Two waiting for the guide to escort him to the ball. Anywhere else and he would have had two or three drinks beforehand to numb the forthcoming pain. He'd represented his country at numerous events such as this. Over the last five years he'd begun to wonder if it was the only thing he was good at, pretending to have a good time. The more objectionable he'd been in the cabinet meetings, the more overseas missions they sent him on. Anything to get him out of sight. There was nothing those politburo boys liked less than having someone disagree with them. Politics had changed him. He probably couldn't tell a plough from a shear these days but he could name any cocktail from a hundred metres.

And then came the retirement. It had been touch and go for a while whether they'd put him out to pasture or wrap a blindfold round his head and shoot bullets at him. Both had their good points. But thanks to Siri his fall from grace had one or two padded cushions beneath it. And here he was, a year later, still upsetting everyone. Making a nuisance of himself. And still they had him handshaking, head-nodding, gorge rising on the cocktail circuit. He hated it. But, at least he had Siri with him. Nothing ever seemed so dark when friend Siri was around. He could have used the old boy's sunshine to brighten up the dull afternoon at the state farm.

'This is an orange,' the commentary had begun. 'It achieves its bright orange glow from the combination of fish entrails mush and fertilizer blended from our own chicken manure. The orange, a tropical fruit, originated in . . . et cetera, et cetera.'

They'd given everyone a slice of orange to suck on. In spite of all that shit blending and offal mushing, it had tasted like any common or garden bloody orange. And Civilai had looked along the rows at all the bananas and papayas and mangoes and lemons and pomegranates and jack fruit and star fruit and he knew what a lot he had to look forward to and how much more fun this fruit cocktail party would have been with his brother at his side. And would that he were with him now. There was something sinister about this country. It wasn't a comic parody of a socialist state, it was a deadly serious parody. It was as if they believed that this was how it was supposed to look. They'd read the Communist Manifesto and missed the point. Just as Christian and Muslim extremists found hatred and vengeance that didn't exist in their respective manuals, these Red Khmer believed Marx and Lenin had called for the obliteration of personality and pleasure and free thought. Believed that blind allegiance was the only way to proliferate their doctrines. Civilai had never read it that way because that wasn't how it had been written.

So far, he'd only seen what they wanted him to. Yet, instinctively, he knew that something unpleasant lurked below the surface. He felt it in his heart and he wanted to have Siri around to talk through his theories. He wanted to know what the little lunchtime drama had been about, whether Siri had learned anything more about this weird place. But, most of all, he wanted to be sure his friend was safe. As far as Civilai was concerned, their departure the following day couldn't come a moment too soon.

He was startled by a knock.

'Siri?'

There was no answer. Civilai hurried to the door and threw it open. Comrade Chenda stood there, pale and flustered.

'It is time to go down,' he said.

'But what about Siri?

'Comrade Siri might join us later.'

'Where is he?'

'He's . . . It's time to go.'

'What is it? What are you not telling me?'

'It's time to go down.'

'You've already said that. Now perhaps you'd do me the courtesy of telling me what you know about—'

But the young guide had turned on his heel and was heading back towards the staircase.

'Everything will be explained,' he said. 'In due time.'

Phosy had spent the day interviewing, phoning, knocking on doors. He had all his notes spread around him on the floor and sat at their centre like a frog on a white lily pad. He had become more confused as the day progressed. Malee lay on the bed gurgling and laughing at the stars-and-planets mobile circling above her head. Her parents noticed she was particularly fond of Pluto. Phosy crawled across to the bed and took hold of his daughter's hand.

'What would you do in my situation?' he asked.

Dtui burst in through the door and threw her bag on the floor.

'If I have to go to one more Nurses for a Better Future meeting I'll scream,' she said. 'I hope you two aren't talking about me.'

Phosy looked up at her with the hopeless expression of a pig on its way to the slaughter.

'He didn't do it,' he said.

'Who didn't do what?'

'Neung. He wasn't the one.'

'Malee told you that?'

She squeezed her husband's shoulder as she walked to the kitchen corner of the room.

'In a way, yes. Neung's wife was away on the weekend of the murders. He was looking after their son. He's six. Now, whoever killed those three women had gone to a lot of trouble, put a lot of planning into it. But there he was babysitting all weekend.'

'So?'

'So why didn't he get his mother-in-law or a neighbour to look after the boy? He could have pretended to be working over the weekend. Why risk your son waking up in the middle of the night and not finding his dad there? Crying the damned house down? And how would he do it? Put the boy to bed, run off to K6 in the early morning, have a romp in a sauna with his boss's wife, stick a sword in her, drive home and kiss his son good morning?'

'He might have sent the boy off to a minder somewhere,' Dtui suggested, pouring hot water on her instant noodles.

'That's what I assumed at first. But the neighbours remember hearing the boy at various times over the weekend. Someone else recalls seeing them at the market on Saturday. His wife said he'd come by the school to pick up their son on Friday. That wouldn't work out. To kill the first victim he would have had to be inside K6 at night. They wouldn't have let him in if he'd turned up late. What kind of electrician works at midnight? He had to have been there inside the compound, hidden away somewhere after his regular day of work.'

'The wife might have been lying.'

'I thought wives didn't lie.'

'Good ones don't.'

'Well, his wife's been camped outside the jail day and night since Neung was arrested. She refuses to leave. She knows he was having a relationship with one of the victims but she's still there supporting him. I'd say that makes her a good wife, wouldn't you?'

'Dr Siri's got to you, hasn't he?'

'There are just too many "Why would he?" questions. Why would he murder the women in places that could all be traced back to him? After all the planning, why would he not cover his tracks? And then there's motive. What reason did he have to kill them? I didn't find any conflict. He doesn't strike me as the type of person who'd kill just for the thrill of it. And this murderer really has to be some kind of psychopath.'

'Somebody must have had a motive,' Dtui said. She put a flat plate on top of her noodle bowl and let it sit until all the chemicals and flavouring and inedible carbohydrates decided to become food. She sat on the edge of the bed and stroked her daughter's hair. 'If Neung didn't do it,' she said, 'someone must really hate him.'

17

Z

The following day, Dtui's comment, 'Someone must really hate him,' was at the front of Inspector Phosy's mind. The rains were holding back but Vientiane was a swamp of mud. All the citizens he passed wore clogs of red clay like Frankenstein boots. Bicycle tyres swelled to tractor-tread thickness. Street dogs had become two-flavoured, caramel above, cocoa below. With all the slithering and sliding, everyday activities had turned to slapstick. The famous Lao sense of humour, bogged down in the socialist depression, found an outlet. Laughter could be heard all around the town. Bicycle-skid victims sat in the middle of the road and howled with delight. Children giggled as they skated across Lan Xang Avenue in their flip-flops. Big-boned ladies held on to each other as they attempted to ford a muddy lane, screaming with merriment.

Phosy witnessed this new mood as he drove back and forth across the city in his four-wheel-drive jeep. He recalled the days when laughter was as common as the chirrup of crickets and the clack of the wooden blocks of noodle sellers advertising their wares. He liked this Vientiane, and on any other occasion it would have cheered him up, but today he had a sombre mission. He had to find another suspect in a case he'd considered closed. He had to put together enough evidence to prevent an innocent man from facing the executioner. In his note, Siri had asked about the morphine elixir. *Who was taking painkillers and why?* Neung had no obvious injury, but one man on his list did. Comrade Phoumi, the security chief. Could Phoumi have injured his wrist in the first attack and been taking morphine to deaden the pain? It was his left wrist so he could still use his sword hand.

Then there was Major Dung, sword expert. He'd lied about his contact with épées. He was a ladies' man. Didn't like to be rejected. A career soldier, a trained killer. He didn't have respect for women, Lao women in particular. The alibi for both of these suspects, impossible to verify without Prime Ministerial intervention, was that they were asleep in their respective dormitories at the time of all three murders. Phosy decided it wouldn't have been beyond either of them to frame a Lao engineer for murders they'd committed. But again he was missing a motive.

Then, next on his list was Comrade Chanti, the husband of the first victim. A reply – long time coming – had arrived from Houaphan that morning. It was handwritten by the signatory at the military wedding of Chanti and Dew back in 1969. The writer was a colonel in the North-eastern Region 7 and a distant, and apparently not loving, relative of Dew. He wrote,

No idea why they bothered. They couldn't stand each other from day one. Definitely an arranged marriage. Parents wanted their kids to appear normal, I suppose. Put pressure on them to produce grandkids. Maintain the family name. Not sure how they ever got around to that. Wouldn't be surprised if the boy was a fairy. Lot of them around these days . . .

So, Chanti; resentful at being forced into an arranged marriage, then deserted. Left with the responsibility of paying for the children's upkeep. No mother around. The marriage obviously a façade. But how would that play out in a mass-murder scenario? Why would he need to frame Neung? Siri always encouraged Phosy to paint elaborate hypotheses. The accusation was only the view of an old soldier but how about this? Possible homosexual connection? Chanti meets Neung at the government bookshop and flirts with him? Neung mocks him and . . . Phosy always had a problem hypothesising himself into homosexual relationships. He was old school. He had a hard time imagining that such tendencies were possible. They certainly weren't natural. But, in this permissive age, even such an unpleasant concept had to be kept in consideration.

Who else did he have? He looked at the fringe players; Neung's wife and his father, the bookshop clerk, other members of the security detail, other readers at the bookshop. He had to admit, with such a clear-cut suspect it wasn't going to be easy to find anyone better. So he focused on Siri's list. He began with the question, *Did Kiang see her affair with Neung the same way he did?* He drove to Kiang's house to talk to her mother. The woman was cheerful and open but she denied that she had ever heard the name Neung. She assured Phosy that if her daughter had been involved in any relationship, she would have been the first to know.

Kiang's younger brother Ming was at home and Phosy found an excuse to talk to the boy alone. Once they were out of earshot of his mother, the brother admitted his sister was involved with a man. She'd sworn the boy to secrecy but even so, this confidence hadn't allowed him access to details. The brother didn't know the man's name or anything about him. All he did know was that the lover was very much like her old boyfriend, Soop. It was as if the dead soldier had come back from heaven to be with her, she'd said. Kiang had never been happier. The boy didn't know why his sister would want to keep the relationship a secret from their mother. Phosy did. He was certain the old lady wouldn't have taken too kindly to her daughter flirting with a married man. Everything fitted. Kiang did have a crush on Neung. His version of events was accurate.

Phosy mentioned another name, Comrade Chanti. The Electricité du Lao chief had denied knowing Kiang but he'd given them all the feeling he was lying. And, sure enough, he was. The brother recognised the name. Before his sister left for Bulgaria, Chanti had called several times at the house. Not quite the coincidence it sounded with so few educated women available to the large pool of unattached men. There had been a number of suitors, none of whom Kiang showed any interest in. Chanti had been very persistent in courting Kiang. But, although the mother had liked him initially, she'd made the astounding discovery that the blackguard was married and had two children. She'd sent him packing with a few choice words and they'd never seen him again. One homosexuality theory out the window. One suspect struck off the list, one more climbing the charts. Things were looking promising.

Phosy drove to Lycée Vientiane where he eventually found teacher Oum sneaking a cigarette behind the science building. She told him, although it was far from a hundred per cent accurate, that the test she'd administered on the stomach contents from victim number three, Jim, suggested traces of morphine elixir. It was quite possible she had taken, or been administered a large dose of the drug. This put paid to Phosy's theory of Security Chief Phoumi using the morphine to deaden the pain of an old injury. It also opened the possibility that Jim had been drugged. Neither Phosy nor Oum had medical training and they didn't know what effect a large dose of morphine might have on coordination or mental capacity. They needed Dr Siri to answer that one and he was off having fun overseas.

Phosy had reached the item on Siri's list which asked, *What was the timing of Neung and Jim's respective arrival in/departure from Berlin?* To answer that he needed to check the transcripts on his desk. It should have been a flying visit, but his return to police headquarters rendered all his other avenues of inquiry null and void. He would never get around to answering Siri's question. Sihot was at his desk with a banana fritter suspended in front of his mouth between his stubby fingers. He was so engrossed by the book open in front of him that he'd apparently forgotten it was there.

'Am I disturbing something?' Phosy asked.

His voice would normally have alarmed Sihot but the sergeant's head remained bowed over the text. The battered banana hovered.

'Sihot!' Phosy yelled.

The sergeant looked up, slowly.

'Yes, Inspector?'

'I trust what you're reading has some bearing on the case?'

'I don't think there is a case any more, sir.'

Phosy approached the desk and saw what had taken control of Sihot's attention. It was a thick exercise book whose pages were filled with small, neat handwriting.

'This arrived from the East German embassy just after you left, Inspector,' Sihot said. He flipped the notebook closed and Phosy stepped behind him to read the front cover. In Lao were written the words 'MY GERMAN DIARY' then something written in German followed by the name 'SUNISA SIMMARIT'. This was Jim's journal.

'Evidently it arrived a few days ago in a box of personal items Jim had sent from Germany,' Sihot said. 'She'd sent it surface mail addressed care of the East German Embassy, Vientiane. They didn't realise what it was till they'd opened it.'

'So why are we only just getting it now?'

'Jim wrote in German. When he realised what it was, the attaché took the liberty of translating the lines he thought would be relevant to the case. I have to say they're very into this investigation, the Germans. He said if there's anything else they can do just get in touch with him. The diary starts off pretty basic, he said, but as she gets more confident with the language, she starts to write more about her thoughts. The lines they translated are nearer the end.'

Phosy took the notebook to his desk and flipped through the pages. The first translation he found was about ten pages from the end. It was written in red ink. The corresponding German was underlined.

Z has asked me again. He's very persistent, it read.

Two pages on was the line, *I know that Z really wants me to be his lover here. He makes no secrets about it. He pretends to be interested in teaching me fencing but he makes comments often about my looks and my figure. I should be flattered but it makes me uncomfortable sometimes.*

The next page. *I know he's married but he comes to me almost every day now.*

And the next. *What do I have to do or say to persuade Z I'm not interested? He was here again today.*

Phosy looked up at Sihot who smiled. The inspector

skipped a few pages until he was almost at the last entry. The red ink was everywhere now, in the margins and above the original lettering. Z had clearly begun to dominate her life. The entries had become less girlish, darker.

Please stop. Please stop. Please stop. I can't accept you. Your passion is killing me. I can't think. I can't study. Your shadow is darkening my life.'

Then the last entry.

Z has taken my virginity. I am spoiled. He forced himself on me in the most awful way. He was inside me. I begged for him to stop but I was a delicate flower pressed beneath him. His strong muscular body was too powerful for me to resist. I still smell him on my skin, his aftershave, his sweat, his passion. It is all over. This country is stained with the memory of this event. I have to leave here. My soul can never be free as long as he is in my world. But what if he follows me back to Laos? How can I ever escape him? He is the devil and he has ruined my life. I fear what he has turned me into.

At the bottom of the next empty page was a signature and a note in red from the attaché saying that this was a certified translation and offering further help if there were any more questions. Phosy looked up and tapped his fingers on the page.

'Bastard,' he said.

'Her life must have been hell there at the end,' Sihot agreed with a mouth full of banana fritter. 'And then he does that to her. A lot of sick people in this world.'

Phosy looked at the piles of paperwork on his desk, the charts, the pages of hypotheses, the interview transcripts. Until this moment they'd been shards of pottery that didn't fit together into any sensible shape. There was always one piece too many or one too few. But now, as he reread the last entry of an unfortunate woman's diary, all those fragments clicked into place and formed a most beautiful solution. The case of the three épées was solved.

18

LOVE SONGS FROM A SHALLOW GRAVE

When the unscheduled China Airlines flight touched down at Wattay Airport at two in the afternoon, the pilot was surprised to see a crowd of people waiting beneath a colourful copse of umbrellas in front of the dismal little terminal. If he'd known them, he would have recognised Dtui and Malee, Mr Geung and Mr Bhiku, Mrs Nong and Madame Daeng. But he didn't, so he was only left to wonder how news of the flight had made it around Vientiane so quickly.

It was a Lao whisper which, unlike a Chinese whisper, becomes more coherent as it's passed on. Somebody from Agriculture went home for lunch at K6 and was out feeding the chickens and mentioned to the neighbour that she had to hurry out to Wattay to receive a parcel from Peking. The neighbour was a secretary at Foreign Affairs. She knew that there weren't any flights scheduled from Peking and guessed it might have been the representatives returning from Phnom Penh. She was a friend of Mrs Nong, Civilai's wife who had recently returned from a stay at her sister's. The secretary rode her bicycle to Civilai's house and told Nong that her husband might be arriving on a flight sometime after lunch.

Mrs Nong finished unpacking her suitcase, inspected a spotlessly clean kitchen, and walked along the street to Comrade Sithi's house. The maid knew her well and let her use the telephone. Mrs Nong called the Mahosot Hospital and had the clerk pass on word to Dtui that her boss could be arriving on an early-afternoon flight from Peking. The message Dtui received said, 'Siri arriving 2 p.m. Wattay.' And so it continued. It had been almost a week since the two old fellows had left on their Kampuchean junket. That wasn't such a rare thing in the region. Flights were unpredictable and communication was poor. But it didn't stop friends and family from feeling anxious.

So there they stood in the rain. None of them was really sure why they'd come. Siri and Civilai had flown back and forth, hither and thither countless times without so much as a crow on a fence post to see them off or welcome them back. But as they gathered, the welcoming committee agreed there was something different this time. None of them could explain what it was but they had all felt the same energy that inspired the decision to make the arduous journey through the mud to the airport.

The Shaanxi Y-8 touched down at exactly two p.m. It skimmed along the runway like a flat stone across a pond, then turned abruptly and taxied towards the terminal. Everyone watched as a portly middle-aged man in a plastic jacket, shorts and bare feet wheeled the portable steps to the plane. In an instant, the passengers began to disembark. A flock of Chinese somebodies alighted first and were met on the tarmac by ministry people with umbrellas. Then came Lao and Chinese in dribs and drabs. Then a pilot with a small suitcase. And only then, once those waiting had all but given up, Civilai poked his head from the aeroplane doorway and walked down the steps.

It took him thirty seconds or so to reach the terminal but, for the entire time, all eyes remained trained on the exit of the plane. Even when Civilai stood directly in front of them, dripping, he still didn't have the reception committee's full attention. Madame Daeng hadn't looked at him at all.

'Welcome home,' said Mr Bhiku.

'Forget somebody, uncle?' Dtui asked.

'What?' Civilai replied without looking surprised at the question. 'Oh, Siri? There was a slight hold-up. Diplomatic thing. He'll be catching a later flight. Decent of you all to come out to meet me on a day like this, though.'

His words were a little too rehearsed. His smile too politician. His overacting seemed to chill the crowd more than the rain. It was as if he'd spent his entire time on the flight composing a light greeting.

'They didn't come to meet you,' said Mrs Nong, stepping forward to brush raindrops from his shoulders. 'I was the only one daft enough to come to welcome you back. This lot's all here for the doctor. Now they'll have to make the trip again tomorrow.'

There was an awkward moment of silence.

'No, Madame,' said Bhiku at last, 'I am equally as joyful to greet elder statesman Civilai.' He handed over the lotus he'd been holding and somehow the evil spell that hung around them was blown away. They smiled and patted Civilai on the shoulder. They all milled around him and spoke at the same time but, as they walked to the taxi rank, first Dtui, then Daeng looked back at the plane.

It was late afternoon and Civilai and Nong were sitting at their kitchen table sampling the sugared dumplings he'd been given before leaving Peking. Nong had described her sister's attempts to grow straw mushrooms in her backyard. How the place smelt like a stable the whole time she was there and only two collar-stud-sized mushrooms to show for all that manure. Civilai had talked about their arrival in

Peking and the food and their act for the hidden camera. He was delighted to see that his apology and promise to be a better husband had brought his wife home to him, but neither of them had been able to speak about the subject that smouldered in the background. Until suddenly there was no choice.

'Anybody home?' came the unmistakable voice of Madame Daeng. Neither of them was surprised by this visit. In fact they'd expected it earlier. Daeng's gauzy figure stood outside the mosquito-wire door.

'How did you get out here?' Nong asked.

'Siri's Triumph,' she replied, kicking off her shoes and pushing past the flimsy door. 'The idiots made me leave it at the gate. That one walked me over here in the rain.'

She indicated the armed guard standing at the front fence. He nodded to Civilai and went on his way.

'They always get super vigilant after a bombing or a murder,' said Nong. She accepted Daeng's bag of *longan* with a nod of thanks. 'I suppose that's always the way, isn't it? Putting the lid on the basket after the snake's out.'

'Have you talked about it yet?' Daeng asked. There was obviously no space for preliminaries.

'Not yet,' said Civilai.

'Then, where should we sit?'

They opted for the outside lounge suite with a view of the gnomes and the two-foot windmill. A plastic sunroof overhead showed the faint outlines of flattened leaves. Rain clung to low clouds. Daeng refused both small talk and a drink. Her determined eyes bore into Civilai's like steel drill-bits.

'I'm not supposed to—' he began.

'I don't care,' she said.

'I know.'

He leaned forward and rested his skinny elbows on his skinny knees. He began his story with their visit to the Lao embassy in Phnom Penh. That was the last time he'd seen Siri. He reached the May Day reception without interruption. He hesitated then, not for effect, but more like a visitor at the Devil's front door. Daeng egged him on with her eyes.

'It was obvious the guide knew something,' he continued. 'And I pushed him as far as I could to get it out of him. But all he'd tell me was that there'd been an incident. He led me down to the reception. I thought I might get some information there. The Lao ambassador was in the room but the minders were shepherding the crowd. They were deciding who should stand where, who should talk to who. I had my Lao-speaking guide all to myself and he'd obviously been told to stick to me. I was introduced to a couple of bigwig Khmer but I couldn't tell you who they were. They were as focused on not answering questions as the guide was on not translating them. They paraded us all through to the dining room and sat me at a table with people I didn't know, and, for the most part, couldn't communicate with. I doubt they could even—'

'Civilai!' said Mrs Nong, firmly.

'Yes, sorry. I wanted a chance to talk with Ambassador Kavinh alone. I could see him on the diplomatic table on the far side of the room. He made eye contact often. But there followed an hour of interminable speeches. Once they were over and the food was to be served, all us weak bladders made a run for the toilets. I saw Kavinh head that way and I followed. I thought my boy would insist on coming with me but he didn't. The ambassador was in the bathroom. There was a crowd in there, including the ambassador's minder. Kavinh greeted me and asked me how the afternoon went. He shook my hand. As he did so he palmed me a note.

He was a very nervous man. Even jumpier than he'd been that morning. I got the feeling he feared for his life on a twenty-four-hour basis. He used the urinal and left. I queued for a cabinet. Once inside I read the note. I only had time to go through it once but the gist was this:

"Your comrade knows the truth about this place. He broke out of the embassy compound. They're looking for him. If they find him they'll kill him. Only diplomatic channels can save him. Tell the Chinese as soon as you get out of the country. It's your only hope."

'Oh, Siri, no,' Daeng said, quietly.

'I was in a panic. I destroyed the note and went back to the reception. There were Chinese everywhere but I hadn't met one who could speak Lao or French or who would admit to speaking Vietnamese. I can't speak a word of Chinese. I honestly didn't know what to do. I didn't know who to trust. It's hard to describe to anyone who hasn't been there. There was an oppressive charge in the air like science fiction. The Khmer Rouge weren't . . . they weren't human. You couldn't talk to them. They were frightening robots.

'I endured the rest of the evening and they let me go to my room. There were mud footprints outside on the carpet. The lock of my door had been picked and left unlocked. I went inside with trepidation. I don't have what you might call luggage but nothing appeared to have been disturbed. I went across to Siri's room. That wasn't locked either but there was no sign of forced entry. There were no muddy footprints inside. Siri's bag had been upended onto the bed. He travelled light too but I remember he had a book with him.'

'Camus,' said Daeng, her voice crumbling like river salt.

'That's right. It was gone. Plus a notebook he kept. I don't know whether he'd taken his travel documents to the embassy with him but they weren't there either. I was lost.

At first I felt outrage. How dare they do this to us? I decided that anger might be the key. Beasts respond to violence. I went down to reception. I made a lot of noise. Kicked over a pot or two. Insisted on talking to a senior official. Insisted on a translator. But, of course, nobody could understand me. When I tried to leave the hotel, the guards grabbed me roughly and spat some insults at me. I looked into their eyes, Daeng, and I saw my death. And I saw the death of others. I saw it so clearly it was as if I had already been killed. I went back to my own room and wedged a chair against the door knob. I was afraid. My legs were shaking. I was afraid for Siri but I was afraid for myself, too. I thought they'd be coming for me. If Siri was up to something they were sure to think I was involved. I didn't grab a gun and hold it to the head of one of my captors . . .'

Civilai's eyes had become as grey and damp as the evening clouds above them.

'That's what heroes do,' he went on. 'But I crept to my bed with the light blazing and I lay there all night wide awake. I lay there quivering like a coward. I considered all the things they might do to me. I'd seen the look of fear in Ambassador Kavinh's eyes. I had no weapon, only one last resort. They said they had no use for money but I didn't believe them. And I had dollars. At least I thought I did. I hadn't checked my secret stash. I took the bag into the bathroom and locked the door. I sat on the tile floor and couldn't stop my hands from shaking. It was half an hour before I was calm enough to peel through the layers of cloth in the strap of my satchel. And that's when I found the letter. It consisted of three single sheets. They had been folded and refolded into a three-centimetre square and wedged into a little plastic coin bag. Somebody had put it into my secret dollar compartment but they hadn't touched the money.'

'Siri,' said Mrs Nong.

'He's the only one it could have been,' Civilai agreed. 'The only one who knew. I thought about the footprints and the picked lock and I imagined he'd found his way back into the hotel somehow and come to leave me the note. That's what I wanted to believe. But the sheets were written in Khmer. The handwriting appeared to be from three or four different sources with signatures at the end of each segment. The last side comprised of musical notes on uneven, handwritten bars. What looked like lyrics were written below. It all meant nothing to me. I wanted to scream my frustration.'

'Calm down, brother,' said Madame Daeng. Mrs Nong had hold of her husband's hand. It trembled as he recalled that awful night. 'There really was nothing you could have done.'

'There was so much I didn't understand,' Civilai went on. 'If he'd found his way back to the hotel, why didn't he come down to the reception? Surely with so many people around he would have been safer than wandering alone through Phnom Penh. I had far too much time to think. I refused to go on their ridiculous irrigation tour the next morning. I told the guide I'd been asked to pay my respects to the Chinese ambassador. Of course it was out of the question. So I stayed in my room until it was time to board the flight to Peking. Even before we took off I was hustling the Chinese on board. I found one woman, one of the official journalists. She spoke Vietnamese poorly. During the flight I did my best to convey to her everything I knew and everything I didn't. She passed my story on to the Chinese delegation. Once we landed, at last I was able to agitate. I still carried a little clout in China from my politburo days. Some people remembered me. The Lao ambassador to Peking came to see me and together we went to the central committee where I repeated

my story in the presence of an official Lao–Chinese interpreter. The committee members seemed, not upset exactly,
more . . . frustrated. Like the parents of a naughty child.'

'Would the Khmer listen to the Chinese anyway?' Daeng
asked. Her voice was calm but not even her tightly clasped
hands could disguise the shaking.

'They're the only people they would listen to. All their
funding, all their weapons, all their credibility . . . it all
comes from China. Their influence is enormous there.'

'So enormous they could bring the dead back to life?'
Daeng asked.

'Now, stop that,' said Mrs Nong. 'They aren't going to
harm a delegate from an allied country. The worst that can
happen is they arrest Siri for stepping out of bounds and put
him in prison. They want to be seen to be strong. With
Chinese intervention they'd have him out in no time. Right,
Civilai?'

Her husband's face didn't convey the confidence she'd
hoped for.

'What of the note?' Daeng asked. 'The Khmer letter.'

'We found a translator,' he told her. 'There's no shortage
of Khmer royalists holed up in Peking. The Chinese like to
hold on to different factions from this or that country and
offer them immunity. They collect them like elaborate chess
pieces in case they might come back into play somewhere
along the line. They've got old Sihanouk sitting—'

'Civilai!' said Nong.

'Yes, right. Right. The translation. I'm not sure, as it
stands, if it could be called evidence and I don't get the
feeling the Chinese were particularly surprised by its
content. But it made a lasting impression on the ambassador
and myself. It was written by officials at the old royalist
Ministry of Communication. They wrote of atrocities they'd

witnessed and their treatment at the hands of the Khmer Rouge. I suppose it can be best summed up by the words of one young man, the one who wrote the song. He said his name was Bo something-or-other. His note was dated April the twenty-first, 1975. He was a musician and a junior official at the ministry. He said that he and many of his colleagues were patriots and that they remained at their posts even after the invasion in the hope that they could offer their expertise to the liberation forces. At first, the revolutionaries were kind to them and welcomed them into the new brotherhood. Bo and his fellows explained their work and taught the newcomers the skills they needed to operate equipment.

'On the second day of occupation the troops took the managers for what they called reorientation. They told the juniors it was necessary to teach them the ways of the new regime. Bo said he heard gunshots every day and night, not from a battle but from what sounded like firing squads or single shots. The young soldiers wouldn't let them leave the ministry building to go home to their families. Bo said that the Khmer Rouge were not like them. They were country people who had never seen cars. Never had electricity. It was as if they saw Bo and his kind as the enemy and Bo began to realise his life would be a short one. That was when he began to collect the testimonies and signatures.

'On the third day he watched them shoot his office mate in the forehead for no apparent reason. The guards left the corpse sitting there at his desk as a "reminder". Bo's final words were that he loved his country and he believed that this was a temporary madness, but he felt sure he would never see his fiancée again. She lived in Battambang and he prayed that the insanity hadn't yet spread that far. He wrote that his only regret was that he would never be able to watch the expression on her face as he sang her the song he had written for their wedding. "It's a poor substitute," he wrote, "but I have written the tune and the melody on the rear of this note. If somebody finds this letter, I would like her to hear it. I would like her to know how much I love her. And I would like the world to know what craziness has descended on our beautiful city. These people are not Cambodian."'

Civilai sighed and slouched back on his seat.

'You think Siri found this note somewhere?' Daeng asked.

'So it would seem. And thought it important enough to risk his life getting it out of the country.'

'But Siri couldn't read Khmer,' said Mrs Nong, drying her tears with a tissue. 'He wouldn't have known how significant it was.'

'He would,' Civilai and Daeng said at the same time.

'It's possible somebody gave it to him to pass on,' Daeng told her. 'But my husband had instincts other men don't possess.'

Of course she'd meant to say 'has'.

19

THE THERAPEUTIC EFFECTS
OF DYING HORRIBLY

Time has lost its meaning. Misery has lost its edge. The sounds I hear no longer bear any human elements. They are ornaments. They are jingles. They are pleasant, almost enjoyable bursts of spontaneous birdsong. My clarity has become a giddy drunken clarity. I see everything as a joke. A funny thing happened to me on my way to the cemetery clarity. As Civilai liked to point out, my smart-arse thyroid is playing up again. Somewhere inside I'm aware this is a symptom, the result of endless light and lack of sleep and poor nutrition. But there's really nothing I can do about it. I'm experiencing madness and it's funny. Move over Rajid.

What good has all this conservation of energy done me? I mean, honestly. What can I do? When they nabbed me leaving Civilai's room at the hotel, that was my chance. I had stashed my evidence and was on my way down to join the party when the black-suited monkeys were on me. I didn't see them coming. But I was fit then, still burning calories from Peking. I could have done a James Bond. There were only two of them. Thugs, perhaps, but I could have felled them with well-placed karate chops. A sprint and a dive headlong through the window at the end of the corridor. Parallel-bar routine through the branches of the strangler fig tree and head for the border. Blew that one.

Very weak now. Perhaps they'll do me the favour of killing me quickly. Perhaps they'll tire of the toenail-plucking and eye-gouging and just put a bullet in me. That would be nice.

And where have you lot gone to? One by one you lost souls drifted away, off through the walls, east, west, north or south. No direction. No leadership. See if I don't desert you some day, you traitors. But, dear ma, you're still with me, my sweetheart. Too bad mothers have no choice. Even if they can't see a hope in hell for their offspring they have to sit it out till the bitter end. Isn't that right, my mother angel? Yes, chew your betels. Spit your blood. Perhaps we could chat about the old days when I come acr—

A key in the lock. Why do they . . . ? Never mind. And there you are, the dungeon keeper. Thirty-six, thirty-seven? Either way, half my age but skinny. Skinny as the Chinese ideogram for tree . . . written in biro. I could take you, you poorly written character. How dare they toss a twig into the lion's den? No, Siri. Badly mangled metaphor. What would a lion care of a twig? I'll work on that. But meanwhile you walk into my lair with your pail and your tin mug. It's quiet beyond the door, and black. Are you the night watchman? What are your orders, twiggy? Keep him alive till morning. We'll kill him properly then. How hard can that be? Feed me and keep me away from sharp objects. But you don't look that bright, do you?

So I lie still and I stare. I stare into the hypnotic glare of the strip light. My tongue lolls from my mouth like that of a sleeping sloth. My breathing stops. I am clearly dead. Call me a liar. Yes, you dare speak to me. Your words sound like 'Is a saucepan under a yellow?' in my language. You dare. You dare come near enough to look into my cloudy eyes. You dare lean close to my face to hold the back of your hand against my nose. And I have you. Snap. I grab hold of your head and I pull it into my stomach. No pain from my broken wrist, just a disorganised out-of-order feeling. I grip you with my arms and legs and I use what strength I have to hold you there. I am a vice. You writhe. You kick and punch. But you're in no position to do me any damage because – you seem to forget – I am dead.

It feels like a lifetime that I hold you to me. Two weak men in a macabre horizontal tango of death. I imagine the music. I think of fresh baguettes. And at some stage during these reveries, you have withdrawn from the dance. You are a bolster in my grasp. But I hug on. I hug until every last memory is squeezed from you because I know one day you will seek the man who took your life. With luck you'll understand I had to . . '. I had to. But I lose consciousness and the bats and the moths come flocking.

I come round some time later. I feel like death but, presumably, I'm still alive. But not you, twiggy. You lie across me in a show of post-mortem affection. You seem heavier without life as I push you off. I apologise to your mother. She probably had something better in mind for you. I search you and realise you have no pockets. What type of fashion would leave a man nowhere to put his handkerchief, his pen, his keys? I look around to see if you dropped them in our little tug of death. And then I see them. They are three metres away, dangling in the lock of the open door. Where is a plan B when I need one?

It's been ten minutes and nobody has come so perhaps there is nobody. I have been brooding over the dilemma of keys out of my reach. Even by extending my chains to their fullest and my joints to beyond their limit, I am still two metres from the door. It's the funniest thing. I wipe sardonic tears of mirth from my eyes. Why do I never have a long pole with a hook on the end when I need one? I shall make a point of including one in my travel kit on my next journey.

You have no belt, my jail keeper, but you have a standard issue black and white checked scarf. It's almost as poor quality as you. I rip it into strips and tie them together, all the while trying to recall the movie that taught me the skill of lassoing. It doesn't come to me. I am amazed at how complicated it is to tie knots with one hand. I attach your tractor-tyre sandal to the end of my rope and I toss. Half a dozen times I toss and my aim gets more wayward and my laughter becomes more manic. If anyone were outside the room they would have heard me by now.

Then I catch me a key. The cloth snags on the bunch and I have a victory of sorts. Except the key is at right angles to me and no end of tugging will remove it from the keyhole. So I work up a rhythm and swing the whole kit and caboodle – door, keys, sandal – left and right, left and right until I'm certain the lasso will slip its mooring. But the keys drop to the tiles with a mighty clang they could hear half a kilometre away.

I sit and wait once more for the invasion of guards. And again it doesn't happen. So I cast my line towards the floor-bound keys and I drag them to me. A bunch worthy of a Dumas dungeon. Door keys, cupboard keys, keys to some ancient vehicle, but nothing small enough to unlock me. Then I see it. A little black hex key. Annoyingly simple. I could have fashioned one myself out of my own shin bone after a year or so. If only I can keep my hand still enough to . . . and it clicks open. And the same key unfastens the chain at my ankle. I could probably open every door and safe and heart in the world with this cunning metal L.

Twenty minutes have passed. I couldn't stand. My knees had become welded lumps. I had to massage the life back into my legs. I had the option of crawling out on my hands and knees but that lacked ... dignity. I wanted to make my escape attempt at least look like that of a biped rather than a tortoise. The feeling slowly came back to me and I staggered through the door and onto an open balcony. The night air was like a blast of freedom. Below was an overgrown stretch of grass that had perhaps hosted football matches in better times. It was illuminated by the odd electric bulb strung along a wall. But, beyond that was a sea of black. My school was the only lit building. I might have been at the end of the world.

I am in the stairwell now, sitting on a step among other debris like myself. I feel like I have been dragged across broken masonry by a team of drunken asses. Indeed I have. My dance with the twig took more out of me than I have to spare. My journey thus far has taken me past three classrooms whose bright lights chiselled out the shape of the doors. From one I heard sobs. The others were silent. Then I passed the room with Teachers' Common Room written in French in grand letters above the door. That was the room they'd taken me to. The business room. It was dark now. Torment is obviously a nine-to-five job. The torturers had hung up their claw hammers and headed off home to play with the kids. Stroke the dog. Kiss the wife.

'How was your day, dear?'

'You know. The usual.'

They don't need night sentries at a place like this. One old twig should do the job. The guests are either dead or broken. My feet appear to be bleeding. I should have taken the jailer's sandals. Smashed glass everywhere. My jungle-hardened feet have become soft after two years in Vientiane. Soft, like my old head. I bleed and I sit and I breathe and another burst of energy arrives. Perhaps I can make it to the ground floor.

LOVE SONGS FROM A SHALLOW GRAVE

As I work my way down I wonder what they'll ask me at my interview as I pass through the other world.

'So, Yeh Ming, we see you almost got out of S21.'

'Yeah. I killed a man.'

'Just the one?'

What kind of a question is that? Of course just one. Surely they don't count death by omission? Damn it. I bet they do. They're tough, these overlords. And they're right, of course.

I brought the keys with me in case there's a gate or another locked door but it takes me another ten minutes to get back to my corridor and to the burning lights. I know I'll regret this decision but it wouldn't be the first time. I'm mad, don't forget. Irrational. They'll smudge over this in my obituary. I open the first door like Alice, not knowing what world I'll find there. There are three men inside. One is awake and alert. He looks at me with surprise. Another is only half-conscious. He seems to come round as I walk into the room. A third looks dead.

I smile but I'm unable to answer their questions. I hand the hex key to the first prisoner and I check the pulse of the third. Prisoner one unlocks himself and his colleague but there is no point in freeing the third man. I recognised his spirit amongst my classmates. I believe the only chance we have of escape is for us to stick together but I can't convey this thought to these men. The second prisoner, now conscious, ignores me and limps from the room. I personally think this is a bad option but look where my decision-making has led me. That leaves me and prisoner one, whom I shall call Thursday. I have no idea what day it is but Thursday was my birthday. It's also the day Madame Daeng puts special number 2 noodles on the menu. It's a good day.

Thursday and I go together to the second room. Adrenalin has recharged me and my hands are steady now. I can unlock the door without dropping the keys. Inside is a pitiful sight. A woman in her late twenties. Beside her, chained to the same pipe is a child of around three. Both mother and child are bruised. Thursday unlocks them, whispering words of encouragement as he does so. He helps her stand and carries the child out the door.

The stench from the third room tells me that it probably isn't a good idea to go in. I gesture for my fellow escapees to stand back and I open the door. I'm a hard man to astonish, really I am. But the sight I see there takes away what final breath I have. Chained to a floor pipe at the centre of the room is my heavy monk friend. He looks up at me with those same pitiful eyes. But I can tell you, this isn't one of his staged dramas. This is as real as it can be. Piled around the room like stacks of tapped rubber are twenty, perhaps thirty bodies in various states of decomposition. Two are attached on short chains to the big man's ankles. He has been beaten. His fingers are bloody.

He speaks first in Khmer, then in French,

'Help me?'

I glare down at him. I hate the man with all my heart but I am not given to revenge. I remove the key from the chain and place it several metres beyond his reach. I tell him how to retrieve it and walk to the door. Nobody deserves to be punished without humanity in this life. He will meet his demons in a future incarnation. I turn back and look at the bodies and I am embarrassed to think of Voltaire at such a moment. I'm afraid that by evoking the words of the writer I might condemn him to the same fate as the books from the library, and the Catholic cathedral and the dove that was just feathers on a rib cage. But he was right.

'One owes respect to the living but to the dead, one owes nothing but the truth.'

I wonder how long these dead souls might have to search for that truth or whether they will understand it when it's found. I don't ask the monk what he's doing there because, in my mind, I know. The gaolers are turning on their own kind. The monster has already started to consume its tail. It's only a question of time before there is nothing left.

We are at the bottom of the staircase now, me, my man Thursday and mother and child. The effort of reaching the ground floor has drained me dry. My breath sounds like waves hitting a pebble beach. I don't think I can go on. I need a nice glass of port and eight hours on a soft bed. But the omens bode well. We haven't heard the sound of our desperate prisoner friend being cut down in his escape. In fact we haven't heard anything. I'm starting to believe my skinny guard was the only man on duty this night. There are no lights on this level. We pause at the rear exit. Thursday seems to be in charge now. I'm glad. He listens then gestures for us to follow across the muddy yard of the school. The grass is up to our knees. I can't feel my feet but I have a rhythm now. And we are making good time when Thursday suddenly stops and looks down. I catch up and I look down also. Lying in the thick grass in front of us is a body with a bayonet wedged between its shoulder blades. The blood is still fresh.

Thursday looks at me and sighs. We both know who it is. His cellmate hadn't made it to the fence. I hear a laugh from the shadows of the building behind us and a very slow, drawn-out 'tut, tut, tut' like a disappointed clock. I turn to see the smiley man illuminated only by the lights from above. He is swaying like a boatman. He is shirtless and my talisman hangs around his neck and swings from side to *side. He walks slowly towards me, uncoordinated, drunk, and I stagger forward to intercept him. Perhaps I can give my comrades a chance to get away. In silhouette against the dimly lit school, the smiley man would make a remarkable cover for a French noir comic book. The pistol solid in his hand. Black blood specks across his chest. No features visible on his head save a grey smile. Yes, sir, he's a natural.*

'You are a terrible disappointment, Dr Siri Paiboun,' he slurs.

I laugh. Perfect. What an epitaph. What a way to go.

The smiley man takes one more step, so close now I can smell booze on his breath. He hooks one arm around my neck and pulls my head to him. He lifts his gun and shoots. The last thing I hear is the explosion. It thumps into my temple but I feel nothing. It's all over. One second you are, and then you aren't. Is this the way it's supposed to be, my spirit fellows?

20

HAUNTED

After several days of pressure from the Lao politburo, the Democratic Kampuchean embassy in Vientiane was finally prepared to make an announcement. Those in attendance were representatives from the Ministries of Defence and Foreign affairs, Judge Haeng from Justice, a clerk of the central committee, an interpreter, Madame Daeng and, at her insistence, Comrade Civilai. For two days they had been haggling over a location for the meeting. As the Lao refused to go to the shopfront embassy of the Khmer, and the Khmer Rouge ambassador refused to be dragged 'like a goat' in front of the Lao, their first secretary and a soldier arrived at the Ministry of Foreign Affairs with a typed statement. This was the first and only comment on the disappearance of Dr Siri.

The Khmer secretary was an older man who sagged from the distress of being alive. He made a brief apology for the ambassador's absence but didn't bother to make it sound authentic. Then he read:

'The Republic of Democratic Kampuchea offers its respect to the representatives of the People's Democratic Republic of Laos. We are two nations who share a common heritage and are striving to achieve true democracy in our region. This announcement is in regard to the disappearance of Lao national, Siri Paiboun in—'

'He's a doctor,' said Daeng loudly. 'It's Dr Siri Paiboun.'

The secretary ignored her and continued, 'in Phnom Penh in May 1978. The Republic of Democratic Kampuchea has diligently and fairly carried out an extensive investigation with regard to the whereabouts of Lao national delegate Siri Paiboun. It is our duty to inform you that the citizen in question is dead.'

There were no sighs or murmurs of shock at that disclosure as, after ten days, they had all arrived at that conclusion. Following Civilai's revelations, the Vietnamese had been invited to share their own intelligence of the situation inside Kampuchea. On this occasion, the Lao had been more prepared to listen. The rumours from refugees and defecting Khmer Rouge soldiers were not fantasy. Cambodia really had gone to hell. Siri and Civilai, being expendable, had been sent to test the temperature. Only one of them had returned. The secretary continued to read.

'Despite a number of warnings about the dangers of venturing beyond designated zones, it appears that Siri Paiboun illegally entered a part of the city of Phnom Penh not yet cleared of live ammunition dropped by the pitiless American imperialists during the Revolutionary Army of Kampuchea's liberation of our capital. He was killed when stepping on an unexploded bomb. The Republic of Democratic Kampuchea sends its condolences to his countrymen and to his widow, and we—'

'Where's his body?' Daeng interrupted.

The secretary attempted to complete his reading but she cut him off again.

'His body!' she said, loudly.

The Khmer soldier who had thus far remained silent and immobile spoke loudly in Khmer to the secretary, staring all the time at Daeng. The Lao translator was about to interpret but the old man did so himself.

'Our ambassador regrets that the explosion did not leave any trace,' he said.

'Convenient,' said Civilai.

'I'm sure the Khmer are doing their best,' Judge Haeng assured them. 'This is a very delicate matter and we don't want it to affect the relationship with our southern neighbours.'

'No it isn't,' said Daeng. 'It isn't a delicate matter. It's a big thumping noisy matter that's being handled delicately. Why are they still here with diplomatic status, calling themselves ambassadors and first secretaries?'

'Madame—' Judge Haeng began.

'What are they doing in our country?' she continued. 'Haven't you lot heard enough? Send the bastards home. Better still, lock them up.'

Haeng and the clerk were making a move towards the distraught woman. She stood and lunged at them and they fell back.

'If either of you goons so much as touches me I'll break every bone in your hands,' she said.

'And she can,' Civilai confirmed.

Daeng stepped back and knocked over her chair. She sneered at the Khmer secretary and spat at the soldier and pushed past the officials on her way to the door. Civilai nodded and followed her out. Judge Haeng finally broke the silence.

'She's upset,' he said. 'You know what women can be like.'

It was midnight and Daeng sat in the Dr Siri memorial library plodding through Inspector Maigret. She couldn't understand why her husband had been such a fan. She invariably knew who killed whom and why a minute after all the characters had been introduced. Sometimes before. Perhaps it was a French thing. Perhaps there were nuances she lost because she had a dictionary open on her lap the entire time. Or perhaps it was one of those peculiar male traits. It played up to their big male egos to think they could solve a mystery, imagine nobody was as smart as them.

It had been six weeks since Siri had left for Wattay Airport. Six weeks since she told him not to forget his noodles. She hoped they didn't have show-and-tell nights in the other world or wherever he'd gone.

'And, Dr Siri, what were the last words you heard from your beloved wife?'

She knew she'd have to reopen the shop again soon. She had money put aside but with this crowd in power, her savings were shrinking before her eyes. Perhaps she'd shut up shop and move back south. At least there she'd be spared the sympathy. They had all come to see her. Nice people. They invited her to visit. To stay over. Even offered to move into the shop to keep her company. Brought presents. Yes, nice people. She hated every one of them. Did she really need to know how much they loved her husband? Did she care how sorry they were? Eventually she'd been forced to lock the front shutters and shout her conversations from the upstairs window. And then she stopped shouting and they stopped coming.

She walked along the upstairs landing and into the bedroom. She didn't bother to turn on the light. She knew where the bed was. She'd lain awake in it for a month. The heroin she'd secreted in her altar to give her relief from rheumatism was currently dulling her grief. It stopped the tears and fuzzed reality, but it robbed her of sleep. She went to the window. The rains had moved south, flooding all their silly collective paddies and creating brand-new disasters for her country. And there was more to come. Monsoons were lashing China to the north and filling her darling Mekhong. Only June and all the sandbanks had sunk and logs sped past her shop with a menace that suggested her river was in a foul mood.

'Don't even think about swimming to freedom,' it snarled.

Crazy Rajid was back. She could see him in the shadows. He sat on his Crazy Rajid stool under his Crazy Rajid umbrella. She wondered if he was the only sensible one of the lot of them. He hadn't found anyone. And what you don't find you don't lose. He'd slept behind his father's house when the rains were at their worst but, as far as she knew, he still hadn't spoken to Bhiku. And she understood. She knew exactly why he held his tongue. Rajid had loved his mother and his siblings and they'd drowned. In his head it was quite obvious that his love had killed them. So how could he continue to love his father? Hadn't he killed enough people? He had to hate his father because he loved him so much. Just as Daeng hated Siri.

She waved but wasn't surprised at all when he didn't wave back.

'Good man,' she said. 'Keep your distance. Love stinks.'

She walked to the bed and, fully dressed, curled herself onto the top cover.

He sat on his stool and looked up at the window. His thoughts were slow and his memory affected but he couldn't forget that sweet woman, Daeng, who was admiring her river. He could understand what she saw in it. It was different every day. The water that passed you this minute would never come back. One chance to see the fallen tree. One shot at the bloated buffalo carcass. Everything was new. It didn't have or need a memory. He loved the river too but today it had almost taken his life. It wasn't a valuable life but he'd decided it was worth hanging on to. He was wet through and exhausted. And he was crying. Not many people had seen him cry. Some thought he had no real emotions. Thought he was cold. But that wasn't true. He was nothing but emotions. His body was just a skin to hold all the emotions in. That's why he was such a weakling. Why he had to pretend to be what he wasn't.

He stood, lowered the umbrella, tied the drawstring and walked towards the shop. He'd started to feel the cold and he knew the chill was coming from inside him. It wouldn't be long before a fever took hold. He needed to eat. He needed dry clothes. But, most of all, he needed to be wanted. He stopped on the pavement beneath her window. A bin for rubbish – half an oil drum – stood there. In it were the broken remnants of a spirit house and an altar. Someone had tried to set light to them but nothing burned in this weather. He stepped up to the grey shutters and a massive sigh shuddered in his throat.

'What if she hates me? What will I do then?'

But it was too late to consider the negatives. He raised his fist and banged on the metal. Not one or two polite knocks but thunder, banging so hard that if she didn't come down he would pummel his fist-prints into the steel. He'd hammer a hole in the metal and step inside.

Daeng might have found rest but she hadn't expected to find sleep. And when the hammering began she gave up on both. Why didn't they leave her alone? She put the pillow over her head. It was musty from the stains of tears. If she couldn't hear the noise perhaps it would eventually stop. But it went on, gnawing through the kapok, 'thump, thump'. And she might have let it continue but for the memory of Rajid on his stool. The possibility that he might be hungry, or ill.

She went to the window. He wasn't there. She leaned over the sill.

'Rajid, is that you?'

The banging continued.

'Rajid?'

The sound stopped.

'Rajid! I'm up here.'

Because the view was blocked by the awning, a visitor had to step back into the road to talk to someone at the upstairs window. But he didn't step back.

'It's all right, Rajid. It's me, Daeng. Can I help you?'

A figure stepped from beneath the awning and stood in the deserted roadway, and the breath was sucked from Daeng in one single gust, stolen from her. She fell to the floor fighting to breathe. She bloodied her elbow against the table leg. She felt the tingling of her nerves at her finger-tips and in her toes. Her stomach cramped. She was angry, no, furious.

'How dare you?' she called, and climbed to her feet. 'I mean, just how dare you?' She staggered to the window. The figure was still there, brazenly haunting her. 'I'm not one of you,' she cried. 'You can't do this to me. Go do your scary stuff somewhere else. It won't work here. I'm past you now.'

'Daeng?' the figure said.

'Stop it!'

Her tears had come despite all her efforts to hold them back.

'Stop it and leave me alone.'

'Daeng, it's me.'

She glared at him through her tears, expecting him to ignite, at least dissolve, something dramatic and ghostly.

Something worthy. But he stood in his inappropriate T-shirt and Bermuda shorts and dripped onto the roadway.

'I could really use a spicy number two,' he said.

21

VERY GREEN TOURISM

How word got around so fast, nobody knew. But even before the first cock crowed, before the first hornbill cooed, the visitors started to arrive. Some suggested the actual crazy Rajid had seen Dr Siri emerge from the river and had sounded the alarm. Others cited dreams, or instinct, or just an urge to stop by Daeng's noodle shop to see how things were going. They were all shocked but nobody was disappointed with what they found. The loss of weight didn't hurt the doctor's looks any, they agreed. The women said he was even more irresistible. Gaunt was in this year and the scars on his shaved head gave him a rugged demeanour. His timing and coordination might have been off just a tad. He took a moment to consider before answering questions, if he understood them at all. Perhaps he stuttered here and there and gave more inappropriate responses than he used to. He'd only had four hours of sleep before they started arriving.

In fact, he found all the excitement bewildering. Faces jumped in and out of his vision like camera flashes. Some he recalled but most were faded photographs in a forgotten album. Dtui was in focus and clear, as were Phosy and Geung. But when Judge Haeng turned up at nine, Siri was respectful and didn't make any sarcastic comments, which perhaps frightened everybody most. They all agreed that Dr Siri must have walked through the burning peat fields of

Satan. They were glad to have him back even if he was . . . a bit odd. Odd was better than dead. But when they pushed him on what had happened there in hell, Madame Daeng was always around to deflect the questions.

'He'll tell you when he's ready,' she said.

The only private conversation she allowed her husband was a brief interlude with Civilai. The old friends stood together in the backyard, staring at the chicken droppings.

'I have something to say, but you're a bit of a moron right now,' Civilai said.

'Yes,' Siri agreed.

'A bit like taking advantage of a . . . well, anyway. I suppose "I'm sorry"s as good a place to start as any. I'm sorry I deserted you. Sorry I didn't do more to find you. Sorry I acted like a . . . Are you laughing?"

'Yes.'

'At me?'

'N'yes.'

'Why? May I ask?'

''Cause yours an . . . you're an arse.'

'That's probably the medication talking. I'll let it pass.'

'It's me talking, you arse. You don't if. I mean. If, the Rouge nabbed you, do you thought I'd have done something else? Something different?'

'Yes, you're a hero. You'd have strolled into the hotel dining room with an AK47 and poked it in Big Brother's belly and insisted they release me.'

'Then we . . . we both be dead. Dumb idea. Doing nothing's not worse than doing something stupid, isn't it? You used your brain. I didn't. I de . . . deserve to be . . . you know.'

'I just feel—'

'You did everything that was humanly poss . . . possible.'

They stood for a few more seconds studying the drop-pings. Civilai coughed and turned back towards the shop.

'Nice cliché,' he said.

'I'm b . . . brain damaged. It's the bes . . . bes . . . best I can do.'

Before ten, to the vocal displeasure of a shop full of people, Daeng decided that the circus was over. The doctor needed his rest. When the last hanger-on was shoved into the street and the shutters were closed, she took Siri by the arm and led him up to the bedroom.

'I could tell them,' he said.

'You aren't telling anyone anything until I hear it first,' she told him. 'I don't care if the president himself arrives by helicopter. I'm not letting him in. Come! To bed with you.'

Siri laughed.

'I don't think—' he said.

'Oh, wipe that conceited smirk off your face, Siri Paiboun. Look at you, scrawny bruised old man that you are. You think I'd be interested in anything but watching you sleep?'

'I've had . . . I mean, I've slept enough.'

'Four hours? That was barely long enough to get those puffy eyes closed. You've barely the energy to speak. You have a month to catch up with. And I want you rested so you can keep something down. I won't have a man throwing up my noodles in my own shop.'

'I'm sorry.'

'I forgive you.'

'But I want, I mean . . . I want to talk about it.'

'And you will, my hero. As soon as I'm ready to hear.'

'I'm not treated.'

'What?'

'No, tired, I mean. I'm not tired.'

'Good. Then lie down here beside me and hold my hand.'

He had barely tucked his fingers between those of his wife when sleep poured over him like liquid cement. He slept through the rest of that day and into the night. He missed the dog-howl chorus at ten and the midnight transformer explosion somewhere across the river. It was four a.m. when he finally stretched and groaned and rolled onto his side to see Daeng beside him. The night was bright but the light came from an open room along the hallway. His wife was smiling.

'I dreamed the world was an awful place,' he said.

'It wasn't a dream,' she told him. 'How are you feeling?'

'I don't know. Heavy,' he said.

'Do you want to eat?'

'No, Daeng. I want to talk.'

And so he began. His speech was still slow but sleep had reorganised his mind. He told her how he'd discovered the letter clutched in the hand of the corpse of the young man from the Information ministry. How he'd decided to pass it on to Civilai because his friend hadn't broken the rules and had a chance to get away. But Siri himself was a marked man. His hours of freedom were numbered. He had been captured leaving his friend's room. He told her how he'd been dragged to the S21 torture camp and charged with spying and subversion. He left out a lot of details, facts he was sure she'd be able to insert herself, but even the abridged version frightened both of them. By the time he reached the night of his escape his whole body was shaking like an old water pump. Daeng had her arm over him to anchor him down.

'The heavy monk had become the enemy already,' Siri said, staring his story into Daeng's eyes. 'One minute he was running the show, the next he was chained to corpses and soon to become one of them. Everyone was aware that they could be next. I don't know how long the smiley man had been nursing his bottle of Johnnie Black on the back porch. He'd just put in a solid eight hours of torturing his colleagues. A man has to have doubts about job security when that happens. There's nothing like Johnnie Walker for showing a man how fleeting his stay on the earth might be.

'When he saw the first prisoner fleeing across the backyard I assume it was instinct rather than conscientious duty that made him grab a bayonet and go after him. He was so drunk I'm surprised he made any contact at all. But I doubt the kill gave him any pleasure. I'm sure the hopelessness had eaten into him by that stage. When he saw me and Thursday and the woman, we were just more walls tumbling down around him. End of optimism. End of life. He had the gun in his hand even before he reached me. There's an old saying, "Only a fool sits next to a man with a gun to his head". Well, I was that fool. He pulled me to him and I didn't have the strength to push him away. I'm sure he had it in mind to do away with me as well as himself.'

'You can take a break if you like,' Daeng told him. Siri's sweat had soaked her clothes. She wiped his forehead with a cloth.

'He pulled the trigger. I heard it click,' Siri went on. 'Then all I remember was being in the middle of this ball of energy, like . . . like watching an explosion from the inside. I don't know what deflected the bullet – his thick skull, a metal plate in his brain, or just his wayward aim. I don't know. Whatever . . . it was kind to me. All I got was a face full of cranial matter and this.'

He ran his finger along the scar that slashed across his forehead like a cancellation.

'It's very masculine.'

'The noise had deafened me and I was in this blissful, pristine silence. Everything seemed so peaceful. I looked up and saw this figure leaning over me. I wondered whether it was one of the angels come to collect me but it was Thursday. He pulled me to my feet and cleaned off my face and half-carried me into the darkness beyond the school. I'm sure there was a lot of wildness going on around us then, guards alerted by the gunshot, people searching, tentative shots into the shadows, I don't know. But it was all such a dream that I felt I was floating off. And they were all around, the spirits of the dead. There were thousands of them lounging about in the deserted suburbs. Slouching in doorways. Crouching by the roadsides. They watched us pass like crowds along the route of a royal motorcade. It was all quite beautiful, I remember. Moving.'

He seemed to be reliving the moment with a smile on his face.

'How did you get out of the city?' Daeng asked.

'Him. Thursday. He was one of theirs too. A Khmer Rouge. He spoke some Vietnamese. He'd been stabbed in the back in one of their purges. He'd been a colonel in the Region Eight command. He knew the city. Knew which parts were occupied, which were deserted. We stayed the first few nights in his relative's house. There was nobody there. The whole suburb was uninhabited and untouched. It was bizarre. We stayed long enough for us all to recover from our respective injuries and illnesses. There was canned food. We boiled water. My hearing returned. The child somehow shook off a malarial fever.'

'Who was she, the woman?'

'She was nobody. No threat. No reason to be interrogated at all as far as I could see. Her husband had been a school-teacher. Chinese descent. She had no more idea of what was going on in that place than anybody. Now, Thursday, he was our saviour. His home town was Siem Reap. He had people there, family. It was perhaps a reflection on the oppressive cloud hanging over us that led him to question whether he could trust them. But we had no choice. That's where we headed. It's over two hundred kilometres. It took us a week just to get to the outskirts of Udong. Foraging, stealing food, avoiding soldiers. We slept in the day and travelled at night. To our favour, there was chaos everywhere. Nobody knew who was in charge. None of the soldiers had orders. On the few occasions we were discovered, Thursday sprang into Khmer Rouge colonel mode and talked us through. It worked. Most of the young cadres in the villages were desperate for authority figures. There had been so many purges there weren't enough chiefs for all the Indians.

'Then, one day, we got lucky. Thursday marched us into a village and took over the place. When a supply truck passed through he talked us on to it. I think if he'd set his mind to it, he could have taken over the country all by himself. When we got to Siem Reap we met up with Thursday's brother and father. They were commanding officers in charge of large units around Angkor Wat. Thursday told them I'd saved his life and that of the young woman and her child. They were nervous about having me there but they agreed they owed me a debt of gratitude. They had to find a way to smuggle me out of the country. And here, my darling Daeng, we arrive at one of the most peculiar elements to my whole story.'

'It couldn't get any odder, Siri.'

'Trust me, it did. I learned that there are only two air routes into and out of Cambodia. One is a fortnightly flight from Peking. The other is from Bangkok to Siem Reap.'

'You're not serious?'

'All this while, all through the slaughter and the genocide, they've continued to run tourist flights to visit Angkor Wat. It's absolutely true. Well-heeled Europeans and Americans pop up to the temple, take a few snaps, buy their souvenirs, eat ice cream and none of them are any the wiser that the population around them is being decimated. "Honey, did you hear that? It sounded like a gun." "Don't be silly, doll. Probably popcorn." It's all part of the KR public relations campaign to make the outside world believe everything's fine and dandy there. I tell you, Daeng, if I wrote this in a story nobody would believe it, but I saw it with my own eyes. I watched them stroll around the ruins and not thirty kilometres away there were graves with bodies four deep.'

'And how did they get you out?'

Siri sighed.

'They shot a Japanese tourist.'

'Siri!'

'I'm not proud of it, and I was in no position to stop it. They didn't tell me until it was done. Thursday's brother was in charge of security around the temple. They found a Japanese tourist on one of the guided trips who looked vaguely like me. He was travelling alone. They separated him from his tour group and put a bullet through his head.'

'How could they?'

'Life has no value to these people. It was like slaughtering a chicken. They handed me his clothes and his passport, decorated me in dark glasses and a hat, and put me on the Thai Airways flight back to Bangkok. It was as simple as that.'

Daeng wiped the tears from Siri's eyes with her finger then attended to her own.

'They gave me the man's wallet as well. He had Thai baht. Lots of them. In Bangkok I strolled through immigration.

The officer stamped the passport without even bothering to look at me. I found a bus to Nong Kai then travelled out to Si Chiangmai. I sat for a day opposite your shop, Daeng. It seemed so far. It should have been the easy part but I didn't know how to get across. I talked to fishermen. None of them was game to chance a trip over here. They'd all lost friends to Lao bullets. So I studied the current. I walked three kilometres upstream and selected myself a log and dived in.'

'You poor man. You've only had four swimming lessons.'

'That's true,' he laughed. 'But I graduated from the leg-kicking class. I was trusting the log to do the rest. Even so, it's a lot easier in a pool than at the mercy of her highness, the Mekhong, and this broken hand didn't help. I almost didn't make it. I was flying past your shop and I was still three metres from the bank. I made the mistake of leaving my log and attempting to splash my way ashore. I was sure I'd performed all the regulation arm and leg movements but they didn't appear to stop me sinking below the surface. I kicked like a mule, took in several litres of water and was washed up in front of the Lan Xang Hotel. I walked back here along the bank. I was a little confused by then. I couldn't remember where I lived until I saw the beach umbrella.'

'I thought you were Rajid.'

'You'd be surprised how much we have in common.'

22

MY MAMA SOLD THE BUFFALO AND
BOUGHT A ROCKET LAUNCHER

The second coming of Siri was generally considered a miracle in Vientiane. He was met by smiles wherever he went. In fact, the doctor had returned to a more caring city. His Vientiane had a far greater appeal once it was compared to Phnom Penh. Yes, the regime had been infected with the same corruption as its predecessors. Yes, they incarcerated old royalists and killed the odd dozen here and there with hard labour. Yes, they were driving the Hmong from their homes. Yes, they forced everyone to study Marx and Lenin and no, they didn't have a crumbling clue how to run a country. But, odd as it seemed, deep down they had respect for their fellow man. It showed itself in peculiar ways, but the Lao – even after being slapped about by this or that oppressor for a century – still held on to their humanity.

Siri had seen the dark side. He'd retrieved his amulet from a headless corpse in a high-school playground and he'd dug the body of a poet from the ground with his bare hands. He'd killed a man who probably didn't want to be doing what he was doing and the life of an innocent Japanese man had been taken purely for Siri's own convenience. And now, he'd had enough of death. It was time to step away from the spirits. Dr Siri had submitted his resignation along with his official report every month since the end of 1975. Every month it had been rejected, or, more accurately, ignored. But when he strode into Judge Haeng's office, slapped his resignation onto the desk and said, 'You have three months to find a new coroner or do without one,' nobody had any doubts that he was serious. Siri had earned his retirement. He had survived the killing fields. He was on life's overtime and nobody had the nerve to begrudge him.

Police work? That was a different matter. That was fun. That wasn't messing with the dead. It was, in many respects, striving for the rights of the living. They couldn't keep a good closet detective down. It was a Saturday evening and Siri and Inspector Phosy were seated on a mat at the back of the evening market. Four glasses stood at various angles on the uneven ground in front of them, two were half full. Two Thumbs had obliged them by lowering their umbrella. There were stars in the sky at last and the drinkers wanted to see them. The first rule of cigarette and alcohol stall management was that the customer was always right until they ran out of money.

'It looks like we're still recognizing the Khmer Rouge,' Phosy said. He hadn't known whether to broach the subject of Kampuchea but he had questions he wanted answered.

'Their embassy's still open but I've been smelling the odd scent of combustible chemicals from Daeng's kitchen,' Siri smiled. 'So, don't be surprised if you wake up one morning and there's a mushroom cloud where their embassy used to be.'

As often occurred in these encounters, Phosy was only half certain that was a joke so he ignored it.

'It's hard to believe all that horror is going on right next door,' he said. 'But you've recovered from your ordeal remarkably. I thought you'd be a wreck for months after what you went through.'

Siri smiled and looked around. He *had* recovered quite remarkably. Since that first morning back he'd averaged twenty minutes sleep a night. And those tiny pecks of sleep were crammed so full of the most horrific nightmares he got more rest when he was awake. He hadn't been able to keep food down so he was on a diet of rice porridge. Anybody passing his bathroom would swear some farm animal was being strangled inside. He still couldn't write with his right hand and he was deaf in one ear. At the slightest unexpected sound he'd jump a foot in the air and his heart would race for five minutes before it could be stilled. He would put his hand to his face and find tears on his cheeks and, at any time of the day or night, images of the dead Khmer were inside his head. Quite a remarkable recovery.

'There used to be an expression,' he said. '"There's always someone worse off than you." But when you get to the Khmer, you're at the end of the line, Phosy. It now reads, "There's always someone worse off than you, unless you're Cambodian." They call the system there Angkar. It's a political machine that has everyone hypnotised. Mindless. I can't believe there's any place worse than Kampuchea, Phosy.'

'How did . . . ? Ah, never mind.'

'Go ahead.'

'How did you occupy your mind through all those hours of being locked up?'

'It's pretty much the same as enduring political seminars. You've been through it. Songs. I sang a lot of Mo Lum country songs to myself and made up a few dozen more in my mind.'

'I'd like to hear them sometime.'

'I doubt that. Unless the title "My mama sold the buffalo and bought a rocket launcher" appeals to you. Then there were word games and mathematics puzzles. Not to mention solving real life mysteries. I have to say there was a long period there when you squatted in my mind, Inspector Phosy.'

'Me?'

'I was very afraid of the outcome.'

'Of the three-épée case?'

'I was afraid you might miss the clues. I underestimated you, and for that I apologise deeply.'

'No need to apologise. You had every right to be afraid. My investigation concluded with half-a-dozen bullet holes in Comrade Neung. End of case. It wasn't until I started to think like you that I saw things the way they really were.'

'We can't think the thoughts of others, Phosy.'

'Maybe not. But we can open our minds and let other people's thoughts in.'

'I'm sure Comrade Neung will be eternally grateful you did. Tell me, at what point did you work it all out?'

'When I read the diary. There were a lot of thoughts at the back of my mind. I'd wondered about the monogram. They'd called Neung Zorro over there. It was a sort of playful joke. But Neung was embarrassed by it. He certainly didn't give me the impression he was so proud of it he'd use it as his signature. He didn't tell anyone when he came back. Not even his father. So I wondered who'd know about it. It had to be someone he met in Germany.'

'So, by this stage you'd dismissed Neung as a suspect?'

'Not out with the garbage exactly but certainly not at the front of the queue.'

'But it was while you were reading the diary that it came to you?'

'As clear as day. The whole tone of her writing felt wrong. I mean, she was a dull, average-looking, short woman on the heavy side. And she's writing about a jock, a good-looking jock who's after her. Basically, a nice guy. I mean, she should be so lucky.'

'There are those who might accuse you of sexism with such a view, Phosy.'

'Stuff them. Human nature is human nature and I didn't see anything about Jim that would make a man leave his senses. She wasn't exactly the fascinating type. She didn't seem to have an enchanting personality. And he was a fencing champion. If he'd been that way inclined he wouldn't have gone after a girl from his home town. I'm sure he could have had all the hanky-panky he could find time for. And there was something eerie about her diary.'

'What do you mean?'

'Well, I only got the translation, but it was like reading fiction, Siri. According to what she wrote she'd just been raped and she was using all this flowery language and smelling his sweat on her skin. I've never met an abused woman who'd rush off to write about it in her diary without taking a shower and a few days to recover. And she's calling him the devil taking her soul and, I don't know, it was just too much. And I started to wonder who was stalking who.'

'Bravo.'

'She'd known him since K6. She was a kid following around this good-looking smart older boy. Budding crush material. She knew what he liked to do. Where he went to school. Knew about his dad teaching him fencing. And he goes to study and she goes off to work at the clinic up north. And she's good. Smart as shit. Everyone knows she'll make a hell of a doctor. But the Americans flee the scene and Jim has the option to move to America. They offer her a scholarship. But she stays on at the clinic. Why would she want to do that? Love for the nation? Or love for something else?

'Our people are desperate for doctors. They find this girl

running a clinic. They turn a blind eye to the fact she was working with the Americans and offer to send her off to study medicine. The Russians offer her a good deal, the Cubans, the North Koreans. But it's not till they offer her a place in Berlin that she accepts. And why? Guess who'd gone to East Germany six months earlier? The love of her life. But he's got himself married since she went away, and has a child. Yet still she believes she's destined to live her life with Neung. She sees it in the stars or somewhere. Already we start to recognise the obsession.

'I still have no idea where or how she taught herself fencing. I wonder whether she might have badgered Neung's father into teaching her after his son went off to study in the north. That would be ironic, wouldn't it? I haven't had a chance to ask him. But it's through Neung's fencing club that she "accidentally" bumps into him again. He's kind. He tutors her. They spend time together. Her crush develops into a growth, a cancer. She wants him more than she's ever wanted anything. But she's a Lao woman. The advance has to come from him. And it doesn't come. She keeps a diary and through that diary her fantasy becomes real. Neung is pursuing her. She is the victim of his love. But time's running out. His course is coming to an end and she still hasn't turned her fairy story into reality. That's when the writing in the diary becomes darker. Neung becomes this unknown evil character, Z. She's becoming more and more deranged. The whole rape scene sounds like a trashy Thai novel.'

'How do . . . ?'

'Not that I've ever read one. The point is she has to justify to herself why she's quitting her course. She couldn't imagine being in Germany without her fantasy lover so she deliberately fails her exams and gets thrown out. She blames it on some mysterious stalker. People feel sorry for her. So she . . . Siri, would you stop staring at me like that.'

'I'm sorry, Phosy. This is the detective I've been searching for all my life.'

'Sarcasm is the lowest form—'

'Believe me, Phosy. I've had the last of my sarcasm beaten out of me. I'm a recovered sarcaholic.'

'Good, whatever, anyway, they're both back in Laos. Home territory. Jim besotted beyond reason. Beyond sanity. Neung still clueless. Jim follows Neung to the bookshop. He goes there often. She signs up also. By now she's built up the courage to confess her love. She tells him they need to talk. But he's too busy. He doesn't call her back. She stalks on, and that's when she sees Neung with Kiang. Probably follows them out to their love hotel. Bang. Her already troubled mind explodes. She wasn't that stable to start with but now, the man she's been in love with for fifteen years, the man she gave up her future and her dreams to follow home, Neung has a lover. A wife's one thing, expendable. She knows that men with wives take on lovers. Happens all the time. But this is an attractive single woman and Jim could smell the love in the air. It was all over for her. Revenge was the only option. Neung works at Electricité du Lao. Jim follows him around. She learns he's in a work team at K6. Coincidentally, the nurse attached to the K6 clinic breaks her leg. It appears someone pushed her off a balcony. They didn't ever find a culprit but I'm sure we all know who it was. And so she started to assemble her murder trilogy.'

'If I'm allowed to say,' Siri smiled, 'that was a brilliant piece of detective work. There I was, afraid an innocent man was about to be shot, but you had it all worked out. If I'd known, I could have concentrated on my incarceration with a lighter heart.'

Phosy wore a glow, not only of illegally imported Mekhong whisky, but of a policeman's pride. It suited him.

'But I was still a pace or two behind the amazing Dr Siri, wasn't I?' he said.

'How do you mean?'

'You worked it out without the benefit of the diary or information from Germany.'

Siri blushed and lowered his voice. Two Thumbs had been edging his chair closer to keep up with the conversation.

'I had nothing conclusive,' Siri admitted. 'Just a series of hunches.'

'Like the towel?'

'Like the towel, yes. Covering Dew's lap with the towel after killing her seemed really incongruous. If you hate someone you don't give a damn about their modesty. It seemed like a gesture of apology. "I'm sorry I had to kill you." And it occurred to me as being a particularly feminine act. That's when it first entered my mind that the encounter in the shower might have been a homosexual one and that the killer might have been a woman.'

'The Vietnamese security people were convinced of it,' Phosy said. 'The Vietnamese girl on their bodyguard unit had quite a reputation for . . . lady to lady . . . you know. Someone had seen her together with Dew earlier that evening. When they found Dew's body in the sauna, they were sure it was their girl who'd killed her.'

'Which explains why they were so keen to cover it up,' Siri nodded. 'Now I see. And Dew's inclinations would also explain the relationship with her husband. Her parents had wanted her to get married and have children to continue the family lineage. It's really important for some people. They knew they'd be raising the children by themselves. It's all about face. Oh, I don't doubt they thought being married

MY MAMA SOLD THE BUFFALO

and having children might shake those silly gay ideas out of their daughter but it didn't work. I feel sorry for Comrade Chanti. He was duped all the way along the line. Can't say I blame him for shopping around for a new wife.'

'Do you think Dew and Jim were actually . . . ?'

'I doubt it. It was more likely that Jim, the medic, found out about Dew's leanings and decided she could take advantage of the situation. Dew's husband was Neung's boss. It was as good a start as any. The first nail in Neung's coffin. She had a narrow avenue of time to work in. She found out Neung's wife was away for the weekend and he'd be stuck babysitting. He wouldn't be able to run around building up alibis. It wouldn't surprise me if Jim hadn't built up a list of other potential victims, all of whom could be tied to Neung.'

'But Kiang had to be at the top of the list.'

'She'd certainly have to be one of her victims. I imagine Jim met Kiang at the bookshop and became friendly with her. She would have talked about fencing, perhaps suggesting that any man who fenced would be impressed with a woman who knew the fundamentals. Something like that. She offered to teach Kiang and said she'd be in touch when she was free. That way she could bring Kiang into play at any time. "Hello, Kiang, I'm free this evening. Would you like a lesson?" We'll never know for certain how it all came together, but there had to be a lot of planning involved.'

'And all for revenge. And she didn't even have the opportunity to sit back and gloat. You'd think a murderer would want to observe. To see whether their plans worked out.'

'Well, I . . .'

'What is it?'

'I mean, I read your report. It was very thorough. Very well done.'

'But?'

'My conclusion wasn't exactly the same as yours.'

'About what?'

'It's really a very small thing.'

'About what?'

'Your opinion was that Jim had committed suicide.'

'She ran a sword into herself. That's not suicide?'

'It's only suicide if she dies as a result. I believe she didn't intend to kill herself.'

'Dr Siri, you're a real pain in the backside, you know that? How do you impale yourself on a lump of metal and not . . . ? OK, go on. This better be good.'

'All right. I'll do my best. Yes, she impaled herself with an épée. But she did so very carefully. Look at the other victims. Épée straight through the heart. Jim knew her heart was on the wrong side. She must have done. If she wanted to do away with herself she could have run the épée straight through her right breast. But she went to great pains – pains against which she took a large slug of morphine – to insert the specially sharpened sword in such a way that it looked as if it had been aimed at her heart. She'd studied medicine. She knew where her lungs were. The blade passed in front of her lung and out the side. The marks on the wooden upright suggested she'd steered the blade by pushing herself against the sword. It was like a very large-scale injection. It looked awful and probably hurt like hell despite the elixir, but it wasn't life-threatening if she got to hospital in time.

'Her mistake was the Z cut in her thigh. On the others she'd used a knife, made the cut after death. But for her own murder she had no time to conceal a second weapon. So she had to write with the tip of the épée. Don't forget she'd sharpened it to a fine point. It had no edge. She'd been wary of slashing a lung so she'd smoothed down the blade. Cutting into her thigh would have been like slicing across an orange with a needle. It would have been very messy and bloody. I imagine the morphine had started to work and she didn't notice how deep she'd made the cut. She certainly didn't notice how much blood she was losing until it was too late. She was intent on getting the blade inside her. My guess is that she envisaged a complete recovery and the opportunity to give evidence against the man who'd rejected her. She wanted to drain every last drop of revenge out of it. I think her own death came as a terrible disappointment to her.'

Phosy downed his drink but didn't reach to refill the glass.

'I hear they're looking for labourers at the salt farm,' he said.

'I heard it plays havoc with the complexion. Do you have a point to make?'

'Not really. Just that I should be looking for a new line of work. I complete what I believe is my finest investigation, I free an innocent man and I get a rare handshake from the minister of justice, but you still manage to trump me with a hidden ending.'

'Hardly worth giving up a career for. It's all academic anyway. No murderer to build a case against. No witnesses. And without corroboration this is all conjecture. In fact, I'm surprised you were able to present enough hard evidence to convince Judge Haeng to drop charges against Neung. Haeng isn't known as a man in possession of an instinct.'

'Ah, but you see? We did have hard evidence. Evidence that put Jim at the scene of the first crime.'

'There was no—'

'I admit I had to break into your morgue to requisition some property you'd stolen.'

'The épées?'

'Correct.'

'And what possible . . . ? Oh, Phosy. The fingerprints.'

'Can't argue with modern science.'

Siri laughed.

'The prints I couldn't identify on the first épée belonged to Jim, didn't they?' Siri said. 'Of course. I didn't check those prints against those of the other victims. Eureka!'

Siri raised his glass and howled like the ghost of his dead dog. Two Thumbs and most of the drinkers turned their attention to the old man with a cancellation scar across his forehead.

'Good luck,' Siri shouted.

'Good luck,' everyone repeated.

'So finally it worked,' Siri laughed. 'Only a hundred years since the invention of fingerprinting and Laos uses it to solve a case. Who knows? In under ten years we'll be comparing blood samples. The heated rush of technology.'

'What are you two so excited about?' came Daeng's voice from the plank walkway leading from the market. She and Dtui, with Malee at her hip, ducked beneath the few erect umbrellas, took off their sandals and sat with Phosy and Siri on the grass mat.

'Science has triumphed over superstition once more, madam,' Siri told her.

He took one of the plastic bags from his wife and removed the boiled duck eggs to the plate in front of him. Daeng upturned a second bag of lethally spicy papaya salad into another. Two Thumbs had no food so patrons were encouraged to step into the market and buy their own. He was, however, extremely generous with plates and cutlery.

'Eating, then?' Two Thumbs called. Such was the colour and depth of his repartee. Phosy took three eggs and presented them as an offering to the proprietor. Daeng and Dtui clinked together their empty glasses, a signal for Siri to do something about it. He set to his task.

'When we planned this we actually had something a little bit more extravagant in mind,' Dtui said as Siri poured the tea-coloured Thai brew into their glasses.

'You mean like brunch at the Bangkok Oriental?' Daeng asked.

'More like a nice restaurant with tables,' Dtui lamented.

Siri handed the ladies their filled glasses.

'You said we could choose,' he reminded her.

'Yes, I know. But you chose the cheapest place you could think of.'

'And where's the fault in that?' Siri asked. 'You go to some fancy, overpriced place and with every spoonful, every glass, you feel wretched with guilt at all the necessary things you could be spending the money on. You worry so much you end up burning all the calories you've eaten and by the time you get home you weigh less than you did before you left home.'

'And we love it here,' Daeng added. 'It's like a second home to us.'

Phosy rejoined the group. He had a new bottle of Mekhong.

'Was that in exchange for the eggs?' Siri asked.

'Charity isn't in Two Thumb's vast vocabulary,' Phosy told them, and sat beside Dtui. She put baby Malee into his lap and the youngster grabbed at his shirt button.

'Any more news of Mr Geung and his lady love?' Siri asked.

'More chance of the national football team going ninety minutes without conceding a goal from what I hear,' Phosy told him. 'Isn't that right, Dtui?'

Dtui was still sulking.

'We wanted to take you somewhere special,' she said.

Daeng put her hand on Dtui's knee.

'Special is where friends are,' she said.

Siri laughed. 'You got that from one of my old greeting cards.'

'I know. So what? The point is it's the being invited that's important. The place doesn't matter.'

'OK,' Dtui conceded. 'In that case we have something to say. Phosy?'

'Why me?'

'It'll mean more coming from you because you're a policeman.'

'What's that supposed to mean?'

'It means nobody expects you to feel anything. It's shock value. You say something from your heart and it traumatises people. They never forget it.'

Phosy frowned.

'In that case . . .' He put both hands on Malee as if she were a conduit. 'What we want to say,' he began, 'is . . . well. I suppose it's . . .'

'You're doing great so far,' Dtui told him.

'Give me a minute. I want to say this right. Dr Siri, Madame Daeng, Dtui and me . . . we didn't . . . we were so sure we didn't deserve to be loved that when it came along we didn't believe it was really there. It took you two to make us see sense. Thanks.'

'Thanks?' Dtui laughed. 'That's it?'

'I think I've covered the main points,' he told her.

'And I say he did a splendid job,' Daeng agreed.

They toasted the moment.

'I want to add one thing,' Dtui said. 'We were all, I mean, all of us, for five weeks we were living a life that we believed didn't have a Dr Siri in it any more. And it wasn't the same life. It was lonely and empty. It was missing something important. So . . .' She raised her glass. 'Thanks for not dying, Doc.'

They toasted Siri not dying and his belated birthday and refilled the glasses because the best was yet to come. Daeng reached into her shoulder bag and produced an envelope.

'This came for you yesterday,' she said. 'I sneakily held it back. I thought this would be an appropriate occasion for you to open it.'

Siri looked at the envelope. It was stamped 'Ministry of Information. DHC'. He looked up and smiled at his friends. It was an amazingly fifth-birthday-party smile for such an old man. Dtui squealed with excitement. They all raised their thumbs at the proprietor who gave them his trademark salute. Everyone around them cheered at the sight. Siri tried to be nonchalant as he opened the envelope but it was apparently made of some linoleum-like material so he ended up ripping it apart with his teeth. He withdrew the single sheet of paper and looked around before reading aloud.

'For the attention of Dr Siri Paiboun. Reference to consideration of your nomination for the status of National Hero, Level Two. The committee of the Department of Hero Creation has reviewed your credentials and we are most impressed with your many years of medical dedication to the well-being of our comrades.'

He smiled again.

'Yey for dedication,' Dtui shouted.

'We admire your forty-seven-year continuous membership of the Communist Party,' he continued, 'and your willingness to take on the role of national coroner at short notice. However, the committee was less than impressed ... was less than impressed with your poor attitude towards authority and your constant blatant disregard for rules and regulations. We feel that younger generations would be inclined to ape such behaviour if we condoned it by approving your elevation to national Hero status. The DHC therefore regrets to inform you that your nomination has been rejected on the grounds that you, Dr Siri Paiboun, are not an appropriate role model.

We thank you for cooperating with us on this matter and wish you the very best of health and a long and productive future. For your information, we are enclosing two documents. One is a review of the amazing advancements in collectivism in the People's Democratic Republic of Laos. The other is a leaflet which outlines the characteristics of New Socialist Man and his role in furthering the development of the republic. We hope they will prove useful to you and help you to contribute more to the advancement of your country. With respect, Minister of Information.'